R0200518074

10/2019

PALM BEACH COUNTY
LIBRARY SYSTEM
3650 Summit Boulevard
West Palm Beach, FL 33406-4198

HIGH
STAKES

Also By John F. Dobbyn

Neon Dragon

Frame-Up

Black Diamond

Deadly Diamonds

Fatal Odds

HIGH STAKES

A KNIGHT AND DEVLIN NOVEL

JOHN F. DOBBYN

OCEANVIEW PUBLISHING

SARASOTA, FLORIDA

ISBN 978-1-60809-355-7

Cover Design by Christian Fuenfhausen

Published in the United States of America by Oceanview Publishing

Sarasota, Florida

www.oceanviewpub.com

10 9 8 7 6 5 4 3 2 1

PRINTED IN THE UNITED STATES OF AMERICA

DEDICATION

After six novels, I can still say with absolute certainty that not one of them would have ever come to life in print if it had not been for the constant inspiration of the one who is my complete love, my best pal in all the world, and the one I admire more than any person on earth—my bride, Lois.

She has been my reason for writing, my writer of all titles, my publicity director, and the first editor of every word I have, or ever hope to write.

This dedication, with love and admiration, also goes to our third musketeer, our son, John. He is an indispensable member of our trio as a constant source of encouragement, as the second editor of every word, and as our brilliant director of technical publicity.

HIGH
STAKES

CHAPTER ONE

As the lone passenger in a tiny gondola grinding its way to the top of a ski slope deep in the Carpathian Mountains of Romania, I had nothing but time to reflect on one plaguing question. If I could relive the previous week, what could I have done to avoid the precipitous drop from heaven-on-earth into a raging version of hell?

The week had been launched in the cock-fighting pit of Judge Abramowitz' courtroom. The goal was to convince his honor that the "borrowing" of a car by my teenage client—Danny Liu—was not the equivalent of hijacking an airliner. Judge Abramowitz, who had had a somewhat checkered boyhood himself, had always considered teenage car swiping as a "boys will be boys" rite of passage. That attitude suffered a wrenching reversal the morning Judge A. left his home in Brookline to find his Lexus missing. From that day on, car theft became a capital offense in his court.

Despite three days of hostile witnesses and cynical remarks from the bench, I managed to convince the jury that my teenage Chinese defendant had been under life-threatening compulsion by the youth gang of the local tong.

The jury foreman's words, "Not guilty," brought an audible "Thank God for juries" from my lips and one more withering glare from the bench.

The case had another surprise turn—an invitation from Mr. Han Liu, the father of my defendant and head of the Chinese Merchants Association, to a celebratory feast at the China Pearl Restaurant on Tyler Street in Boston's Chinatown.

What I expected to be a cozy dinner with Danny and Mr. Liu turned out to be an extraordinary feast, at which, I'm beginning to realize, I was ultimately to be served up as the main course.

I should have caught on. My mind had been too numbed by the ordeal of a week under Judge A.'s raining sarcasm to catch the significance. I found myself seated center stage in the China Pearl's private dining room. I was ringed by Mr. Liu, no lightweight himself; Mr. Chang, president of the Central Bank of Chinatown; and Mr. Lee Tang, concert master of the Boston Symphony Orchestra.

The fifth member of this eclectic cast was a tall, athletically built Chinese enigma who sat in silence, beaming cold inhumanity from unblinking eyes.

The banquet of at least a dozen courses, each served with a taste of some form of Chinese wine, had settled me into a state of unsuspecting nirvana. The fatted calf was ready for the roasting.

I was vaguely aware that all eight eyes were fixed on me, when, after the final course, Mr. Liu began to effuse gratitude for his son's "liberating verdict." By way of further reward for my "hard-fought victory," Mr. Liu offered with some insistence a week's retreat, fully paid, in his personal idea of Shangri-La, a resort hotel in the heart of the Carpathian Mountains of southern Romania.

My immediate response should have been, "Thank you, but no thank you."

Before I could speak, Mr. Liu held up a hand. "You were married last year, Mr. Knight. A lovely lady. Terry, yes?"

I felt on safe ground saying, "Yes."

"She, of course, would be included. If you thought of refusing for yourself, could you deny this gift to her?"

In a haze of temptation, I recalled the previous year's unrelenting trial schedule that left us little but ten p.m. dinners and a few hours together on Sundays ever since our honeymoon. I mentally scanned my schedule for the next week—and the mouse bit the cheese. The trap sprung. I found myself expressing grateful acceptance of the offer. Mr. Liu was ecstatic. The others were smiling like Cheshire cats, with the exception of the chisel-faced member of the cast. And I, God help me, was oblivious to the second shoe about to drop. In fact, I naively initiated the drop by asking if there was perhaps something I could do for Mr. Liu.

Mr. Liu leaned close. He was smiling, but his tone of voice had a bit more steel behind it.

"Perhaps a small service, Mr. Knight. No more than an hour or two out of your week. There's a small violin shop in the town of Tesila. It's in the mountains, less than an hour from your hotel. It's owned by an elderly violin maker, Mr. Oresciu. You'll find him delightful. He has a special violin for our Mr. Tang here. If you would simply pick it up and bring it home with you."

"Harmless." That was the word that ran through my mind, a mind so into overload at the prospect of a second honeymoon that I'm surprised that I even thought to ask, "Wouldn't it be safer just to have it shipped and insured?"

That brought smiles, again except for Mr. Cast-in-Stone.

"I might have been guilty of understatement when I said this violin is 'special.' I've seen the care you took when my son's life was in your hands. Mr. Tang's concert schedule prevents him from making the trip. Mr. Chang's bank is financing the purchase, but his time too is limited. We three agree that the violin would be safest in your hands."

Again, the alarm bells in my mind were muted by my raging desire to get home to tell Terry what had fallen into our laps. Especially muted was the bell that suggested asking what stake the man with soulless eyes had in this venture and why his name was never mentioned by Mr. Liu.

I asked, jokingly, "What is this violin—a Stradivarius?"

Mr. Liu simply said in a whisper, "Yes."

Mr. Liu told me he would send an introductory message to Mr. Oresciu and that he would make arrangements through the banker, Mr. Chang, to transfer full payment for the violin once I had met with Mr. Oresciu at his shop. Mr. Oresciu would then entrust the violin to me for delivery to Mr. Liu when Terry and I returned home a week from Sunday. The very heart of simplicity. What could possibly go wrong?

* * *

The Carpathian Mountains, like the Alps and the Rockies, wrap around you in such spiritual majesty that you scarcely want to blink lest you lose sight of them for an instant. You sense that God is enfolding you in his protective arms.

For the first two days, Terry and I were bathed in that serene beauty. The hectic year between the time of our marriage and those moments vanished. We were newlyweds again in paradise. No other world existed. Until Wednesday.

That morning, I left Terry by the pool of the Hotel Regal in the mountain village of Sinaia. As she relaxed, I drove a rental car about ten miles through winding mountain passes to the town of Tesila in the valley of the Doftana River. At the end of the short Strada Carierei, I found a small, neat building only slightly less aged than the mountains. The model of a violin suspended above the door made it clear that the plan was dead on course.

One of those old tinkle bells announced that I had entered the main room of the shop. The aroma of freshly chiseled wood matched the sounds coming from the second room behind a cloth curtain. I scanned the variety of violins hanging from each of the four walls, while labored sounds of feet stirring and the words "*Indata, Indata*" came from the next room.

An elderly figure under a shock of white hair limped through the curtain. He could have been the model for a garden gnome. His soft blue eyes peered over wire-rimmed glasses while he said something in Romanian.

I crossed the floor with my hand out and said, "Michael Knight, Mr. Oresciu. I'm here from the United States." Every wrinkle in that old face blended into a welcoming smile.

"Ah! You found me in my little kingdom. Sit. Sit. I have coffee. Could you refuse a bit of Romanian pastry?"

His sparkle was enhanced by his clipped Romanian accent. I have to admit, his smile made me smile. "How could I, at the hands of such a gracious host?"

He laughed and took my hand in two of the strongest hands I've touched since I last shook hands with a jockey.

He motioned to a chair by a small table. "Please sit. My wife just brought strudel, and Romanian coffee is always strong and hot."

"Thank you, Mr. Oresciu. May I look around?" I nodded to the surrounding violins.

"Certainly. An old man's toils. Do you play?"

"Not the violin. But I appreciate a fine creation."

He nodded. The warm smile never left his lips. "You are kind, Mr. Knight. Take down any one you like. They're more to be touched than seen."

"And best to be played. I'm sure you know why I'm here. Have you ever met the concert master, Mr. Lee Tang?"

"Ah!" His eyes went to the ceiling. "It was two weeks ago."

He took my arm in one hand while he pointed to one of the violins on the wall. I could see moisture in those eyes of ninety-some years. "He came into this very room. We talked. He put that violin to his chin. It was . . . Mr. Knight, it was as if an angel was filling the room with the sounds of heaven. Out of this instrument."

"That your hands created."

The words seemed to catch as he just nodded his head.

Within minutes we were sharing an apple strudel that would have been worth the flight over. Mr. Oresciu seemed to delight in every sigh of ecstasy I couldn't repress with each bite.

We chatted about many things, and the longer I was in his presence, the more I wanted to take him, shop and all, back to Boston with us.

At some point I asked, "This instrument that I'm to deliver to Mr. Tang. Mr. Liu said that it was a Stradivarius. Am I right?"

The smile lingered, but a seriousness seemed to set in. "Yes. Do you know what that word means, Mr. Knight?"

"My research says that it must have been made by Antonio Stradivari in Cremona, Italy, somewhere around 1700. It's still apparently the Cadillac of violins, to use an Americanism."

He shook his head. "No, Mr. Knight, those are just facts. Do you know what it *means*? In these few minutes I sense that music is . . ." he touched his chest . . . "deep in your heart. Then you'll understand when I say that no one before or since, has created an instrument with the tone, the resonance, the power to lift music to such heights. Do you understand?"

"I think so. May I ask?" I looked around at his handmade violins. "Not even you?"

He shook his head firmly. "Never."

"Why not?"

He shrugged. "Some say that between 1645 and 1750 there was a minor ice age. It stunted and slowed the growth of trees in Europe.

The wood grew much more dense then, especially the spruce, which is the heart of every violin. We will never have that material again." Once more he gave a shrug.

"You don't accept that?"

"I accept it the way I accept that things fall because of gravity." He leaned closer to lower his voice. "I believe, Mr. Knight, that God put something into the soul and the hands of Antonio Stradivari, a gift that has never been given before or since."

The smile was back. "Just the musings of an old man."

"I'll carry those musings with me for a long time, Mr. Oresciu."

He gently touched my arm. "Good. Then I feel happy to show you something. Come."

He led me through the curtain to the room where he had been at work on three wooden forms for violins. He drew the curtain fully across the door before he moved his workbench away from a floorboard in the center. He lifted the floorboard and took out of the recess an ordinary violin case.

He opened the lid and gently lifted a violin out of the case. He put it to his chin and took the bow. I stood there in the grip of the sound he brought out of that instrument. He closed his eyes and played a section of the *Violin Sonata in D* by the Romanian violinist and composer George Enescu.

When he finished, he laid the violin back in its case. I could find no words. He saw it in my face, and the light in his eyes expressed more than words that the same thoughts were passing between us.

He said quietly, "And that music . . . from these rough old fingers. Do you see now what the word 'Stradivarius' means?"

I nodded. "Mr. Oresciu, someone once asked a great American musician, Louis Armstrong, what jazz is. He said, 'If you have to ask, you'll probably never know.' I know what he meant."

He nodded. "I feel sure you do. Now to the business. You and I are apparently just the conduits here. I'm instructed to see that the money is transferred to the real owner before I hand you the instrument. I'm sure you understand."

"Of course."

"I'll contact your Mr. Liu and tell him that I have had the most delightful morning with his emissary. We are ready to do the business. It should all be done and ready for delivery by, shall we say, two o'clock this afternoon. You might enjoy the shops of our town to pass the time."

"I will. And thank you for a morning I shall probably never forget."

* * *

I enjoyed wandering through the small shops of the town until two o'clock. I actually found myself looking forward to spending a few more precious minutes with Mr. Oresciu.

I reached the door to his shop with his name on my lips to let him know I was back. Perhaps that was one of those forks in the road that could have changed the outcome. Though at that point, the die was cast. From that moment until I found myself alone on that ski gondola, I can think of no other path I could have taken.

CHAPTER TWO

THERE ARE MOMENTS that so shatter your expectations that they squeeze the breath out of you. I walked through the door of that shop practically hearing in advance bright, welcoming words from Mr. Oresciu. What I saw drove my mind into overload.

Most of the violins that had brightened the walls were smashed to pieces and scattered from one end of the floor to the other. The table where we had had coffee was upended. Drawers were pulled out of cabinets and thrown across the room.

I was frozen to the spot until I heard a low, gasping sound from the workroom. I ran to the door. The curtain had been pulled from the rod. My eyes darted to the hunched form lying on the floor, rocking slightly back and forth and moaning with each barely audible breath.

I ran to kneel on the floor beside him and lifted his head gently off the hard floor. The gashes on that gentle, sweet face broke my heart. My chest was so tight, it almost stopped my own breathing.

I put my ear to his mouth. His breath was weak, barely detectable. When I tried to move him into a more comfortable position, he moaned in pain.

Once my desperation settled into rational thought, I took off my shirt to make a pillow. Before I could lay his head on it, his eyes flickered open. I made a move to call for help, but his hand held me for a second. I put my ear back close to his mouth. With an effort that brought a wrench of pain, he forced a whisper. It was just one word, but he forced it out twice. *"Centru . . . Centru."*

The pain took him either to unconsciousness or what I feared more. In either case, I laid his head on my bundled shirt and ran to the phone. I dialed zero, yelled for help, for an ambulance. Thank God, the voice responded in English.

In minutes that seemed hours, an ambulance with men in medical uniforms arrived. With no waste of time or motion, they had my friend on a carrier, on oxygen, and connected to an intravenous tube. Within minutes of their arrival, Mr. Oresciu was in an ambulance in full flight.

For what might have been ten minutes, I stood in that room, trying to connect the scene in front of me with the morning I had spent with that gentle soul. I recalled the word he had forced out on the floor—something like *"Centru."* It suddenly became obvious that, even under the circumstances, his thought would be for the Stradivarius violin, probably the first one he had ever seen. It had been under the floorboard in the center of the workbench—probably what he meant by *"Centru."*

The workbench had been overturned, but the floorboard was still in place. The thought occurred that if the violin was still there, whoever turned the place inside out to find it might be back for another go at it.

I pried up the floorboard, and with mixed feelings, found the violin, the center of this vortex, in its place. There was an old burlap bag in the corner of the shop. I lifted the violin in its case carefully and put it into the bag. My wits had returned enough to add one more precaution.

There was a window in the back of the workroom large enough to let me avoid walking out the front door in plain view. I went through it and began making my way down the alley behind the shop. The idea was to pass behind several buildings before coming out on the main street.

My plan was apparently one step behind. I had barely started walking, when I found two men blocking the path ahead of me. They each had a hundred or so pounds on me, an athletic build, and more to the point, handguns.

There was no point in running. I froze on the spot. When all else fails, a lawyer resorts to his primary weapon—his mouth. I could only hope we shared a language.

"What do you want?"

"I think you know what we want. Just place it on the ground in front of you. Gently."

The heavy accent sounded more Russian than Romanian, but this was no moment for linguistic analysis. Both guns were now pointing in my direction.

Not to tip any delicate balance, with both hands showing, I slowly and deliberately opened the burlap bag. I lifted the violin case out of the bag, set the case on the ground, and stepped back. The one who did the talking waved the gun in a motion that I anticipated. I bent down and opened the violin case to show that it wasn't an empty case.

I responded to the next wave of the gun by closing the case and fastening the snaps. When I stepped back this time, I had a clear understanding that my usefulness to these thugs had expired. My mind was groping for any move that could evade what was clearly their next intent.

I could see the thug who did the talking raise the gun to eye level and take aim. Again, when your mouth is your only resource, use it.

"Before you do something we'll both regret, you'd better take a look behind you."

The talker grinned. He assumed, as would I, that it was a desperate trick. To my astonishment, it wasn't. As I was straightening up, I saw a third giant move into the alley about thirty feet behind the two in front of me. The third giant also had a gun. Thank God, he chose that moment to use it.

Within less than a second, he fired a shot that dropped the vocal Russian on the spot. The second Russian spun around. He got off a shot that twisted my rescuer backwards. The second Russian seized the moment to grab the violin case and sprint down the alley.

My rescuer pulled himself to his feet, holding his oozing side. He ran limping toward me. He would have pressed on for whatever slim chance he had of catching the escaping Russian, but I grabbed him by the arm. The wound in his side weakened him enough to allow me to stop him.

He was close enough now, even in the shadows of that alley, for me to recognize the Chinese, steel-cast face of the silent man who had been at the dinner in the China Pearl Restaurant.

He pulled away and started to limp in the direction of the Russian. I called to him, "Let him go. He doesn't have it."

He looked back at me with an angry, questioning expression, and started off again. I said it louder, "He didn't get it. Look."

He turned back. I picked up the burlap bag and took out a second violin case. As a precaution against whatever might happen, when I put the Stradivarius in the burlap bag, I also put one of Mr. Oresciu's violins that was lying unbroken on the floor into a violin case and put it into the bag with the Stradivarius. The one the Russian escaped with was not the Stradivarius. That would become obvious when someone opened the case and found only a slightly damaged violin made by Mr. Oresciu. But for the moment, it gained us a respite.

My rescuer abandoned the chase and walked back. I remembered asking Mr. Liu the name before we left the China Pearl that night.

"You're Mr. Chan, right?"

Still stone silent, but a slight nod.

"Come on. My car's out front. I'll get you to a hospital."

I almost jumped when a voice came out of him. "See to yourself. And your wife. When they come back, you'll need more than a bag of tricks."

He was right. The slight sense of victory dissolved. That was just round one. I needed to be ready for round two. My first move was to search the pockets of the dead man. I found and kept his Russian passport.

My second immediate move was to call Terry at the hotel. Fortunately, I caught her in the room. There was too much to explain on the phone. I just told her that it was extremely important that she leave the hotel right away. I remembered seeing a hotel a few blocks away from the Hotel Regal. I told her to catch a cab to the Hotel Cota and check in. I'd make a reservation by phone.

I suggested that she take just what was necessary for the moment. We could pick up the rest of our clothes later. I promised to meet her in the room at the Hotel Cota within an hour.

Terry most certainly had questions, but she was also familiar with the types of hair-raising situations that have tended to catch up with me in the course of my law practice with an alarming frequency. I knew I could count on her to move at full speed. Hopefully, there would be time for questions later.

I have no idea of the speed limits on Romanian highways, but whatever they are, they were fractured on the drive back to the Hotel Regal in Sinaia. I walked directly to the smiling and professionally composed clerk at the registration desk.

"Good day, Mr. Knight. I'm sorry you're leaving us."

"Then I assume my wife checked out."

"She did."

That was a relief.

"We're under a bit of pressure at the moment. Could we leave our suitcases here and pick them up in the morning?"

"You certainly could, but that won't be necessary. Mrs. Knight took your luggage with her."

That was a stopper. "How could she handle the suitcases and small bags herself?"

"Oh, she had help. The two gentlemen with her were happy to carry the luggage. In fact, they insisted."

I could feel that one in my stomach. "Did you see where they went?"

"I saw them as far as their automobile at the front entrance. A black Mercedes, I believe."

My temperature, pulse, and blood pressure were beginning to rise off the charts. "What did these men look like?"

"Well, they look much like the young Russian tourists we have here in ski season. Strong, athletic, mid-thirties."

"Why do you say 'Russian'?"

"We conversed in Russian."

"Did they give any idea where they were going?"

He thought. "None that I can recall. Is anything wrong? Would you like me to call the authorities?"

It was tempting, but I needed more time to get a grip on the situation. My first priority was to make no move that would endanger Terry. At least more than I already had.

"No. I'll check back with you in case they leave a message."

"Oh, dear, how could I forget? They left this for you."

He handed me an envelope with the crest of the Hotel Regal. I wondered for an instant if they had taken it from our room. That led to imagining a scene between them and Terry that would not have helped me to think clearly about the next move.

I walked into the bar and sat in a booth. The letter shook in my hand. I'd opened letters like this under similar situations, but the life at stake had always been mine—not Terry's.

I took thirty seconds to will all of my mental functions to a state approaching control and tore open the envelope. The scratchy hand-writing got right to the point.

> *No more games. We have her. You know what we want. You will bring the real item this time. You will meet us at the top of the ski gondola on Mount Sinaia at four o'clock this afternoon. If you wish your wife alive, unharmed, you will follow directions precisely.*

My mind was racing to glean everything I could about these people to formulate at least a vague plan. They were undoubtedly Russian mafia connected. Given the object they were after, they were probably at a level of intelligence, even at the street-soldier rank, that was above that of the drug and human trafficking thugs who wouldn't know a Stradivarius from a refrigerator. The use of the English word "precisely" in the note was both confirming and troubling in terms of the level of sophistication it suggested.

I spent the next hour putting together an approach that might level the playing field. One thing was certain. If I underestimated this crowd, Terry and I would never see the reunion that was at the top of my wish list.

CHAPTER THREE

I WAS THE only rider aboard the Sinaia ski-lift gondola at 3:45 that afternoon. The mice gnawing holes in my stomach on the climb were actually a relief from the ones I'd been living with just waiting.

The man at the bottom who operated the lift for summer tourists gave me the discomforting word that two Russian-speaking gentlemen and a "pretty young lady" were his only customers. They were all still at the top.

The gondola bumped its way slowly over support wheels up a nearly vertical face of the mountain. I learned from the operator who controlled the starts and stops that the cable passed over the crest and slowed briefly at the top to allow skiers to step off. The cable made a U-turn and descended by a parallel path.

Between every rattling bump of the cable, I went over my "plan" with less confidence in every replay. I knew two things. Once I handed the burlap bag with the violin over to the Russians, Terry and I would both become liabilities as witnesses. The only question was how we'd be terminated. The solitary location could not have favored their side more.

The second thing, the only straw I could find to grasp, was my gamble that these particular *mafiosi* were on a different plane from the average low-level Russian thugs. The drug dealers and human traffickers I've had the displeasure of knowing had no attachment to the product they peddle. It's all money. My wishful thinking was that either these particular thugs or the ones who pulled their strings actually cared about the survival of the violin, for whatever reason.

It took twenty grinding minutes to reach a point fifty feet from the top. I scanned the ledge at the top for a glimpse of a human head. Still nothing.

At forty feet, I made cell phone contact with the man who controlled the gondola at the bottom. A large enough wad of American dollars had passed to his welcoming hands to keep his attention focused on my every wish.

By thirty feet from the top, I was in near panic mode. The only slim advantage I could muster would run out if the gondola crossed the ledge.

Ten more agonizing feet and my sun finally broke through the clouds. I saw the head and shoulders of a man who could be sent by central casting to play a Russian mobster. The gun in his hand was pointed dead-on in my direction.

He was cautiously edging up to the rim to look down at the rising gondola. I could have been just seeing what I wanted, but he looked as relieved to see me in the gondola as I was to see him. Enemies have never looked so good to each other.

I gave the word by cell phone to my well-paid controller at the bottom. The gondola broke to a sudden, swaying stop. I was fifteen feet from the edge, hanging over a dead drop of at least a thousand feet above jagged rocks.

The grin on the Russian's face froze. An unhealthy redness climbed from his neck to his hairline when the gondola stopped fifteen feet from his grasp. He still had the one trump card that counted above everything—Terry. I knew I had to seize that brief moment while he was still flummoxed by the sudden interruption of his plan.

I threw open the side door of the gondola and threw out a ten-foot length of rope. I gripped the top end like a lifeline. I could see his eyes shoot down to the other end of the rope. As soon as he realized that a violin case was suspended there, a thousand feet above disaster, his eyes were burning into mine.

He yelled something in Russian to someone behind him. I could see him reach back to grab something. My heart nearly seized when I saw him grasp Terry by the arm and hold her close to the edge of the cliff.

Terry looked down and caught my eyes. She must have been terrified, but the only sign of it was a pleading, questioning look. I nodded a "yes" signal to give her some hope. She must have caught it. She gave me a faint smile that fortified my waning courage.

The guttural Russian turned to English. "You have ten seconds to pull up that rope. And do it carefully. If that violin is harmed in the slightest, she goes over the cliff. I'm counting. One . . . two . . ."

I summoned enough grit to steady my voice. "And you have five seconds to back up and let her go. At the count of five, I drop the rope, and there's one less Stradivarius in the world. One . . . two . . ."

I prayed intensely that I was right that he had personal reasons to care for the survival of the violin. It was my only hope of leverage.

I grabbed the gondola rail with my free hand and leaned further out over the abyss than I actually dared. He could see that a bullet that hit me would send the violin case into free-fall. My eyes were fixed on his to see who would blink first.

I saw a flicker of panic cross his face. At least he'd stopped counting. I had one major advantage. I'd been analyzing this moment since early afternoon. He'd been thrust into the dilemma in the last instant. I counted on his being quick enough to realize that if he carried out his threat of killing Terry, his leverage to get the suspended violin would die with her. He had no other card to play. I had the violin, and the chances were at least fair that his life depended on his bringing it intact to those who sent him.

I needed to move him off of dead center while he still felt stymied. I gave the rope a quick jerk. The violin jumped at the end of it. He almost leaped for it. His expression spelled instant panic. It was time to press the moment.

"Understand this. I tied a loose knot in the rope. The next jerk could pull it free. You want to play another round of Russian roulette?"

His mouth was open, but no words came out. The drops of sweat were not from the summer sun.

"You have one chance to get this violin. Do you hear me?"

There was no answer, but the desperation in his face said he was contemplating the price of failure.

"Leave the girl there. Take your hands off of her and back up. I promise you. It's your only chance to get the violin."

I snapped the rope. The violin case danced at the end of it. It brought his voice back. "How do I know I can trust you?"

"You don't. It's your only choice. Or you can stand there while I give this rope a few more jerks. That's about all it will take." I gave the rope a bounce for emphasis.

"Here's the deal. You back off. You leave the girl there. She gets into this gondola. When we reach the bottom, I leave the case, rope and all, with the man who runs it. You understand?"

He tried one last move. He thrust Terry's arm over the edge until he was all that was holding her balance. I was more terrorized for Terry than I'd ever been for my own life. I clung to one thought. I'd dealt with the Russians before. I had some idea of the kind of death he'd face for failure, and he knew it better than I. I responded with one more solid jerk of the rope that bounced the violin case halfway up to the gondola. We could both see the knot slip down to the last inch of frayed end.

He gave an involuntary scream of panic and pulled Terry back. He let go of her arm as if he'd been holding a time bomb. He took two small steps back.

That put confidence back in my quiet, steady voice. It was more powerful than if I were shouting. "Move back. Twenty feet."

He took two more steps and stopped. He was forcing control of his voice. "If that violin is not there when I get to the bottom, there is no place in the world you can hide from us. Both of you."

"I understand that. That's why I want this over with. Completely."

That seemed to have a settling effect. He took ten more deliberate steps backward and stopped. I used my cell phone to have the controller below start the gondola slowly forward. When I barely cleared the ledge, I had him stop it.

Terry ran to the open door and jumped in while I kept the rope dangling over the side of the cliff. I gave the word to the man below. The gondola started in reverse toward the bottom.

I yelled over the side, "One more condition. You and your buddy stay at the top until this gondola stops moving at the bottom. One move before that, and all bets are off."

As soon as I pulled up the rope and retrieved the case into the gondola, Terry and I were clinging to each other like life itself.

I watched the Russian stare at us until we finally dropped out of sight. I had no idea if he'd wait the full time before getting into another gondola, but we had enough of a head start to make a run.

Fifteen minutes later, we reached the bottom. I handed the case, rope and all, to the attendant with directions to give it to the man behind us. Terry and I ran to where I'd parked.

I hit nearly triple-digit speeds on the road through Sinaia. When Terry came unfrozen enough to let go of my arm, she glanced at a violin case on the back seat. "Michael. What's that?"

"It's our insurance. If I gave them the violin they wanted, they'd never let us live to tell about it. I promised him the violin case and the rope. I didn't say the violin. I picked up a spare case in Sinaia this afternoon."

"But won't they come after us again?"

"I'm sure they will. But I have to end this for both of us. When I turn the real one over, it has to be on my terms, not theirs."

I'm sure that left more questions than I had answers at the moment.

* * *

I knew the lead time we had could vanish in an instant depending on how many Russians they had on our trail and where they were staked out. By then, the man on the mountain would have alerted their agents in Sinaia.

We did the eighty miles to Bucharest in about fifty minutes. We skirted the city limits before dropping down to something approaching the speed limit. The choice from there was between the airports of Belgrade, Serbia, and Sofia, Bulgaria. It was a coin-toss. I chose Sofia for no reason other than wishful intuition.

We headed south. Terry gave in to exhaustion and slept against my shoulder during the five-hour drive. I drove into the center of Sofia and located the shipment office connected with FedEx. I watched while the agent boxed the violin case with the real Stradivarius as physically secure as possible. It was like a thousand-pound weight off of our shoulders when we left the object in their hands. I left the office almost smiling at the irony. My initial suggestion to Mr. Liu was to ship the violin by public carrier.

I had two points of vulnerability to the Russians. The violin was one—and it was now beyond my control. The other—the most important—was Terry. I explained everything that had happened from the time I left her at the hotel pool in Sinaia to our reunion in that gondola. Like it or not, and in spite of my promise the day we married to avoid any more life-threatening situations in my practice, I was back into another fine mess, and Terry was totally engulfed with me.

Rather than agonize over how we got there, I focused on how to cut all ties with the people who continued to threaten our lives. It had to end, or we'd be running for the rest of our lives, with practically no idea of whom we were trying to escape. Hiding was not a solution.

I convinced Terry that since I'd been in positions like this before, I had some notion of how to climb out of it. It could best be done if I knew she was out of harm's way.

After a quick supper in the Sofia Airport, I saw Terry off on a flight to JFK in New York, with a connecting flight to Manchester, New Hampshire. Once she arrived, the plan was for her to rent a car and drive to the tiny town of Milton. A cottage beside the Tri-Echo Lake had been owned by my parents for many years. I had used it for those times when seclusion and peace were the only antidotes to the pressures of criminal trial practice.

I caught the next plane for Atlanta with a connection to Providence, Rhode Island. There was a chance that the Russian mob had stake-outs around Logan Airport in Boston.

Before taking off, I dialed the phone number of the one who put this chain of calamities in motion, Mr. Liu. The surprise showed in his voice.

"Michael. You're early. I didn't expect you till Friday. Is everything alright with the . . . object?"

"There are several ways I could answer that, Mr. Liu. You and I are going to talk face-to-face. I believe you left a few details out of our last conversation."

"What do you mean? Is it alright? Do you have it?"

"In a manner of speaking."

His voice lowered. His tone took on a sharpness he'd never exposed before. "What does that mean? This is more important than you realize."

"So it would seem. I got that impression from your Russian competition."

Silence for several seconds. "Did they get their hands on the object?"

"Not quite. They did however get their hands on my wife and me. I believe you forgot to mention that possibility."

"Where are you now, Michael? Where is the object?"

"The damned thing is a violin. Could you at least be honest enough to call it that? And I have no intention of telling you where I am over the phone. My wife and I are, however, both alive. I'm sure you were about to ask."

"Of course. When can I see you, and when can you—"

"One question at a time. I'll meet you at nine thirty tomorrow night."

"Fine. Shall we meet upstairs in the China Pearl Restaurant?"

"Not this time. I need someplace more neutral and more public. At nine thirty, I'll be in Public Garden on the bench by the dock for the swan boats. I suggest you come alone."

"Will you have the . . ."

"Violin. It's a Stradivarius violin. If you'd been tiptoeing around it like this last week, I'd at least have been forewarned."

"Will you bring the . . . violin?"

"Let's talk. Perhaps then I can decide whose side I'm on."

I could hear his voice start to reach a higher pitch just before I hung up.

CHAPTER FOUR

I DROVE A rented car from the airport in Providence, Rhode Island, to a parking lot a few blocks from my office at 77 Franklin Street in Boston. On the elevator to the seventh floor, I could feel the juices of self-confidence welling up more strongly with each passing floor. Just being on home turf made life seem more in control—whether it was or not.

I made an immediate right turn off the elevator for the corner office. For nearly four years now, it had been the proudest point of my existence to be the junior partner of a man who stood like Gulliver, towering above the many Lilliputians who did battle with him in the courts of Suffolk County. Lex Devlin is a sheltering oak for the defendants he chooses to represent; he is the formidable lion of the defense bar to prosecutors who face him in court; and he is my senior and only partner in the firm of Devlin and Knight—and more to the point, he is the man for whom I would unflinchingly walk off a cliff.

Mr. D. was due to leave for court, but when he looked up and saw me, I saw the light of a father's eyes for his returning son. His court date would suffer a delay for our reunion, but there would probably be no repercussions. Judges of both federal and state courts granted him such small concessions for a long and highly honorable career of service to the bar.

"Michael. You're home early. I didn't expect you till Monday. Is everything alright?"

I gave a sincere smile and an equivocal nod. I took my accustomed seat to the left of his desk, while he had his secretary notify Judge Janet Levy that he was unavoidably detained.

In terms as short as I could make them, without underplaying their seriousness, I filled in the significant steps that had turned a second honeymoon into a disaster on greased wheels.

The creases in his forehead grew deeper with each incident I related. "What can we do about this, Michael? Whatever you need."

I loved the "we." No matter how dangerous the situation, he was instantly fully into it on my side.

"Thank you, Mr. Devlin. Right now, it feels like Terry and I are caught between Scylla and Charybdis."

"The Russian mafia and the Chinese mob. Damn. How can I help?"

"Somehow I have to get us out of the cross fire. Then there's that violin. I wish I could just toss it up between them like a jump ball."

"How do we bring it off?"

"I have a way to get a line on the cast of characters on the Chinese side. I'll work on that this morning. But I need to get a handle on the key players on the Russian side."

"I see where you're going. Let me see if I can set something up. Lunch today?"

"Perfect. The sooner, the better."

He grabbed the phone and punched in numbers that bypassed the office staff and went directly to the deputy district attorney, Billy Coyne. Mr. Coyne and Mr. Devlin were like two well-matched gladiators. The innumerable times over many years they had been paired in combat as prosecutor and defense counsel had bred a deep mutual respect and, though they'd never concede it, an abiding affection.

"Lex. Aren't you due in court? One of my young assistants was in my office this morning griping about having to face the lion without a whip and a chair. He wanted advice."

"And you told him what?"

"Just play it straight. I told him that if he tries bluffing or bull crap, he'll find himself up against the master of both. That was a compliment, Lex."

"And a fine one, coming from a man who must have kissed the Blarney stone twice. Billy, even more than your wit and wisdom, I need some information."

"And I take it it's for your ears only."

"And Michael's. Can you meet us at the Marliave for lunch?"

"Noon?"

"Can we say one o'clock? I'm stretching Judge Levy's calendar as it is."

"Done. And, Lex . . ."

"What?"

"Go easy on my young assistant. Leave him some self-respect."

"He shall leave the courtroom with his feathers unruffled. I may even let him score a few harmless points for your sake."

* * *

My next check-in on the way down the hall to my office was my faithful, occasionally long-suffering secretary, Julie Benson. In her case, "secretary" covers everything from my irreplaceable right arm to my doting, twenty-four-year-old "mother" figure. On occasion, when I have time to think about it, I dread the day when some Prince Valiant will finally come to his senses and marry her out of my professional life.

"Michael, why are you back early? Are you alright?"

"Never better, Julie."

"Good. Then here's the list of the calls you owe. I ranked them in order of the amount of heat coming through the phone. That top one could warm a ski lodge. The rest are semi-rational, for lawyers. Shall I start calling from the top down?"

"Not yet. Give me about half an hour."

I could see her smile fade away. "Don't worry, Julie. In half an hour I'll take the heat."

I was walking toward my office, but suddenly a thought stopped me cold. "Julie, that one at the top of the list. Did he have an accent?"

"Definitely."

"Russian?"

"I don't know. Possibly."

"What did he say?"

"It didn't make sense. Michael, some of your clients are stranger than the lawyers."

"This one's not a client. Did he leave a message?"

"Oh yes. He said you *must* call him at the number I wrote there. It wasn't a question. He didn't say it, but I got the strong implication of '*or else.*' Michael, why do you deal with these people?"

I wanted to say, "Damn little choice"; but instead, "You have to play the cards you're dealt, right?"

"That's gibberish. Do you actually know that man?"

I wasn't sure. The current supply of Russian gangsters seemed inexhaustible. "If he calls back, put him through right away, even if I'm on the phone."

I needed the half hour to make a call to a resource I've tapped more times than I could count and never come up empty. Harry Wong and I go back to a house wrestling team as sophomores at Harvard College. After college, while I went the law school route, Harry rose from student, through an alphabet of degrees, to resident genius at MIT down the Charles River. The first criminal defense case I had under the guiding hand of Lex Devlin put me back in touch with Harry for information and personal life-risking that put us both in the inner sanctum of the Boston Chinese tong.

I got him on his cell phone.

"My dear friend Harry."

"My dear friend Michael. Why is it every time we greet each other that way I wind up risking my skinny neck to save some unworthy client of yours? Please tell me this is just social."

"Social it is. And just to prove it, I'm inviting you for dinner. My treat. How about James Hook on Atlantic Ave.? We haven't been there in a while. Six o'clock?"

"Why not? And this *is* purely two old friends for a good lobster dinner. Nothing more terrifying, right?"

"Harry, my friend, what would life be without surprises?"

"Michael, this sounds like—"

"Gotta go, Harry. Six o'clock." Click.

The phone hardly hit the cradle when I got an intercom buzz from Julie.

"It's him, Michael. The Russian accent. He's creepier than ever. How about if I tell him you're out of town. No idea when you're expected?"

"Put him through, Julie. You can't outrun the devil."

"What does that mean?"

"It means put him through. I can handle it. And hang up. No listening in."

"Michael, when have I ever—"

"Every time you think I need protection. Put him on."

There was a pause. I heard a click for the connection and waited for the click that meant Julie was not on the line to hear something that would enflame her motherly instinct.

"Hello. This is Michael Knight."

I expected a growling, bombastic Russian voice threatening me, my family, my dog, and everyone I'd met since kindergarten. I was braced for it.

"Mr. Knight. So nice to reach you in person. I trust you had a pleasant return from my country."

The voice was shockingly cordial. It caught me off guard. I did put together the heavy accent with the reference to Romania as "his country." I remembered hearing while I was there that the breakup of the Soviet Union left a large block of the old Russian guard still in permanent residence.

"Thank you. You could say the trip had its interesting points." I was thinking of the old Chinese curse: "May you have an interesting life." His quiet laugh indicated that he got the point.

"I'm sorry for any unpleasantness. I hope we can put all of that in the past? You and I have a great deal in common. Shall we concentrate on that? We can bestow on each other more benefits than you realize."

One more reassessment. This was not a garden-variety Russian thug. Thug, perhaps, but with composure and some refinement, at least on the surface.

"You could begin by telling me your name."

This time the laugh was heartier. "Of course. You may call me 'George.' That will do for now. Michael and George. That's the beginning of a working relationship."

"And, George, what exactly will this relationship be working on?"

"Ah, directly to the point. I like that. I would think you could guess. There is an object, a musical object. It's in your possession. The point of our relationship would be to transfer it to our possession, my possession."

"In exchange for?"

"Still to the point. Good. Let your heart dream. You may name your price, Michael, within reason. I'll be straightforward. I have a very serious need to acquire this object. The price you name may be concomitant with that need."

My mind was bouncing between thoughts like a pinball machine. For one, I'd given my word to turn this thing that nobody wanted to call "a violin" over to Mr. Liu. On the other hand, I decided that his duplicity in not mentioning "complications" with the Russian mob had nullified that bond. A second factor that favored giving it to the Russians was my personal ultimate goal of a "normal" life for Terry and me—i.e., no Russian assassin around every corner. On the third hand, if I turned this albatross over to the Russians, Terry and I might incur the fire-breathing dragon of the Chinese mob. No easy out. I needed time.

"Perhaps you and I should meet, George. Some things are discussed better across a table."

"I could not agree more. When?"

I thought of my list of meetings with Billy Coyne at one, Harry Wong at six, and Mr. Liu at nine thirty. Perhaps the information I'd get from that trio would give me an idea of how to deal with George.

"How about tomorrow morning?"

There was a pause. "I'd hoped you'd realize that there is some urgency here. Perhaps this afternoon. No later."

"Not possible. Tomorrow morning. Eleven o'clock."

Another pause. "And where did you have in mind?"

My mind was racing. Someplace public, someplace where a threat could not be carried out with an easy avenue of escape.

"I'll be at the Skywalk on top of the Prudential Building tomorrow morning at eleven. I'll be alone. And you?"

"Of course. I hope you'll keep an open mind, Michael."

My mind ran back to the scene with Terry at the top of Sinaia Mountain. My thought was, "Open, yes. Unprepared? Never again."

I simply said, "Till then."

I hung up and dialed the cottage in New Hampshire. Terry caught it on the second ring.

"Michael, are you alright? Where are you?"

"I'm fine. I'm at the office. How about you?"

"Good, but worried. They could find you there."

"I've taken precautions. I'm working on a resolution of this thing. I'll keep in touch. Meanwhile, you'll have to settle in there. I'll let you know as soon as we can both go home. Hopefully, it won't be too long."

We talked a bit, but kept it brief. I knew that the Russians must have known I was in my office. I needed mobility, and I still didn't know if I could trust the chummy tone of George.

* * *

I took the elevator down and walked straight out the door. I hit a good pace in the midst of the midday walkers for the few blocks to the Arch Street Shrine of Saint Anthony. It had been my local drop-in refuge from any number of pressures over the years. In that sidewalk crowd, it was impossible to tell if I was being followed. My instincts told me that I was.

A few legal favors for the Franciscan Friars over the years had led to a close relationship with Friar Mike Griffin. A number of late-night chats over some good Benedictine brandy gave him an insight into my erratic professional life. He showed no surprise when I asked for an unusual favor.

Five minutes later, in a friar's robe with the hood up, I walked up the center aisle of the church and out the front door. I passed two men in the back row who practically had "Russian mob enforcer" tattooed on their foreheads. They glanced at the robe, but showed no sign of recognition.

The walk to the parking lot where I left the car was actually liberating. People I passed in the friar's robe mostly smiled or nodded. I almost regretted taking off the robe when I reached the car.

I had over an hour before meeting Mr. Devlin and Billy Coyne at the Marliave for lunch. I used it to drive through the Callahan Tunnel to the Winthrop shore just north of Boston Harbor. Terry's father had built a house by the ocean decades before. Terry was living alone there when we married. Since we both loved the location, we chose that as our first home.

I drove down Taft Avenue. Fortunately, my rental car was less recognizable than my own Corvette. As a precaution, I managed to coast by Andrew Street slowly enough to spot a car with two bulky men staked out with their eyes on the house. That gave me multiple creeps. The two possible "Russians" in the back of the church could have been my own overactive paranoia. But if George and I were now shooting for team players of the year, why did he have my home clearly staked out by thugs?

I drove another block and parked the car. I jumped the sea wall and walked along the beach until I was in front of the house. The view of the stake-outs was blocked by the house. I was able to scramble over the sea wall and approach the house from the ocean side undetected.

I scrambled down the bulkhead and came into the house through the basement. I was now free to roam through the house as long as I was careful of windows facing the stake-out.

When I opened the door from the basement, I paused for three seconds. I felt the blood in my veins freeze. There was a chilling silence. Terry had a five-year-old Shetland Sheepdog she called "Piper." He was the love of her life before we met. The first time I picked Terry up at home, he ran to brace me with a thorough sniff-test. Then he just sat down at my feet and looked up at me. I kneeled down, and he just jumped into my arms. Terry had never seen anything like it.

From that moment on, Piper had two humans who had sealed a bond with him. After that, every time I even turned a doorknob to come into the house, Piper was there, twisting and wagging and begging for the hug I always wanted to give him.

When I opened that door from the cellar to stark silence, every alarm in my mind went off. Our next-door neighbor had been coming in to feed and take him for walks while we were in Romania, but at that hour, Piper should have been there!

I ran upstairs and threw open every closet door, looked under every bed, pulled aside every drape—all the time nearly sick with the fear of what I might find.

I exhausted every possibility but one. I went back out the way I'd come in. This time when I walked the beach behind the seawall, I picked up a solid three-foot length of driftwood. I went a block beyond Andrew Street so I could come up behind the stake-out car.

I bent low and eased up to the back of the car. The only possibility I could think of was that the two thugs had somehow grabbed Piper, God forbid, disabled him, and put him out of sight in the trunk of the car. I put my mouth to the trunk. I barely whispered the word, "Piper."

The eruption of instant thumps and barks from the trunk lifted the two goons straight up. Above the sudden barking, I could hear the crunch of the head of the tall Russian on the right against the roof. There was a zesty flow at peak volume of what could only be Russian curses.

The driver yelled something that stemmed the flood of curses. He spat out what sounded like an order. The tall one on the right threw open the door and edged his way out rubbing his head. Meanwhile, Piper kept up the uninterrupted yelps and barks that hid any sound I might have made.

I slipped around to the side behind the driver's seat and ducked below window level. The passenger thug came around to the back. He hit some button that sprung open the trunk. Piper leaped out while the lid was still rising. I could see a mean gash from his ear to the back of his head.

The cacophony of barks and snarls doubled in volume. Another order came from the driver's side. The Russian moved faster than I thought possible. He grabbed Piper in an iron fist by the back of the neck. The bark turned to a yelp of pain. I took two quick steps toward the back of the car and swung the driftwood log as if I were going for a home run over the Green Monster in Fenway park.

The wood connected dead center with the Russian's ribs. The snap, crackle, and pop sounded like a bowl of Rice Crispies. He dropped Piper and rolled on the ground, clutching as many ribs as he could reach.

The driver was out of the car, coming up behind me with a gun in his hand that looked like a canon. I spun around to see the barrel pointed squarely at my chest. It must have been pure instinct. I pointed an arm and finger straight out at the hand holding the gun and screamed, "Get it, Piper."

My eyes were glued to the Russian's finger as it started to move the trigger. In an instant, all I could see was the hair raised on the back of Piper's neck. Instead of a shot, there was only a flow of Russian curses. The gun was on the ground and the Russian was jerking his hand in every direction with Piper's teeth sunk in and gripping.

I picked up my trusty driftwood and planted one more blow, this time to the head of the Russian with the gun. He dropped to the ground unconscious. I pulled Piper away from his hand. I just stood there hugging him for what must have been ten seconds.

I finally got it together and reached into the pocket of the unconscious Russian. I took the driver's license out of his billfold and ran with Piper to my rented car. I drove the length of the Revere Beach Parkway until my pulse and blood pressure came down within range of normal. Piper lay across my lap the whole way.

The first time I glanced at the car clock it was quarter past twelve. I had a one o'clock appointment with Mr. Devlin and Billy Coyne, but Piper came first. I called my faithful Julie. I told her I needed a favor. She came through like a champ. She met me at her apartment on Beacon Street, and was more than willing to take him in.

* * *

I parked under the Boston Common and walked to the Marliave Restaurant. I had a thousand questions to fit into some kind of order before meeting Billy Coyne, but one kept bubbling to the top. Why had the one I assumed to be the top Russian offered an olive branch and the prospect of a George/Michael partnership for the greatest mutual prosperity since Johnson & Johnson, while he was sending his goon squad to invade our house, steal our dog, and do heaven-knows-what to whomever they found there?

The olive branch could have been a trap. I knew that. But for some reason I can't explain, I still had a modicum of intuitive trust.

CHAPTER FIVE

I ARRIVED A few minutes before one at the Marliave Restaurant off Bromfield Street. I was welcomed graciously as always by Tony, the owner/maître d'. I knew the red carpet was for my connection with Mr. Devlin, but it still felt warming.

Tony escorted me to the private dining room just off the kitchen. There had been enough exchanges of private information in that room, sometimes carrying life or death implications, between Mr. Devlin, Deputy District Attorney Coyne, and "the kid" as I will always be to Mr. Coyne, to alert Tony to the necessary privacy protocol even without knowledge of the particulars.

I was relieved to be the first to arrive a few minutes before one. It avoided having to suppress any response to Mr. Coyne's inevitable reference to "the kid's undisciplined generation."

Messrs. Devlin and Coyne arrived at a minute or so past one o'clock. I made certain to be looking at my watch when they walked in. That brought a grin from Mr. D. and a sneer from Mr. Coyne.

Four exquisite courses were prepared personally and served by Tony, our host, who has never let Mr. Devlin even glance at a menu. Between courses, I took center stage. I poured out every relevant detail of my recent adventures, from the meeting at the China Pearl

Restaurant to the knock-down episode with the Russians that morning.

As I expected, Mr. D'.s reaction was heightened concern for me when he heard about the morning's incident. Mr. Coyne's reaction was a look of confusion. I focused on the latter.

"Mr. Devlin told you that we need information that you might be able to give us."

Mr. Coyne pushed back in his chair. He just scowled for about ten seconds before breaking the silence.

"This is a hell of a thing."

"I agree, for a lot of reasons. What's yours, Mr. Coyne?"

"Listen to me, kid. Nothing said in this room leaves this room."

"Goes without saying."

"Well, now it's been said. So remember it."

Mr. Devlin stepped in. "Billy, you know damn well you can trust Michael as far as you can trust me. So to hell with your blustering. Get to it. I have to be back in court sometime this year."

Mr. Coyne just raised his hand in submission and laid his napkin on the table.

"This is disturbing."

I couldn't resist. "You know, I find it disturbing too, and then some."

Mr. Coyne gave me a glance before continuing. "What I meant was we have the Chinese mob, undoubtedly the tong, and the Russians after the same thing. And both of them apparently willing to kill for it. That's off. The tong's prey is usually strictly Chinatown. That's what keeps us out of it. The Chinese extortion and theft victims in Chinatown are afraid to report anything. On the other side, the Russians generally leave the Chinese territory alone. They have the rest of the world to plunder. What the hell is it that gets these two into the same game?"

I leaned over to catch his eye. "You remember I mentioned a Stradivarius violin?"

"Senility has not set in yet, kid. Yeah, I remember. So what?"

"So apparently this particular Stradivarius caught the attention of both of them. With me uncomfortably in the middle."

He looked me in the eye. "Kid, I had a case with a stolen Stradivarius last year. I found out there are over six hundred and fifty Stradivarius instruments in the world today. What makes this one so special?"

"The fact that the Chinese were willing to pay over a million for it?"

"Maybe. But that's the going price for some of them. Sometimes more. If they're willing to pay the going price for it, that's just doing business. Where's the criminal aspect that would attract the tong? You said this Russian, George, was willing to pay an open-ended price for it, too. That leads to the same question for the Russians."

"What are you thinking, Billy?" Mr. Devlin asked.

"I'm thinking the obvious. There's something about this particular fiddle that your boy's holding like a hot potato that puts it in a class by itself. I don't like it. It could mean that a lot more people die in my city before this thing finds a home."

Mr. D. and I looked at each other with the same thought. That number who die could include someone at our table. I thought it best to move on.

"There's another question hanging here, Mr. Coyne. This is what we needed to ask you."

"So speak."

"The Russians have almost killed me three times since this thing began. Before the last time, I got that call from the one who calls himself 'George.' I got the sense that he's close to the top echelon in the organization. I doubt that he's the very top or he wouldn't be so jumpy. He was laying the groundwork for peaceful cooperation between us. Then an hour or so later, I have a run-in with two of his Russian mob staking out my house. It makes no sense. I've heard the Russians follow a strict chain of command or they lose body parts. Does this make sense to you?"

"Maybe. There's a point you could be missing."

"That's why we're here. Would you share it?"

"There is more than one mob out there. You know about the Russian mafia. It's centered in Moscow, but it's all over the world. You also know by now that you damn well don't fool with them. My guess is they're the ones you ran into in Romania and then here this morning. What you probably don't know is that there are other crime gangs that operate in different parts of Romania. They're mostly built around native Romanian family clans. They operate in the poorer sections of Bucharest and in cities all the way to the Black Sea."

"Are they in league with the Russians?"

"Hell, no. All the years Romania was part of the Soviet Union, they were oppressed by the Russians in every way you can think of. When the Soviet troops marched down the main boulevard in Bucharest in August of 1944, it was in some ways almost as bad for the country as the invasion of Nazi troops before. The Romanian people had a hell of a time under the power-hungry communist dictator, Ceausescu. Romanian gangs existed then. They were mostly tight-knit groups with family clan ties for trust. They worked the black market, but they were pretty much stifled by the communists.

"When the Soviet Union finally fell apart under Gorbachev, Ceausescu was killed, and the Romanian counter-revolution took

their country back. Those clan gangs were free to expand and operate like they never could before. But they were still strictly ethnic
Romanian. The old grudges lived on. No Russian would ever be let
in."

"What kind of crimes are they into?"

"Depends on the gang. Some of them moved into drugs, loan
sharking, prostitution."

Mr. D. drew closer. "How does a Suffolk County D.A. know so
much about Romanian gangs?"

"After the Soviet Union broke up, some of the Romanian gangs
went international. A couple of them operate over here. When any
international gang comes into Boston, we work with the FBI."

My turn. "Any one gang in particular?"

"I'm getting to that, kid. My guess is that your new buddy, George,
is part of a Romanian gang that moved into Boston about five years
ago. Their home base is in Constanta in Romania. It's a port city on
the Black Sea. They're no choir boys, but they're not the Russian
mob either. My guess is that you thought this George was Russian
because you couldn't tell a Russian accent from a Romanian."

I found that less than comforting. The odds in favor of a quick
way out of this tangle for Terry and me just dropped a notch. Now
we had three gangs to juggle in dropping that hot potato.

I reached in my pocket and handed Mr. Coyne the driver's license of the unconscious Russian in Winthrop. I also gave him the
identification of the Russian gangster that I took off of his body in
Sinaia when he was killed by my rescuer, Mr. Chan, outside of the
violin-maker's shop. I explained how I got each of them.

He looked at them both for about fifteen seconds. He set them
down in front of him with something between a sigh and a groan.
The lines I was reading in his face were not comforting.

"Kid, you never bring me anything easy, do you?"

Lex leaned closer over the table. He was reading Mr. Coyne the same way I was. "What, Billy?"

Mr. Coyne looked directly at Mr. D. "This business just jumped to a new level."

He picked up the identification that I took in Sinaia. "This one I don't know. But I'll bet my pension he was a low-level thug connected with the Russian mob, probably sent by the boys in Moscow."

He picked up the driver's license from the man on the Andrew Street stake-out. "This one I know. This guy is not street scum. You got their attention, kid. He's with the Moscow mob, but he's local. Ivan Petrovitch. They've got a heavy presence here. Mostly around a section of Brighton."

My comfort level was draining. "You know him?"

"I know his work. He's one of their top assassins. You draw an elite class of enemies, kid. Maybe you should take another trip."

Lex jumped in. "That's not an answer, Billy. Can't you have this gangster picked up?"

"For what? The kid says he was just sitting in his car on a public street."

"How about stealing the dog?"

Billy shrugged. "To what end? Their lawyer'd have him out on bail before the ink was dry on his booking. This is a connected group." He looked at me. "Any chance the blow to the head killed him?"

"I think he was just unconscious. I don't know. Maybe. I swung hard."

"It doesn't matter. They'd just send another one practically as good as him. You stirred up one hell of a hornet's nest. Another trip is sounding better all the time. Let things cool."

Lex and I exchanged looks. He knew just what I was thinking. Leaving town was no answer as long as I had possession of the thing that had them all on red alert. If Terry and I were ever going to have our life back, it had to be faced head-on. My immediate problem was that the enemy was like Cerberus, the three-headed hound of Hades. Which head should I face first, while the other two had immediate plans for my life.

* * *

I left the Marliave with eyes in every direction. I couldn't detect anyone taking an inordinate interest in my whereabouts. That was no gold-plated guarantee, but it was the best I had to work with.

I had a few hours before meeting Harry Wong for dinner. Given all that was riding on it, I decided to give the "fiddle," as Mr. Coyne termed it, a bit more security. I found the FedEx store to which I had shipped it from Sophia. It seemed almost too easy to simply present identification and pick up something that three organized crime gangs would be willing to spill my blood over.

On the theory that an ounce of insurance might outweigh a pound of regret later on, I drove to a little known, but much loved, shop called "Broken Neck Guitar Repair" on Boylston Street near the Berklee College of Music. Lanny McLaughlin fixed me up with the rental of an expensive violin and case.

My next stop was the bank of large lockers in South Station. I chose one large enough for suitcases to stash the "Strad," as I'd begun calling it in my frequent thoughts. I tucked the rented violin and case into the locker beside the one holding the Strad, and left with both keys. At a local stationary store, I bought an envelope and mailed the key to the locker with the genuine Strad to myself at my office. I kept the other key in my pocket. Somehow, all of that juggling gave me a mild sense of pseudo security. As the saying goes, "When in doubt, do something, even if it's wrong."

* * *

It was getting close to the time to meet Harry Wong for dinner. Back in 1925, James Hook and his three sons set up a shack on a fish pier on the Boston waterfront to supply nearly every restaurant in town with those sublime prehistoric crustaceans as endemic to Boston cuisine as the bean. That small wooden edifice is surrounded today by state-of-the-art high-rise hotels and fine dining facilities, but when Harry Wong and I feel that irrepressible yen for boiled lobster done to a wicked perfection, we meet at the corner of Atlantic and Northern Avenues where our pal of many years, the third-generation Jimmy Hook, meets our needs as no one else can.

It was about quarter of six when I sat at one of the open-air tables a safe hearing distance from any of the other patrons. I knew that Harry, being fundamentally an MIT engineer, would arrive precisely at six. I kept the ever-lurking jitters suppressed by chatting with Jimmy Hook about the present state of lobsters off New England shores until Harry arrived—precisely at six.

Jimmy put in our standard order of two boiled lobsters each and two Sam Adamses, and went back to his office. Harry gave me a wary look, at which I just smiled.

"Michael, whatever unbelievable mess you've gotten yourself into this time, and there is one—I know that look—could we please keep Mrs. Wong's boy out of it?"

"Without question, Harry. The only thing on my mind is two good lobsters."

"Good."

"And a bit of information."

"Bad. I count three times now that what followed the 'information' nearly left Mrs. Wong childless."

"Harry, your mother passed away five years ago. God rest her."

"I'm aware of that, Michael. The point remains."

Our two Sam Adamses arrived. I raised my glass for a toast. "My friend, shall we drink to comradeship, like two musketeers—one for both and both for one."

Harry raised his glass, but before the clink, he raised his free hand. "Aha. But the fine point here is that my life never involves anything more dangerous than Boston traffic. May it stay that way. Whereas yours is more frequently out of control than anyone outside of a Lee Child novel."

"Point taken. A revised toast. Here's to a simple dinner and engaging conversation."

He raised his hand higher. "Conversation about what?"

"About the weather, about the Red Sox, about philosophy . . ."

Harry smiled. We clinked glasses. I finished, "About the tong, and in particular, about a man named Mr. Chan."

Harry's face froze. He lowered his glass. His voice was calm and steady, but I could feel the tension. "How do you know that man?"

I owed it to Harry to go first. Once again, I laid out every relevant detail of my odyssey involving the Strad. I paid particular attention to the details of Mr. Chan's appearance and his presence at the China Pearl dinner, and especially his saving of my life at the hands of two Russians in Sinaia.

Harry listened in silence, staring into his glass. When I finished, he just shook his head. There was no humor in his voice. "What do you need to know, Michael?"

"Anything you can tell me. Why is the tong interested in a violin? Why would a tong enforcer—I assume that's what he is—be in the dinner company of Mr. Liu? Of a banker? The concert master of the Boston Symphony Orchestra? And why would he save my life in Romania? Who is he?"

Harry sat back and rubbed his forehead. I could feel his conflict of emotions. I gave him time to sort out his thoughts. In about a minute, he leaned close to me and spoke in a tone so low I could barely hear it.

"I have no answer to most of those questions. You ask me about Mr. Chan. This takes me to a place I said I'd never go again. And I wouldn't. But I see why you need to know."

We were both startled by the presence of the waiter. He set two steaming lobsters in front of each of us, just screaming for cracking and immersing in sizzling butter.

When the waiter left, Harry leaned over. "Let's eat, Mike. It'll give me time to pull this together."

CHAPTER SIX

WE ATE IN virtual silence. When we finished, Harry said, "Let's walk down the pier."

We had it to ourselves. The only sound was the distant high-pitched screech of seagulls harvesting their evening catch of shiners.

I let Harry break the silence.

"The first time you got me involved in one of your escapades . . ."

"*Escapades*?"

"You want to tell this story, Mike?"

"Sorry. *Escapades* it is."

"Bear with me. I'm going down a path here I swore I'd never revisit."

"Take your time, Harry."

He stopped and leaned against the rail looking out to Boston Harbor. I stood close to catch every word without interrupting.

"The first time you brought me into one of these . . . cases, I had to give you some explanation of how I knew so much about the tong in Chinatown. It's no easier to say it now than it was then, but just listen. I need to put this in context.

"When I came over from China, from Hangzhou, I was twelve. We lived in an upstairs room on Tyler Street in Chinatown. My father was kept in China by the communists. My mother and grandmother were away all day working. After a while, I started hanging around a martial arts school down the street. I picked up the moves fast enough to get the attention of the recruiters for the tong. They brought me into their youth gang. I got the full initiation, blood-letting, secret oaths, all the ritual crap that goes with it. I was fourteen. I thought I was king of the hill.

"Then the reality set in. They used me like they use all the kids in the youth gang—to do their violent work. I was ordered to help put pressure on any of the shop owners who balked at paying *lomo*—lucky money—to the tong. When they paid, they were 'lucky' because they wouldn't be vandalized or burned out or worse by the youth gang.

"It was minor stuff at first—tipping over shelves, some spray paint, nothing that couldn't be undone if they paid. I'll admit it. I felt the power of the gang behind me, and I liked it.

"Then they needed to set their hooks into me permanently. There was old Chinese man. He scraped by on a little decrepit shop on Beach Street. He lived alone. Nothing in his life was anything but drudgery except for one thing. He had a glass fish tank of koi. It was the heart of his life. When he wouldn't pay extortion money to the tong, they sent me to teach him a lesson. One of the older kids in the gang stood there. He ordered me to smash the fish tank. It was hell. The old man was crying and pleading while they held him. He was yelling that he'd pay. Then the older kid with me said we had to send a message to the other shops. He handed me a brick and yelled the order. I can still hear the wailing coming from the old man's throat when I smashed the only thing he lived for.

"I ran out of there and kept running. I couldn't get away from the sound of his wailing. I ran, crying like a baby, until I just dropped.

"Every day that I saw the old man on the street after that, he looked closer to death. He died in about a month."

I could see in his face that Harry was reliving every emotion. I put my hand on his shoulder. "I remember you told me that, Harry. You don't have to . . ."

"Yes, I do. There's a part I didn't tell you. The head of the youth gang in those days was the man you mentioned, the one who saved you in Romania. We called him Mickey Chan. I remember him well. He seemed somehow above the rest of that bunch.

"I don't know why, but I felt he took a special interest in me. Maybe it was because I was on a track at school to go to college. The rest of those poor kids in the youth gang were on a dead-end road to nowhere.

"You may not understand what I'm about to say, but I understand it. That business with the old man's fish tank was a major crossroads in my life. I didn't realize it then, but Mickey Chan could see it. I'm sure in my heart that he wanted me out of that gang and away from the tong. What happened to the old man would have happened anyway, but Mickey made sure that I got the order to break that old man's heart."

Harry's words stopped flowing for a minute.

"How was that a favor, Harry?"

"Mickey knew that I was too caught up in the 'big-shot' feeling to leave on my own. He knew that when I followed the order to do the cruelest thing I could imagine, it would have one of two effects. If I was too far gone, I'd just live with it and go on. But if I was still worth saving, it would sicken me of that whole existence. I'd see that life for what it was. I'd do whatever it took to get out."

He stopped again. After all those years, I could see moisture in his eyes.

"I know which road you took. But how did you get the tong to let you out?"

"That man who saved your life, he saved mine too. Mickey Chan put his own life on the line by going to the number two man in the tong. The number one man, the Dragon Head, is only known to the number two man. No one else. Mickey pleaded for me to get them to break an unbreakable rule. I don't know what he said, or what he promised. I only know two things. I was permitted to leave, and Mickey Chan paid a price that I can't even imagine."

"What happened to him after that? I'm assuming he's still part of the tong."

Harry turned to me and just held up his hands. "I have no idea. I never heard his name spoken from that time to this."

I looked out at the ocean with thoughts tumbling around in my mind. My assumptions about Mr. Chan were undergoing some confused revision.

"Thank you, Harry. I know that wasn't easy. For what it's worth, you may have given me an insight that could possibly . . ."

He turned to look me in the eye. "Save your life?"

I just smiled. "Who knows?"

"Mike. What I said before about my getting involved in this. Don't underestimate the tong. They're a hell of a mean lot. If you need my help, I'm with you. All the way. Call me."

The handshake carried a lot more than courtesy.

* * *

It was a little after seven. I had more than two hours before meeting Mr. Liu in the Public Garden. I checked a copy of the *Globe*. The Boston Symphony Orchestra was playing a concert beginning at eight.

I found a parking spot on Mass. Avenue and walked around Symphony Hall to the entrance used by the musicians. My knock on the door brought an elderly keeper of the gate. I asked if I could see the concert master, Mr. Lee Tang. The firmness of his "No. Not before a concert" reminded me that getting to see the concert master of one of the most renowned classical music orchestras in the world during his warm-up before a concert was like dropping in cold for a chat with Bruce Springsteen, Tony Bennett, or Adele ten minutes before showtime—only more so.

I knew the timing was awkward, but my schedule was not exactly flexible. I handed the old gentleman my business card and asked him to just set it in front of Mr. Tang.

Within five minutes, the door opened. Mr. Tang, violin in hand, waived me in. "Mr. Knight. I have just a minute, but it's good to see you."

He led me to a small rehearsal room and closed the door behind us. He motioned to a chair with his bow and sat opposite me.

"Mr. Liu said you had some difficulty. He wasn't specific. Are you alright?"

I was a bit stunned by the fact that he asked for me and not the Strad. "Thank you. I'm fine. I know we have little time. Just a couple of questions, Mr. Tang."

"Certainly."

"What do you know about previous owners of the violin? Let me tell you why I'm asking. Mr. Liu's group is not the only one interested in it. In fact, the competition is . . . intense. At this point, believe me, if I just gave the violin to you, it would come with a bit of a curse. I need to find out why it's drawing more attention than just the one- or two-million-dollar price tag."

His expression said he was honestly perplexed, which led me to believe he had no part in the flaming intrigue.

"I'll tell you what I know. Mr. Liu contacted me during an orchestra tour in Eastern Europe. He said a group of Chinese businessmen were hoping to buy an authentic Stradivarius for my use with the orchestra. He asked me to meet with Mr. Oresciu in Romania. I believe you were to meet with him also."

"I did. Please go on."

"When I first met with Mr. Oresciu in his shop, the Stradivarius hadn't arrived for some reason. I came back two weeks later. Mr. Oresciu showed it to me then and asked me to play it to confirm that it was authentic."

"And it was?"

His eyes lit with emotion. "Beyond a doubt. If you could just hear—"

"Excuse me, Mr. Tang. I don't mean to be rude. We have very little time, and I have to ask. Do you know who owned the violin before it came to Mr. Oresciu."

"I naturally asked where he had found it."

He paused. I could see him trying to bring something back. "I remember him saying something that seemed odd at the time. Something like, 'Why think about that? It's here. Shall we enjoy the moment?' I'd have asked more, but he insisted that I play the instrument without delay. Needless to say, my mind was totally consumed by the tone of the violin. I never thought to ask again."

A rap on the door was followed by a voice, "Five minutes, Mr. Tang."

He held out his arms in a gesture of almost apology. We stood. He held out his free hand. "I wish I could be more help."

"Thank you for seeing me without notice. You've actually been more help than you realize."

"Good. May I offer you a seat for tonight's concert?"

"I truly wish I could. Duty calls."

Another knock on the door. "Yes. I'm coming."

Before he went out the door, I had the chance to say, "Mr. Tang."

He turned with a gracious smile.

"I'm an enormous fan."

The smile broadened. "Take good care of yourself, Mr. Knight."

Again, in a week of violence, I indulged myself in the warmth of someone's concern that went beyond the Strad.

Brief as that was, I'd learned two things. The first was that Mr. Tang was a total outsider to whatever was pulling three dicey gangs into a demolition derby over the Strad. My guess was that he was involved to lend legitimacy to a major Chinese bank's financial involvement in acquiring the Strad for the use of the Boston Symphony Orchestra. Mr. Tang was clearly the only one of that little clique at the China Pearl dinner who could authenticate the violin as a Strad.

I was also curious, as was Mr. Tang, about Mr. Oresciu's dodging of the question about prior owners of the violin, when he could simply have denied that he knew. That part was painful. I'd had a growing sense that at some point, I might have to dig into the previous ownership to find out what was attracting three crime gangs to a violin. If I had no other source, I might have to fly back to Romania to find Mr. Oresciu, if in fact he was still alive. That trip was not on my bucket list.

* * *

With all of my senses on full alert, I was still detecting no trace of anyone on my tail—Russian, Chinese, or otherwise. With unwarranted confidence in my security, at nine twenty, I walked across Boston Common. I took the path through Boston Garden that led to the swan boat dock for my meeting with Mr. Liu.

In the moonless illumination of dim lampposts, I sat on the empty bench in front of the dock. Over the next ten minutes the number of people passing on the path by the bench dwindled from few to zero. The only sound was the slogging of water against the side of the closest swan boat tied to the dock about thirty feet away.

That place, where I had never experienced anything but joy since my childhood rides with my parents on the swan boats, began to take on a disturbing creepiness. Mr. Liu was late, and he was the one who seemed to want the meeting as if his life depended on it.

I gave it another ten minutes with my eyes on both directions of the path. Nothing. I was getting an uneasy feeling that by standing still, I was risking rediscovery by the Russians.

In one final bit of nostalgia before calling it quits, I focused on the silhouette of the closest swan boat instead of the path. I could look back through the years and see my mother, father, and me on the front row of benches in the boat, throwing crackers to the ducks.

The more I looked in that scant light, something was wrong. The shape of the boat's silhouette was off. I focused harder and realized that someone was sitting in the rear where the driver would pedal the boat. He seemed to be staring at me in total silence.

I walked slowly down the dock toward the boat. My wishful thinking was that it was Mr. Liu. When I got close enough, I called his name. Nothing.

I reached the edge of the boat. The tiny light bulb on the dock picked up the outline of a figure sitting like a puppet propped up in a chair. I edged closer until I could just make out features. In an instant of recognition, I felt the air rush out of my lungs. I could see Mr. Liu facing me. His eyes were like the dead eyes of a mannequin. I climbed over the side into the boat and moved to within a few feet of him.

The rest happened in a moment. It's still a blur. In one instant I was skidding on some sticky fluid on the floorboard and catching a flash look at a gash that ran from his ear to the other side of his throat. In the next fraction of an instant, I suffered a hit in the ribs like Tom Brady catching the shoulder of a three-hundred-pound charging lineman. It knocked the wind out of my lungs and propelled me over the far rail of the boat. At that same moment, I heard something like the crack of a gunshot.

There was no time to brace before hitting the water. I went straight down, totally submerged. Two massive arms like steel bands drove me to the bottom. They held me under until I thought my lungs would burst.

I could feel my body being thrust forward through the water as if by a swimmer's strokes. I was just beginning to lose consciousness, when a fist clutched the back of my shirt. It thrust me upward. My head cleared the surface. I was gasping for air, when I felt an iron hand over my mouth.

I heard the whispered words, "Quiet! If you want to live."

I did what I could to muffle the sound of my gasping breaths, but my lungs were uncontrollably trying to suck in air. The sound must have carried. Another muffled gunshot sent something so close to my ear that my breathing stopped by itself.

The hand from behind pushed me back under the water. Slowly, silently, we moved through the water along the bank of the pond another twenty feet before it let go of my neck. My head bobbed above the water for a quick gasp of air. I heard the voice whisper, "Stay here. Stay down."

I was aware of the body beside me lifting itself silently onto the bank and moving like a low shadow toward the trees behind the bench I'd been on. I stayed there frozen in silence until I heard a snap that sounded like bone on bone. The air was silent again.

Within ten seconds, a face was down beside mine. The same voice was whispering. "Get out of the pond. Move fast. Don't trust anyone."

I sputtered out, "Wait. Who the hell are you? Why . . .?"

He stood up. Before he turned, a dim beam from a lamppost caught his face. He was gone before I could call him by the name Harry Wong had given me—Mickey Chan.

CHAPTER SEVEN

I PULLED MY dripping body out of the pond almost as fast as I'd gone into it. Against every impelling urge to do a hundred-yard dash to the underground parking lot in Boston Common where I'd left the car, I stopped to look behind the bench where I'd been sitting. The gunshots had come from that direction, as well as the bone-snapping sound when Mickey Chan disappeared.

The bushes behind the bench covered all but the legs of a prone, still body. I pulled back a few branches that covered the torso and head, joined by a neck that had an unnatural twist. There was a handgun still clenched in the right hand.

I risked leaving fingerprints to pull the wallet out of the back pocket. I put the money back, left the gun, and took the wallet.

The sound of running footsteps made for a quick decision. It could be the Russians. Not good. It could be the police after hearing gunshots. Also not good. I was there alone between two obviously murdered bodies. At best, if it were the police, I'd spend the night at the station answering questions—to which I would have no convincing answers. That would also make me a sitting duck for reattachment of my Russian shadows.

I followed my instincts and cut a rapid retreat through the bushes and across the grass on a roundabout route across Charles Street to the parking lot.

I drove straight up Route 1 and checked into the Towne Plaza Motel in Danvers. I needed a bit of respite on neutral ground. A long call to Terry in New Hampshire had just the calming effect I needed for a night's sleep.

In the morning, I bought a set of clothes on the way back into Boston to replace the ones I'd taken for a night swim. Fresh clothes, two Dunkin Donuts, and a large black coffee stiffened with two shots of espresso recharged my drained battery for what could be an "interesting" day.

Before my morning meeting with George at eleven on the Prudential Skywalk, I needed to get a new read on how many thugs, and of what ethnicity, I had to watch for over my shoulder. I parked on Newbury Street close to the Prudential. Mr. Devlin was still in his office when I dialed his direct number. After I gave him a quick update on the Public Garden episode, which did not sit well with his paternal concern for his junior partner, he called Billy Coyne's secure number and made it a three-way.

"Where were you last night, kid? The bodies are still mounting up. You know anything about that?"

"And the very top of the morning to you too, Mr. Coyne. I think we might do each other some good this morning. Shall we trade some information?"

"Damn, Lex. Now I've got to deal with two of you Irish horse-traders. Go ahead, kid. You lay down your cards first. Then we'll see."

"No time for games this morning, Mr. Coyne. Your police found two bodies in Public Garden last night. I need to know something you might know. And vice versa."

There was a pause. "Keep talking, kid. No promises."

"One of the bodies was a middle-age Chinese man. The other was a gangster. Probably Russian. You found no identification on the latter. I may be able to help you there."

"Like you said, kid, no games. Can you identify the Russian, or not? And how the hell do you know him? Were you there last night?"

"One question at a time, Mr. Coyne. I'm going to give you this much on faith. The Russian behind the bench with the broken neck, his name was 'Sergei Brackovitch.'"

I was reading it off of the driver's license in the wallet I took from his dead body. I heard a low whistle on Mr. Coyne's end. I gave him a few seconds to put his words together.

"To hell with a hornet's nest, kid. You walked into a lion's den. Do you know who he is . . . was?"

"That's why I'm calling."

"Lex, you've got to put a leash on that partner of yours. He is so far out of his league . . ."

"Say it, Billy. What?"

"How do I say this in words you'll take to heart, kid? Brackovitch has been on our radar for years. The Russian mob in Boston answers to the mob in Moscow. Even the Italian mafia doesn't mess with this bunch. This Brackovitch, he was their top assassin. Cold as a clam. Unlike some in his profession, this one's intelligent. We've been after him for a string of murders. Never laid a glove on him."

"Where do these Russians operate? Do they have a center in Boston?"

"Wait a minute, kid. Still my turn. Someone obviously put him out of business last night, at close range. Not an easy move. Whoever did it could be my next most wanted. What do you know about it?"

"Nothing I could attest to. I didn't see it happen. Back to my turn. Where does this Russian mob hang out?"

"They're spread out. After the Soviet Union dissolved, the Russian borders opened up. We got a flood of Russians coming in. Most of them good people. Mixed in were a bunch of the worst gangsters on the planet. Some of them former KGB. They centered on Brighton Beach in New York, but we got more than our share around Boston."

"Where?"

"Lot of places. Mostly Lynn, Chestnut Hill, Newton. Even out in Springfield. Nearly as we can tell, the string-pullers are centered in Brighton, our Brighton."

"Where in Brighton?"

Mr. Coyne paused. "Lex, this loose cannon you have for a partner. If I tell him, is he going to go marching in the front door? People have been killed for less."

"Tell him where, Billy. At least we'll know what to avoid."

"This comes with a warning, kid. Stay the hell away from there. You hear me?"

I gave him the sincerest "I hear you" I could muster.

He lowered his voice. "What I hear . . . the Moscow Café. It's on Beacon, near Market Street. Rumor says—and it's just a rumor—it's like what Angelo's in the North End is to the Italian mafia. People have gone in there and never come out."

"What are you doing about it?"

"Damn little. In that neighborhood, nobody talks, in English or Russian."

That was more than I wanted to hear. I tried to force down the unpleasant premonition that as things were moving, I might someday find myself on the wrong side of the Moscow Café door.

Mr. Coyne picked it up. "The Chinese man who was shot last night in the swan boat. What do you know about that?"

"His name is Mr. Liu. He was the head of the Chinese Merchants Association in Chinatown. He was the one who sent me to Romania for that violin."

"What's his connection with the Russians?"

"I wish I knew."

"Then tell me everything you know about this man who killed him."

"I have no idea who . . . Wait a minute. You ask that like you know who did it."

"Possibly. And every angle I look at with this business, there you are right in the middle of it. Suppose you tell me why the boys in Chinatown wanted him dead."

"What boys in Chinatown? How do you know it was the tong?"

"I'd like to remind you, kid, you're talking to the deputy district attorney. If you have any information about this, you have a legal obligation—"

Mr. D. jumped in. "Oh, for the love of God, stop the official bull-crap, Billy. You're getting as much as you're giving here. Give us an answer."

Billy dropped his voice.

"This goes no further . . ."

"We know that, Billy. It never has. Now answer the question."

"We got a phone tip this morning. Called herself Ming Tan. She has a Chinese grocery shop on Tyler Street in Chinatown. She was walking through Public Garden last night. She saw the man who killed the man you say was Mr. Liu."

"Did she know the killer?"

"Apparently he's known to people in Chinatown."

"Did she give a name?"

"Yeah. Chan. People call him 'Mickey.'"

That was unsettling. I was still trying to get the cast of characters divided between the sheep and the goats. That further blurred both categories. The one thing I knew for certain was that I owed my life twice to the man I knew as Mickey Chan.

* * *

My pledge of confidentiality to Mr. Coyne was a restraint I had to keep in mind. I owed that to both Mr. Coyne and Mr. Devlin. I was walking a tightrope when I called Harry Wong.

"That was fast, Mike. What do you need?"

"I know how sensitive this is, Harry. Believe me, I wouldn't ask if..."

"We've been down this road. Whatever it is, I said I was in. Just say it."

"I need to talk to Mickey Chan."

I could hear the air intake on the line. I filled the pause. "I have no idea how to reach him. I know you haven't seen him in years. Thin as it is, you're my only connection."

Harry's voice was more tense than I'd ever heard it. "Why?"

"I wish I could tell you. I can't."

"Just tell me that it's important enough to have me do something I swore I'd never do in this life."

I gave it a second's thought before I said all I could disclose in two words. "It is."

I gave Harry the silence he needed. He said all he could say in three words. "I'll call you."

* * *

It was time to ride the elevator up to the fiftieth floor of the Prudential Building to what's called the Skywalk. It's a tourist's Mecca with glass walls on four sides of the entire floor. It has a view like the Eiffel Tower. On a clear day, you can almost see the Eiffel Tower.

I was early, but I wanted to be there when the man I knew as George arrived. I also decided to take out a bit of insurance. I called

Mr. Devlin back and caught him just before he left for court. He had a thousand questions after our conversation with Mr. Coyne. Most of them led to direct orders to keep my vulnerable body parts out of dangerous situations. Since I could imagine no future in which that was likely to happen, I gave him my usual assurance that I'd do my best to stay out of harm's way.

Without raising further alarms, I let Mr. D. know that I was about to meet the man called George on the Skywalk. There was some comfort to both of us in Mr. Coyne's guess that he was probably Romanian instead of Russian *mafioso*. I promised a text message that Mr. D. could receive quietly in court as soon as I reached the ground floor intact after the meeting. It probably did nothing for his peace of mind, but having someone in my corner know my whereabouts most certainly helped mine.

My eyes scanned the area when I stepped off the elevator on the fiftieth floor. There were enough tourists clustered in groups at various points around the glass walls to give me comfort. At the same time, there were plenty of empty patches at the windows for a private conversation.

I had a rough mental image of George from his voice on the phone. None of the people absorbed in their audio guides met the image.

As always, I was first drawn to a spot on the west wall to pay homage to the view of Fenway Park—also as always, with a silent prayer for the spirits that still hover there, some alive, others now playing on a different field of dreams. The Splendid Splinter, Ted Williams, always leads off, but Carl—Yaz—Yastrzemski, and lately Big Papi Ortiz get their share. The list goes back beyond my years to my father's tales of the Babe himself.

I felt a gentle jarring from the approaching voices of some young tourists that broke the spell. I moved along the glass wall willingly.

I felt they should not return to wherever was home without absorbing that view.

I found a position at the glass with a ten-foot open space facing northeast. My eyes oscillated between our home on the shore in Winthrop and a constant check on the door of the elevator.

At eleven sharp, a small group stepped off the elevator. It included one who would have been a natural for the role of my imagined vision of George. He was also the only one not to spare a glance at the view. His total attention was given to scanning the scattered crowd. I was a bit jarred when his first look in my direction brought an instant smile of recognition. It was jarring because I was certain we had never seen each other before.

He walked directly over and introduced himself with one word. "George."

I responded in kind. "Michael."

"Yes, indeed. May this be the beginning of a fruitful and trusting friendship."

"Along that line, I seem to be one step behind."

"Oh?"

"'Michael' is my real name, as I'm sure you know."

"Would it surprise you to know that 'George' is my real name?"

I matched his smile. "It would surprise me. But then you also know my last name."

"I think we'll leave the name game where it is. For the moment. On the other hand, Michael, I do want your trust. You have an important decision to make, and to make soon. To whom do you give the object in question? Yes?"

I was struck by the fact that, for the first time, one of the contestants actually suggested that the decision was mine to make. "In terms of trust, George, I notice that you came alone. You scored points there. I'm sure you know that I came alone."

He moved to the window by my right side and seemed to take an interest in the view. His voice dropped to a whisper. "Perhaps not as alone as you think you are."

"Meaning?"

"You have a definite magnetism for members of a certain Russian organization. Don't look immediately. Two young muscular men beside the group of tourists. Twenty feet to your left. Black hair, average height. One tan sport coat, the other a gray sweater on this hot day. What do you suppose they conceal?"

I gave it a few seconds and looked slowly to my left. He was right. They stood out, if you knew what you were looking for.

I could feel a chill set in. "Damn. How could I have missed them?"

"You didn't. They just came up on the same elevator with me. Don't worry about them."

"Thank you for the advice, but they're probably after me, not you."

"They are. Just smile and listen to me." His voice dropped another notch. "I'm sorry that time doesn't permit me to build your trust more slowly. You can appreciate the urgency. It's time you understood the importance of the decision you're about to make. We need to talk. Not here."

He looked straight into my eyes. The smile was gone. "I leave it to you. I have a car waiting. Will you summon enough trust to join me for lunch at the restaurant of my choice? The chef is Romanian. He is beyond excellent. More to the point, we'll be able to speak in complete privacy."

He paused. I had no immediate answer.

"I promise you this. You'll be free to leave at any moment you choose. Your decision. Will you come with me now?"

I knew my options were limited. Staying there with the Russians stood out as the worst choice. Making a run on my own seemed like

the second worst, given that the Russians seemed to have little difficulty in reattaching themselves. That left George.

I nodded slightly in the direction of the two Russians. "What
about them?"

"As I say. Don't worry about them. Let me do you a personal favor
as one more assurance of my good faith."

He inched a cell phone out of his pocket. He tapped a few keys. It
was like watching a plan come together. From four different corners, I watched four men drift generally in our direction. One by
one they appeared to wander until the four were assembled like a
wall surrounding the two Russians.

I heard a quiet, "Let's go." George moved in the direction of the
elevator. Just as I began to follow, I saw the two Russians make a
quick turn together. I noticed the lips of one of the four move. The
Russians froze in place. They seemed to be following an order when
they both turned back slowly to focus on the view outside.

George was holding the door of the elevator from the outside for
me to go in.

"You chose wisely, Michael."

"What would you have done if I hadn't? Left me to work it out
with the Russians?"

He paused as if he were looking for words. "There would be no
'working it out' with these people. You've been lucky so far. More
than you know. Those two at the window. They're both former
KGB. They're professionals in ways you don't want to think about.
They would surpass your pain threshold very quickly. You'd give
them anything you own."

"And then they'd kill me?"

He held his answer while I walked inside and turned to face him.
As I passed, he whispered with no smile. "If you were lucky."

CHAPTER EIGHT

I WAITED FOR George to slip into the elevator beside me. Instead, he held the door open from the outside. We were alone, but he still spoke in a whisper.

"You'll be met downstairs. My man will take you to the car."

"You're not coming?"

"In a minute. I have a bit of business to finish. I'll meet you at the car."

On the ride down, my imagination ran full throttle over what his "bit of business" might be. I could only assume that it involved the unenviable future of the two Russians.

By the time the elevator passed the forty-fifth floor on the way down, I had reached a firm conclusion that my trust in George allowed space for some control of my own destiny. I hit a speed dial number on my cell phone. Over the past four years, when obligations to my clients led me into dark corners, my second resort, immediately after prayer, was to Thomas D. Burns, a private security operative, as he preferred to be called, whose fees would be seen as obscene but for the fact that they were worth every cent.

"Michael, my lad. What craziness are you up to this time?"

"I wish I knew, Tom."

"Probably putting your neck on the block again for some ungrateful client. If I could give you one piece of—"

"Tom! Stop talking. Just listen. I have about one minute. I'm coming down the Skywalk elevator. I'm being met and taken for a ride to some Romanian restaurant. I have no idea where."

"Who's forcing you?"

"It's voluntary. I think. I want to be sure it stays that way. Can one of your boys put a tail on me? I can stall for just a few minutes."

I hit the stop button for one of the floors above ground level. I was alone on the elevator. When the door opened, I held it open.

"No sweat, Mike. I have a man close by. He'll pick you up when you leave the building. As soon as you know which exit, send me a one-word text—*north* or *south*. Give him three more minutes. Now, tell me more."

"It'd take me a half hour to fill you in. I'll be with a man in his sixties, gray hair, a little hefty. The idea is lunch and a chat. I want insurance that someone knows where I am in case it becomes more than that."

"Rest easy. You'll be on my radar as soon as you leave the building."

"You fulfill my every wish. Very important that your man stay out of sight."

"Mikey! What the hell! Do you think you dialed the wrong number?"

"I'm sorry, Tom. I know. You're the best there is. And so are your men. I just needed to say it. My lunch date is a godfather of some Romanian crime gang. As we speak, my guess is he's personally arranging the demise of two ex-KGB killers. Oddly enough, I'm not totally comfortable."

"You do keep the strangest circle of friends."

"They say you can never have too many friends."

"In your case, there's an exception."

"I'll keep that in mind. Okay. Here goes, Tom. Last few floors. Is your man ready?"

"You're covered. Go easy. If things get dicey at lunch, hit the speed-dial. Give me one ring. It'll be like the Marines landing on Okinawa."

A man in black pants and a black shirt was waiting when the elevator door opened. He bowed slightly. As nearly as I could understand through his accent, he was pleased to meet me, and asked me to follow him.

Within a block, I was stepping into the nicely air-conditioned back seat of a black Lincoln Continental. Within another two minutes, the other half of the back seat was occupied by my smiling host.

He said a few words to the driver in Romanian and settled back. "I suggest we relax and enjoy the ride through this beautiful city."

I nodded. As we approached the first traffic light, my host spoke again to the driver—this time in English, I assume for my benefit. "Drive slowly, Gregor. Don't rush the traffic lights."

He turned to me. "We don't want to make it difficult for your man to follow us."

I was about to make a pointless denial. George held up his hand and smiled. "Relax, Michael. There is nothing secretive about where we're going. It's for lunch, remember?"

I had to know, if only to burst Tom Burns' bubble. "How did you spot him?"

The smile was still there. "I didn't. Your man's very good. You can tell him I said so."

"Then how did you know?"

"Two things. Your elevator took three minutes longer than usual to reach the ground floor. I could only assume you used the time efficiently."

"And the second thing?"

"Hah. It's exactly what I would have done. I think neither of us would have lived to this age in our particular businesses without attention to details. Yes?"

I sat back. I was beginning to smile myself. For some reason, I was becoming comfortable in George's company.

* * *

The décor of the Wallachia Café on Centre Street in West Roxbury was warm, relaxed, and distinctly eastern European. The traditional Romanian garb on the bartender and waiters was colorful, but not overdone.

It was clear that George was on his home turf. Within two minutes, every employee in the house found a reason to come by and welcome him.

After an effusive greeting to both of us, the maître d' escorted us to a small, warmly appointed, private dining room to the rear of the restaurant. George was truly in his "Marliave," being treated like Lex Devlin.

An older waiter delivered a basket of bread that could not have been out of the oven over a minute. He placed an unlabeled dark glass bottle in front of George with two glasses. Waving off the waiter's offer to pour, George removed the carved glass top and held the bottle over my glass.

"There is no better way for a Romanian to welcome a guest than to pour liberally from our national libation. Have you ever sampled *tuica*?"

"Never. I like the aroma."

"Ah. That's a mere beginning. *Tuica* is the purest essence of plums, as they can only be grown in our own Romanian soil. To offer it to a guest, particularly for the first time, is to offer our souls in friendship. May I?"

"My pleasure. My honor."

"The honor is mine."

He poured, as he suggested, liberally, for both of us. We raised and touched our glasses with our eyes locked together. And we sipped.

The aroma that reached my nostrils first suggested that the alcoholic content of *tuica* had to exceed fifty percent. That first sip placed the estimate over sixty percent. The taste and texture, however, were as smooth and cushioned on the palate as the finest Vermont maple syrup. One sip led to a second, and a third, until a faint but distinct buzz reminded me that I needed every brain cell intact for what might follow.

What did follow was a procession of courses that could only have originated in the heart of a country that took the culinary arts seriously. My vocabulary and my girth grew simultaneously.

Words and delicacies passed my lips such as *mezeluri*—salami, sausages, and cheese; *ciorba*—soup spiced with the tang of sauerkraut sauce; *sarmali*—stuffed cabbage; *frigarui*—chicken kebabs; *mamaliga*—polenta with sour cream and shredded goat cheese.

The flavor of each morsel was lifted to new heights by another sip of the insidiously smooth *tuica*.

The final blow to any doubt I could possibly have had about Romanian food was the rum-soaked *savarina* under a blanket of freshly whipped heavy cream.

We spoke of nothing from appetizer to dessert, and when the last drop of *tuica* was poured, George settled back and caught my eye. I realized from his tone that everything to that point was prelude. "Do I have your attention, Michael?"

"You do."

"That's important. It's more important than you realize. You have no understanding of what you're involved in. That's why we're here."

I turned to face him directly. "In the last week, I've been that close to being killed four times. My wife was kidnapped and threatened with death. My home was broken into. My dog beaten and stolen. Three people have been murdered. I'm still in the crossfire of three crime gangs. And all of it over a damn violin. It's been a curse since I first touched it. If you can give me a clue as to why, then you definitely have my full attention."

He wiped his lips, from which the smile was gone. "Tell me, what do you know about Dracula?"

My disappointment at where this was going must have shown in my tone. "Ahh. You mean the vampire? Bela Lugosi? Bram Stoker's novel about the so-called 'undead.' All that stuff about garlic necklaces and wooden stakes and . . . ?"

He held up his hand. "No. None of that. I'm talking about the real Dracula, flesh and blood, a very real person in our history. What do you know about him?"

I was somewhat relieved by that turn. "Practically nothing. In fact, absolutely nothing. I didn't know he existed."

"Then listen carefully. It might begin to explain what you've been going through."

He sat back, took a healthy sip of *tuica*, restored eye contact, and began.

"This man called Dracula. The word means 'Son of the Dragon' in Romanian. It also means 'Son of Satan.' He can be defined by three extremes. To most people in his time, he was the embodiment of the most unspeakable, inhuman evil the devil himself could inflict on his victims. Perhaps so. To the Christian people of Wallachia, the Romanian province he ruled, he was . . . no less than a Christian saint, worthy of a saint's burial in the center of an Orthodox

Christian monastery on the river island of Snagov. For the third extreme, we have history, where he is, as you can attest, almost entirely forgotten. Perhaps his reality has been eclipsed by the vampire myths.

"Dracula ruled with the most powerful weapon of subjugation—abject fear. He made use of every extreme practice of sadistic torture conceivable. There were no prisons in his kingdom. Nor any need. The mere suspicion of disloyalty to the prince meant an excruciating death.

"The name, 'Dracula,' was a title. He was known during his reign by his true name, Vlad—Vlad Tepes—Vlad the Impaler. He earned the title. His personal method of execution was to drive a sharpened wooden stake through the victim's torso, entering the lowest natural opening of the body and exiting at a small point in the neck. The stake was then driven into the ground with the victim suspended. His genius was to avoid puncturing any vital organ. Vlad could then enjoy at his leisure the three or more hours or days of suffering it would take for the blood to drain the life out of his suspended victim.

"When his pleasure had ended, Dracula would have the dead bodies removed from the stakes and cast into the river. The bodies would drift downstream to the villages below. They'd be pulled out by villagers who would find these dead bodies, completely drained of blood, with no visible wound but a small hole in their necks where the impaling stake came through. This was the 1450s. What conclusion do you suppose superstitious people in those dark times came to about the prince upstream?"

"A vampire."

"Exactly. The 'undead', who supposedly lived on by sucking the blood out of his victims. Those people were not without imagination. As the legend grew, details were filled in. The vampire lives and kills in the dark of night. He seals himself in a casket during the day to avoid the sun. A clove of garlic around the neck or a Christian cross can drive him away. He can only be killed by driving a wooden stake through his heart. The whole fantasy was ripe for Bram Stoker four hundred years later to turn it into a novel. From that point on, the memory of the flesh and blood Dracula was all but submerged under the tales of the vampire."

"I understand."

"I think not. Not yet. Not the depth of his sadistic depravity. On one occasion, Dracula invited hundreds of *boyars*, the aristocracy of his province, to his palace in his capital of Tirgoviste. He trusted none of them. He sensed that they were taking his absolute reign lightly. It's told that with his eyes flashing with delight, he gave an order. The hall was surrounded. Over five hundred *boyars*, as well as their wives, children, and attendants, were immediately impaled and left to the ravage of blackbirds."

"Unbelievable."

"No, quite believable. The stories abound. Envoys of the Turkish Sultan once brought the official greetings of the Sultan to his throne hall. When they bowed to him, they refused to remove their turbans. He asked them why they would so insult a great ruler. They said it was the unbreakable custom of their country. Dracula replied, 'I wish to strengthen your law so that you may be even more firm in your custom.' He ordered that their turbans be nailed to their heads. Once done, he sent them back to the Sultan with the message that while the Sultan might be accustomed to enduring such shame, he was not."

"I'm beginning to get the point."

"Then I'll spare you any further details. But rest assured, I have scarcely scratched the surface of the ingenuity of his sadistic delights."

"You mentioned another extreme. You said he was regarded as some kind of Christian saint by his people."

"Exactly, and given a saint's burial."

"Your people have an imaginative definition of a saint?"

"Perhaps. But you have to understand the times. Dracula's longest reign ran from 1456 to 1462. In the spring of 1462, Sultan Mehmed II invaded Wallachia. His plan was to turn the Christian province into a part of his growing Muslim Turkish empire.

"The Sultan led his army across the Danube. Dracula knew he was outmanned. He began strategic retreats to draw the Sultan deeply into his territory. As Dracula moved further back into the Carpathian Mountains, he actually burned each of his own cities. He poisoned their wells, killed all of his people's cattle. He left nothing for the Turks to eat or drink in the midst of the most intense heat of the scorching sun.

"During his retreat, Dracula even dressed some of his people who were infected with diseases like leprosy, bubonic plague, and tuberculosis in the clothing of the Turks. He sent them into the Turkish ranks to spread the diseases. Probably the first use of germ warfare. By the time the Turks reached Vlad's capital of Tirgoviste, the plague had broken out widely among the Turkish soldiers."

"And that won the day?"

"No. It was a factor. But what ultimately penetrated the heart of the Sultan, what actually drove him to withdraw from the attack, was a sight that you and I can't even imagine. When the Turkish army passed through the smoking desolation of that abandoned city, stretched out ahead of them was a mile-long gorge, lined on both sides with more than *twenty thousand* impaled corpses. The Sultan realized that he could never win victory over a man who could do such things."

I was stunned. I had no words. I think George, who had probably heard these stories from childhood, was silenced for the moment himself.

The first thought that I could express was, "And this is your idea of a saint?"

"Not mine. But think of the times. This Christian country was about to be overrun by the Muslim Turks. Christianity itself was in danger. Whatever his methods, he stopped it."

"Somehow, I still can't . . ."

"There's more to the story. Earlier, in 1453, the center of the Roman Empire, Constantinople, had been taken by the Muslim Ottoman army under the same Sultan Mehmed II. Pope Pius II saw the twenty-one-year-old sultan as a disastrous threat to the entire Christian world. He made an urgent call at the Council of Mantua to all of the Christian leaders to join his crusade against the Turks. The other leaders pitched in with kind words. Nothing more. Dracula was the only one to pledge his full support to the pope's crusade, military and financial."

I think George could see by my expression that I was still not about to begin praying to this particular "saint." He added one last point.

"He was a complex figure. For example, after he killed one of his mistresses by impaling her for infidelity to him, he provided for the survival of her soul in the afterlife by giving her a full Christian burial."

"How sweet of him. Does this smack of hypocrisy, to use a kind word?"

George was able to smile. "Of course. But he was consistent in this respect. He always surrounded himself with priests, confessors, bishops. He built monasteries and endowed them heavily. These were pre-Lutheran times. People thought that good works and a proper ritual at the time of death could wipe out a multitude of sins."

George looked at my questioning expression. He laughed. "Fear not, Michael. I'm not trying to bring you into his camp."

"Good. You haven't."

"So why did I tell you this distressing tale? There is one point I haven't mentioned. When the Turks entered Tirgoviste, they found it totally abandoned. They also found something else missing. For the six years of Dracula's reign over Wallachia, he extracted immense tribute from his Wallachian people. He received lavish gifts from neighboring rulers—even the Turkish Sultan. His capital city was incredibly rich in holy relics and artistic treasures.

"But, when the Turks arrived, every speck of that immeasurable treasure was gone. Dracula, Vlad Tepes, had taken it all."

"Taken it where?"

"As always, you go directly to the jugular, Michael. To this day, it has never been found."

CHAPTER NINE

THIS TIME I took a healthy sip of the *tuica*.

"At last, a ray of light."

"Indeed."

On the other hand, the thought of an immeasurable treasure at the root of the past week's intrigue only flooded my mind with more questions. George sat back and waited for the floodgates to burst open.

"I don't know which question to ask first."

"Start anywhere you like. I'll tell you anything I know."

I took a minute to let my mind sort out the logjam. George gave me the moments in silence.

"Let's start with the obvious. I take it I'm in the crossfire of three gangs because of some hope of finding Dracula's hidden treasure. So far, so good?"

"So far, absolutely. No question. Go on."

"And the treasure is somewhere in Romania."

"Possibly."

"Dead end there, I see. Do you actually know where it is? Do any of the three gangs know where it is?"

"If any did, it would be long gone, and you'd cease to be the center of attention. Maybe even cease to be at all, depending on the gang. I think you know that."

"Then that brings us back to that damn violin. Is that the connection?"

George leaned back and smiled. "Now you're asking the right question."

He took a small sheaf of papers out of his suitcoat pocket and set them on the table between us, facedown.

"Do I read these?"

"In a minute. Let me fill in some pieces. We're dealing with a span of centuries."

He rapped on the table. A waiter appeared within moments. George held up the empty bottle of *tuica* with a questioning look to me. I considered the buzz already ringing in my consciousness and opted for coffee. What came in a steaming cup was strong enough to walk on, and a potent antidote to the buzz.

The waiter withdrew and closed the door. We were again alone, but George still kept his tone low.

"What I'm going to tell you is part history, part legend, part folk-lore, and part guessing at missing pieces. Remember, we're going back to 1462."

"Understood."

"Let's start with the guesswork. First, as far as we know, Dracula never left today's Romania during the time we're talking about—in particular, the provinces of Wallachia and Transylvania. Secondly, the treasure most likely represented a large physical bulk. He couldn't have taken it far without drawing attention to it. Thirdly, no one has yet discovered where he stashed it."

"How do you know? It's been about five centuries."

"I think you still underestimate the size and value and artistic extent of this treasure. Believe me, if it had been found, it would have been a major event in history."

"Fair enough."

"So what do we know? Dracula's treasure was safe where he had it in his capital, Tirgoviste, until Sultan Mehmed invaded his province of Wallachia in 1462. As I told you, Dracula and some of his faithful fled north toward Transylvania. Mehmet himself gave up the chase in Tirgoviste, but he sent some of his soldiers after Dracula.

"Dracula made it to what's now known as Dracula's Castle on the Wallachian side of the Arges River. The Turkish soldiers caught up with him. They set up a camp around the castle. A Romanian slave of the Turks, one of Dracula's distant relatives, fired an arrow into a window of the castle with a warning note that the Turks would attack at dawn. Dracula escaped by a narrow stairway carved out of the stone in the middle of the castle. It was just large enough for one man to pass. You can still see it there today. It spiraled down into the mountain to a tunnel that put him beyond the Turkish attackers. The townspeople met him and a few of his men with fast horses for their escape. They had even nailed the horseshoes on backward to leave a false trail."

"Did he escape?"

"Yes and no. He managed to cross the impossible Transylvanian Alps to get to his supposed ally, the Hungarian King Matthias. Matthias was ruling Transylvania at the time. You know the words, 'the best laid plans of mice and men aft gang aglay.'"

"John Steinbeck."

"Robert Burns, actually. Matthias had a secret alliance with the Turks. He immediately took Dracula prisoner."

"Bummer."

"Depends on your sympathies. The point is this. It's inconceivable that Dracula would leave behind nothing but scorched earth for the Turks, and yet leave them his greatest treasure. From the time he fled Tirgoviste, he could have taken it with him as far as his castle. When he fled the castle down that narrow winding staircase and rode for his life, there is no way he could have carried the treasure."

"Someone else possibly?"

"Highly unlikely he would have trusted anyone else with his treasure. Not in his nature."

"Are you guessing it's hidden in the castle?"

"Also unlikely. Over the past five and a half centuries, every inch of that castle has been searched."

"You're saying he hid it between Tirgoviste and his castle."

George raised his hands to say, "What other conclusion is possible?"

"But where?"

"That question, my friend, has three very well-armed and determined organizations giving you more attention than you might be enjoying."

"And this relates how to that violin?"

"Ah, that's another story. From the time—"

He was cut off in mid-sentence by a few quick raps on the door and the entrance of our driver before George could respond. The driver came at quick-step to George's side. He whispered in Romanian. It was a bit like wearing a belt and suspenders. He could have been shouting and I'd still have been clueless.

George rose immediately and turned to me. "Michael, come. I want you to see this."

We walked back into the bar area of the restaurant. The tension among the men in the room was at least at level ten. I saw a man I didn't notice there before being held from behind by a large member of George's retinue. One of George's men pointed to a backpack sitting on the floor by the bar. George spoke to the man being held in what sounded like Russian. There was no answer.

George came over to me. "This man is with that Russian gang that seems attracted to you. He came in and ordered a drink at the bar."

"Don't you serve Russians?"

"Yes, of course. They even eat here. But not this one. That backpack by the bar. He left it on the floor when he started to leave."

"What's in it?"

"My guess is enough explosive to blow us all to Bucharest."

"This doesn't make sense, George. If I get blown to pieces with the rest of you, no one will know where that violin is."

"Actually, it does make sense. They must have someone outside with the triggering device. Probably in a car. They'll wait for you and this man to leave. Then they eliminate us. The competition. Probably take you captive."

"What do you plan to do?"

George shrugged. "Let them have their way. Up to a point."

George looked at me with a small smile that surprised me. "Are you up for this?"

With no inkling of what was behind that smile, I matched it and nodded.

George called one of his men by name. He said something to him in Romanian that sounded like a question. Whatever the man said back sounded like a strong "yes."

The man gingerly picked up the backpack and took it back into the kitchen. Within a few minutes, he reappeared in the kitchen doorway and said something that apparently pleased George.

George came over to me. "I know you have a reputation for steady nerves under fire. My men spotted a car parked down the block with a Russian driver. He's probably holding the trigger for this device. What would you say if I asked you to go out the front door and walk toward the car? I'll warn you. He's probably waiting to take you prisoner."

I could feel the gremlins start dancing in my stomach at the thought. "Into the lion's den."

"So to speak. Will you trust me to protect you?"

"Will it advance the cause?"

"It might well."

Some things you do in life defy logic. I remembered John Wayne saying, "Courage is being scared to death, and saddling up anyway."

"Let's do it."

"Bravely spoken. Take this gun. Keep it in your pocket. When I tell you, walk out the door with this Russian in front of you. Keep the gun on him. Turn right and walk slowly toward the black Buick at the end of the block."

"And when we reach the Buick?"

"You'll know what to do."

With the gun in my pocket and the Russian a step in front of me, we walked out of the restaurant and turned right. The Buick was a hundred feet ahead of us. I nudged the Russian and willed my feet to walk behind him.

At thirty feet, I could make out the features of the man in the car. I could see his eyes dilating as I walked into the spider's web. He raised his hand with a gadget that looked like my garage door opener. His eyes darted from me to the restaurant behind.

There was a flash of tension in his face. I could see his grip tighten on the thing in his hand. Instinctively, I hit the ground. I looked back at the restaurant for the blast. It came with a numbing shock to the ears, but not from the restaurant. The blast came from in front of me.

I looked ahead just in time to see the rear end of the Russian's car blown off the ground. The gas tank must have ruptured. Flames shot out of the trunk area. The Russian driver's eyes were the size of his gaping mouth. He threw open the car door and dove for the sidewalk just before the entire car was blanketed in flame.

The Russian who was a step ahead of me had also hit the ground. He scrambled to his feet and ran to pick up his comrade. I looked back to see George outside of the restaurant door, apparently enjoying the scene.

I had the gun out of my pocket. George yelled to me, "Let them go. I want them to report this back to their people."

Since I had no alternative plan, I watched the two Russians break Olympic records in a dash for their lives.

I walked back to the restaurant and gratefully accepted the celebratory glass of *tuica* that George held out to me with a broad smile.

"Well done. I had my explosives expert take out enough of the charges to make it effective but not deadly. The Russian driver was concentrating on watching for you and his partner leave the restaurant before he pushed the button. My man was able to sneak up behind and drop the backpack under the rear of his car."

George beckoned me to follow him back to the private dining area. "Please sit, Michael. There's a bit more that you need to know. Then the decisions are yours."

We sat at the table close enough to speak in a low tone. "Your last question, before we were interrupted, was how this all relates to that violin. You need to know. Then I have something important to ask of you."

That last sentence felt like an unsheathed sword dangling directly overhead. I put it to the back of my mind to better absorb what I hoped would be the first thread of sense I'd heard in over a week.

"I'll be brief, but I have to go back centuries. Bear with me."

I told him I would.

He took a deep breath and a deep quaff of *tuica* while he settled on a point of entry.

"I told you about the conquest of Wallachia by the Turks. Once Dracula was imprisoned in 1462 by their allies, the Hungarians, the

Turks dominated the whole area we're talking about. I'm sure they searched, but there is no record of their finding the treasure.

"Jump ahead. Two hundred and twenty years later, 1683. The Muslim Turkish empire had marched all the way to Vienna, the center of the Christian Hapsburg's Holy Roman Empire. If the Turks took Vienna, Christianity would likely have been wiped out across Europe. In the most momentous battle, perhaps of all time, King John III Sobieski led the Polish Hussars in the largest cavalry charge in history to defeat the Turks at the walls of Vienna. It took sixteen more years, but the Christian armies drove the Turks out of Wallachia and all the way back to the Black Sea."

"Interesting. But what does this have to do—"

"Patience. You've heard of the Silk Road?"

"More or less. It was a trade route."

"From Chang An in eastern China all the way west to Italy and back. It carried everything from silk to Buddhism from China, and even the plague at one point. It also brought the culture of the West to the East, including, sometime around 1695—are you listening, Michael—one particular violin made by Antonius Stradivari."

He now had me on full alert.

"Those were violent times. One route of the Silk Road passed just above Wallachia. It was vulnerable to being hijacked by Turkish bandits."

George picked up the sheaf of documents he had placed on the table in front of us. "I want you to read this. But first, let me tell you this much. A captain of the Turkish army, Captain Suleman, hijacked a caravan on the Silk Road bound for China. One item he took was a Stradivarius violin."

"One I might be familiar with?"

My question ignored, he continued, "There is reason to believe that around the time the Christian armies were driving the Turks out of Wallachia, this Captain Suleman stumbled onto Dracula's treasure. You'll see when you read these papers. Things were moving fast. The Turkish army was retreating. This captain had no time or means to take more than a few small items with him. But here's the point. One item he took was the Stradivarius violin."

"This army captain knew its value?"

"As a violin? Probably not. That's not the point. He somehow placed the key to the location of Dracula's treasure somewhere on or in the violin. Why there? Who knows? Perhaps because it was the least likely place anyone would look. For whatever reason, he did."

That, as the saying goes, actually did take my breath away. That hot potato I'd been carrying for a week took on an entirely new dimension.

George gave me breathing room to pull together the obvious question.

"There's a bit of a gap between 1700 and this week. How do you know it's the same violin? Stradivari must have made . . ."

"About a thousand instruments. So you want to know why three gangs all believe this is the one."

"A reasonable question, the odds being a thousand to one."

"I'm going to leave you here. Read these papers. See if you find the odds reduced."

CHAPTER TEN

GEORGE HANDED THE papers to me as if he were handing over the original Magna Carta.

"Need I say, Michael, I'm entrusting you with something that is more valuable than anything you can comprehend. Understand also, it holds the potential to release more benefit—or more unmitigated evil—on the people it will affect than you can comprehend."

"I understand what you're saying, but you need to understand that I'm making no commitments—none, until I know a great deal more than I do right now."

He bowed slightly. "That's the trust I'm placing in the depth of your character. God help us all if I'm mistaken."

His fingers slowly released the papers into my hand.

"What you're holding is a translation of a section of the personal journal of a ship's doctor from the time he set sail on a Turkish merchant ship trading between Istanbul, Samsun, Constanta, and Odessa on the Black Sea. It was handwritten in Turkish in 1699. The original pages have been tested for authentic dating of both the paper and the ink. With that, I'll leave you. We'll speak when you finish."

George left the room and closed the door. The papers he left with me read as follows:

Personal Journal of Dr. Baran Demir:

Ship's surgeon, Turkish Merchant Vessel Chabal Bahari

March 12, 1699

Our days in the port of Constanta on the east coast of Transylvania were fore-shortened without notice. Instead of the usual trade goods, the cargo we took on under military orders was human to the point of over-loading. In my thirty years of practice as a physician, a-sea and a-shore, I have never seen the human condition reduced to such wretchedness. The soldiers of the Turkish army had been fleeing for their lives in retreat before the forces of the Christian Empire. Exhaustion and near starvation, compounded with disease, required as much treatment as the wounds inflicted in skirmishes even as they retreated.

I make note of one particular soldier. A captain, Ismael Suleman, by name, one of the very few names I had time to learn. The tendons of his right arm had been all but severed by a Christian blade. The matter of more concern was the advanced state of infection, the wounds having gone untreated during his forced march to the shore.

My immediate intent was to remove the arm with the greatest haste. I was in the initial stage of applying scalpel and saw, when he rose out of his state of collapse and delirium. I felt the vice-grip of his left hand on my cutting hand. His desperate pleas to save the arm overcame my sounder medical judgment.

I applied what little I had to combat the infection, so deeply entrenched that I thought my ministrations useless. The pain and fever drove him shortly to a state of protective unconsciousness. I used the time to quickly and temporarily repair damaged portions of the arm to the extent possible.

Throughout that night, I stole moments from attending the avalanche of other casualties to bathe and treat the infection. That done, I could simply commit him to the mercies of Allah.

Whether by the work of my humble applications or, more likely, by the power of Allah, at the end of the second day, the fever broke. The pain subsided, but the delirium had left him. When I saw him that second evening, he grasped my arm with his sound left hand with unexpected strength. His protestations of gratitude brought this hardened physician to tears.

When I stirred to leave him to tend other patients, his grip persisted. He lifted his head and pulled my ear close to his mouth. His rasping words still ring in my memory. "I will repay. I will repay."

The effort proved exhausting. He sank back into unconsciousness. I pried his fingers from my arm. I called on one of the ship's seamen to continue to bathe and re-dress his arm, while I made the rounds of other injured and depleted soldiers.

Midway through the second watch of the third day, I stole a few precious moments of redemptive sun and sea air on deck above my makeshift hospital. Our course from Constanta to Samsun held to an east-southeast bearing in a moderate wind directly a-port. I linger to recall those precious moments of peace, the first in days, and the last I will likely know for what may remain of my life.

That peace was shattered by a clear call from aloft. The voice from the crow's nest stirred us all with that word more dreaded than "storm" or "tempest." Despite the efforts of the Turkish fleet to rid the Black Sea of that plague, the call from above was "Pirate ship! She flies the black flag! Ten points to Starboard!" And worse yet, "She closes fast!"

Our captain was quick to pick up the accursed ship in his glass. I could see him scan the horizon for any path of escape. My own scanning found none. The pirate ship was closing rapidly from a distance, by my guess, of no more than half a league. She was under full sail, and could clearly outrun our bulky, over-laden vessel in a chase.

We all knew the captain's mind. To flee was impossible. To allow closure and fight, fool-hardy given our vulnerability and the bristle of cannon on the pirate ship's every side. To simply surrender and offer up our cargo and stores with a plea for the lives of those aboard, doomed. The black flag came with a history of seizure of merchant ships and the bloody slaughter under cutlass of every living trace of humanity aboard.

I had resigned myself to uttering what would certainly be my last prayer to Allah in this life, when I heard from aloft the ringing call, "A-stern! Warship. She flies the flag of the Turkish fleet!"

The captain spun his glass to the rear. He shouted the orders. "Come full about! Aloft! Full sail!"

Full sail unfurled and secured, we came about. Our sheets caught the wind. We hit the top speed our doomed vessel could muster directly into the protective aura of the rescuing Turkish vessel. The cheers poured out of every man on deck, and must have given spirit to the bedded soldiers below.

My own spirits rose higher the closer we drew to the arc of the range of the Turkish vessel's cannon. The only pause to my jubilance was the fact that the pirate scourge continued to pursue at full speed. When she was all but within range of the more heavily-armed protector ship, she still pressed on into certain destruction. Why?

The answer came with dispiriting clarity when we found ourselves locked tightly between the two opposing ships. The vessel that would be our salvation suddenly struck the Turkish flag and hoisted the black flag of piracy. We had been drawn like a fly into the spider's death trap.

As fast as we had regained hope, the desperation of our situation enveloped us like a cloud. I rushed below to a scene of near panic. Soldiers who could scarcely stand were forcing themselves upright, strapping on sabers. If it were a near certainty that every merchant crewman and officer aboard would be reddening the sea with their blood before the next watch, the doomed lot of the depleted soldiers was beyond certainty.

I made my way for one last farewell through the turmoil below to the bedside of Captain Suleman. He saw me. He beckoned me approach with his strong arm. When I reached his side, he fell back on the bunk. He again drew my ear close enough to hear his final words over the din.

"Listen to me, physician."

I tried to settle him. He just pulled me closer. "No time. I say it once. Believe the words of one who will soon be with Allah."

He coughed up the phlegm that clogged his throat. I tried to say something, but he forced his words through a rasping throat. "You know of the treasure of Dracula. You must have heard. Say it. Say it."

"I've heard, of course. But no one . . ."

"I found it. I was lost, wandering alone . . . in retreat . . . The treasure . . . It's beyond anything . . ." He choked again. Before I could speak, he forced the words. "There was no time . . . Our army was fleeing. They were on us . . . I left it all."

A coughing fit seized him. I tried to settle him, but he pulled my ear still closer to his lips. His voice was barely audible, but with my hand to Allah, these were his words.

"I took one item with me . . . A violin I had seized in a raid . . . Hear me. It's in my bag. Here, under the bunk. A harmless violin . . ."

He pulled me with even greater strength till my ear touched his lips. "I repay as I said . . . It's all I can do . . . Take it."

"But why . . ."

"You're a physician . . . They may keep you alive. Hear me."

He put every ounce of the last drop of strength Allah gave him into his final words. "The key . . . to locate the treasure . . . It's . . . the violin."

His soul passed. I was thankful that he would be spared the slaughter that was coming.

I found the bag where he said it was. I could feel a box the shape of a violin case inside. I took it and my bag of physician's instruments and scrambled through the melee of staggering soldiers up to the deck. I forced my way to the mainmast, and just clung to it.

I tried to close my eyes, but something inside forced me to witness the numbing slaughter all around me. Sabers, cutlasses glinted in the sun, to be bathed in the next instant in human blood. The screams of the dying drowned out the savage curses and war-cries of the pirates, crazed with the intoxication of killing.

I saw the pirate captain, laying waste all in his path, coming toward me. In one last, almost peaceful surrender, I closed my eyes. I held my physician's bag in front of me to absorb a first blow that might fall. I said the last words of my lifetime to Allah.

I waited. It never came. When I opened my eyes, I saw their captain ordering attackers away from me. The screaming and killing went on until I was the only soul of our ship's company still drawing breath.

The massacre was followed, as it had probably been on many captive ships, by a stripping and carrying off to their vessel of everything of any imaginable value. In the midst of it, their captain, whom I assumed by his words to be Russian, seized two of his cut-throats and ordered them to take me and secure me in his cabin. I could only assume, as I later learned to be true, that he recognized my physician's kit as the tools of a trade in desperately short supply among his murderous band.

In the weeks that followed, I was held prisoner in a small room next to the captain's quarters. I was allowed out only to treat the battle wounds of that pirate band, incurred in occasional skirmishes with the pitiable crews of ships taken like our own.

With the exception of the delivery of daily food rations, no one came into the room in which I was held. No one gave eye to the bag of Captain Suleman. I assume that if they gave it any thought at all, they considered it part of my medical equipment.

I had many hours in that room to examine closely the violin that Captain Suleman said with his dying breath was the key to finding the treasure of Prince Dracula, secreted for over three hundred years.

My impression of the violin, being no expert in instruments of music, was first, that it was a piece of impeccably fine handiwork. I was equally impressed that the instrument was of considerably more recent origin by the date inscribed inside than the fifteenth century reign of Prince Dracula.

I had hours—in fact days—to pour over every facet of the grain, the shape, the color of every feature of the instrument. I shone light through the openings in the face of it in search of some clue. Absorption in the puzzle might well have saved my sanity, but it revealed no hint of the treasure's location.

It has been, by my count, six months to the day since my abduction. I can sense by the sounds outside my room that anchors are being dropped. My command of the Russian tongue is scant, but from the words I hear, we are in the port of Odessa.

If I am correct in my assumptions, this plundering voyage is over. If, in fact, we are in the port of Odessa, there are doctors here. My value to these brigands as a physician is over, and I have no other value. I have no reason to believe that my life will not be taken this day.

I have no alternative but to close this journal with a prayer to Allah that it and the violin might fall into the hands of one more worthy of deciphering the key that has eluded me.

I hear them coming. I go to Allah.

CHAPTER ELEVEN

GEORGE OPENED THE door, and I jumped. My mind had been completely absorbed in what I had just read. I was stunned by how, after three hundred years and thousands of miles, it had come to touch my life so deeply.

George held up his hands in a silent asking if I had finished. I nodded.

Again, my mind was almost paralyzed with a congestion of thoughts and questions. Most stunning of all was my first realization of the actual significance of that violin. It added geometrically to the weight of my being the only one on earth who had access to it.

George sat down beside me. He took the lead. "I can see it in your eyes. You're beginning to realize what's at stake. The story continues. Shall I?"

"Please."

"What you read occurred in around 1700. Let me piece together, as well as I can, the past three hundred years. The ship's doctor's personal fate was as he predicted, as far as we know. His bag of physician's instruments was probably sold in the Odessa medical community.

"But the violin. Remember that Odessa was on the northern trade route of the Silk Road. The pirates sold the violin to a Russian trading company in Odessa. They, in turn, shipped it to China to be traded for Chinese silk."

"How could you know that?"

"The Russian trading company kept careful records of all of its trades. Fortunately, the company is still in existence. We have a copy of the record of that trade. Shall I go on?"

"By all means."

He drew his chair closer. "We're dealing in centuries here. The next time the journal of Doctor Demir surfaces is in Istanbul in the 1800s. The pirates had sold it with the violin to the Odessa trading company. Probably for a pittance, since it was written in Turkish. None of them knew what it said. It gathered dust on the shelves of the trading company for a couple of centuries. It was still untranslated. Finally, at that point, some employee there thought it might have value as an historic document. We know from the trading company's records that it was sold to a dealer in ancient documents in Constanta on the Romanian coast of the Black Sea. Being written in old Turkish and in the handwriting of a doctor, it was not easily translatable.

"Again, it collected dust until it was donated in 2017 to the Antiquities Department of the Koc University of Istanbul, where it was finally translated by an expert in ancient Turkish script, Professor Sakim."

"But the violin was still in China, I assume."

"Patience, Michael. More *tuica*?"

"No. More facts."

"Alright. Professor Sakim did what academics do. She published an article, with a translation of the doctor's journal, in an obscure academic linguistics publication. Probably made full professor on it."

"I'm seeing the connections."

"Not quite yet. The reference to the violin being the key to Dracula's treasure was catchy enough to be picked up as a short blurb by some popular media. It was still only a tiny blip on world news for that one day. No one took much interest because no one could easily connect the doctor's journal with a particular violin. Plus, almost no one knew anything about the real Dracula as opposed to the fictional vampire. The stories about his treasure were even more like folk legends."

"But you knew about it."

"Yes. I did. I'd been hearing about it as factual history from my parents since childhood."

"So what did you do?"

"I began an odyssey. I traced the doctor's journal back from the university to the manuscript dealer in Constanta, then to the trading company in Odessa. It cost a few coins, but I got to see the trading company's records going back centuries. I was able to match the entry regarding the purchase of the journal with the purchase of the violin, since they were part of the same deal with the pirates."

"What about the violin?"

"The trading company's record showed that it had been traded to a Chinese dealer on the Silk Road in Guangzhou. I followed it there. I found that it had sat for centuries, probably because the name of Stradivari was still unknown there in the 1700s. It finally moved again when someone in Guangzhou dug it out of a storeroom and recognized the Stradivari seal. It was sold for about half a million dollars to a dealer in Hong Kong."

"And you found it there?"

"If I had, we wouldn't be having this conversation. It was one of those things. I located the dealer just three weeks after he'd resold it."

"To whom?"

"I couldn't find out. Hong Kong had reverted to communist China. To keep it from the communists, the deal was done on the black market."

"Dead end."

"Almost. What happened in between, I have no idea. But I have ears all over Romania. About two weeks ago, I heard a rumor that a deal was being done for a Stradivarius by a small violin maker in the tiny town of Tesila outside of Bucharest. Mr. Oresciu. It was supposed to be a secret deal, but it was more than this little violin maker could keep to himself. I also heard that there was a Chinese connection with the deal, as you know. That was enough to get me curious. But by the time I got back to Romania, his shop had been ransacked. The violin maker was in the hospital barely clinging to life. The Stradivarius was gone."

"Another dead end."

"Perhaps. But then I heard your name. Your visit to that part of Romania. I heard about the interest the Russian mafia had suddenly taken in you. The man who runs the gondola on the ski mountain in Sinaia is Romanian. He shared an interesting story about your adventure on the mountain with your wife—and a violin."

"Interesting."

"Yes, very. I asked myself, could my quest at last be close to fruition?"

He sat back in silence. His eyes were looking into mine. The clear message was that the ball was in my court, and the "ball," so to speak, was clearly whatever I would choose to do with the violin.

I had no immediate response. There were too many loose ends flying. On the other hand, his open recitation of the violin's history entitled him to an answer. All I could do was to lay out the conundrum.

"The best thing I can give you is honesty, George. I'm like a mouse surrounded by three hungry cats. The Chinese—I assume the tong—have paid something over a million dollars for this item. I'm the delivery boy. Their response to my deliberately misdelivering it to you could take on disastrous results—for my wife, Terry, as well. You'll concede this?"

"Please continue."

"In the second corner, we have the Russian mafia making no secret of the worth of our lives if their wishes are not met."

George nodded.

"And here in the third corner we have my host, more gracious than the other two, but with the same objective. My handing over the violin. Would that there were three violins. But, alas . . . Anything I'm missing here?"

"Yes. A great deal."

He leaned back in the silence of his own thoughts. I let the seconds go by. The easy smile was gone. I thought I saw a tinge of anger. He seemed to be in self-debate about sharing his thoughts. I gave him more seconds until he resolved the debate. He leaned forward with more steel in his voice.

"Michael. I'm sorry the weight of this is on you and your wife. But it is. And therefore, you'd better know the stakes. If that Russian mob of gangsters you refer to as 'mafia' get their hands on that treasure, God help Romania and every other part of the world. They'll flood the globe with their drugs, their human trafficking, every other despicable evil this treasure will finance. Don't for a moment think that your country will be spared."

"I can—"

"Hear me out. The Chinese tong is no better. You know it in Boston. That's just one tentacle of the sordid octopus that gives the orders from Hong Kong, and possibly the mainland. Again, if they find the treasure, God help your country and mine. We'll be awash in drugs . . . and other things."

I hesitated to respond, but if ever there was a time for cards-on-the-table honesty, we were in it.

"I'm speaking plainly, George. You've been a perfect host. But I've only heard your . . . organization described as a 'Romanian mafia.' What is there to choose between you and . . ."

"Once more, you have no basis for understanding. You would have to live under the heel of Ceausescu and his Russian communist puppeteers for decades to know why we resorted to black market tactics. Other crimes? Yes, of course. When the essentials of living are denied to you and your people at the hands of the most brutally corrupt . . . I'm sorry. My emotions run very deep."

"I'm listening, George."

His tone became quiet, but no less intense. "My country . . . My Romania has been raped by the Turks, by the Huns, the Mongols, the Romans, the Ottomans, the Christians . . . to name a few. The Nazis did their share, and then there were the Russian communists. They kept us on our knees until that filthy scourge was lifted in 1990 and we could breathe as Romanians."

"I understand what you're saying."

"You understand the words, perhaps. Not the emotion. Not the reality. And in the middle of all of these centuries of being plundered, there was the dictator, Vlad Tepes—Dracula. This treasure we speak of—for the most part, it was bled from the Romanian people. The bleeding kept them under the crushing heel of poverty."

"And you're saying?"

"Forgive my bluntness. If there is any just right to that treasure and all it can do, it belongs to the Romanian people. And to no one else. Your personal well-being in all of this is, of course, a consideration. But there is also a matter of conscience. I'll say no more."

I sensed that our meeting had concluded. I stood up and extended my hand. He rose and took my hand. He held it while he spoke.

"I'll only add this. My driver will take you back to where you left your car. You're free to leave, as I said from the beginning. Ask yourself. If this meeting were with either the Russian or Chinese gangsters, would the same be true?"

I tested his words by following his driver to the rear exit of the restaurant. As I was being driven back through familiar locales— the Jamaicaway, Copley Square, Tremont Street—it occurred to me that the last question George asked about my likely fate at the hands of the Chinese or Russian gangs was for me the most telling consideration.

And yet, something bothered me. George gave the impression of laying every card on the table. I wondered if there was one card he still held close to the chest. Given the number of Stradivarius violins in circulation, and three hundred years of loose historical threads connecting the ship doctor's journal with that particular violin in the South Station locker, did George have some particular reason—beyond mere hope—for his apparent confidence that this violin was the one that held the key to the treasure? If so, and it seemed likely given the efforts he continued to pour into the quest, why not lay that card on the table as well—or even hint at its existence? A small point, but so is a grain of sand in the shoe, and it causes a small but continual discomfort.

*   *   *

It was well after two in the afternoon when George's driver turned onto Boylston Street close to where I had parked. I was about to call Harry Wong, when a cryptic text message popped up on my cell phone. "Three. Ten Tyler. Dressed goose."

Dear Harry. What would I do without him? Those five words were a flashback to the first time I had put his neck beside mine on the chopping block for an entree into the closed circle of Boston's Chinese tong. My recollection of those days and Harry's coding methods gave me a clear translation.

I first needed an update from Deputy District Attorney Billy Coyne. I knew I could only get it with Mr. Devlin's intercession. I called Mr. D.'s office. I reached his secretary, Bev Sheer, without whom, brilliant as he is, Mr. D. would be as lost as I would be without Julie. Bev told me that "himself" was still in court. I left a message, knowing with certainty that she'd get my message to him wherever he might be.

George's driver let me off. I transferred to my rental car. Given the uncertainty of what thug from what gang might be on my tail next, I was at least grateful that my beloved Corvette was sheltered in its Winthrop garage.

I had barely started the car when my phone buzzed. I knew Bev Sheer would come through. Mr. D. was on the line, as requested, with Billy Coyne, who started with, "What do you need, kid? Make it short. I'm not your personal research staff, ya know."

"A hell of a lot of truth in that. On the other hand, Billy-Boy, I'm not yours either. When have you ever given me an ounce of information without getting a pound's worth back? Am I right?"

Actually, Mrs. Knight never raised a son dippy enough to say those words to the Deputy District Attorney—particularly when I needed to tap that source of highly privileged information. My actual words were, "I would never presume you were, Mr. Coyne. But something sizable is brewing here. If you'll help me with one piece of it, I'll put you ahead of the whole thing when I have it together."

"So what do you want, kid?"

"The murder of Mr. Liu in Public Garden last night. You mentioned a tip on a suspect."

"Yeah."

"What's the status? Do you have an indictment?"

There was a pause. "Lex, we're on thin ice here. If that kid ever . . ."

"Billy, for the love of God. Do I have to say this every time? Michael's rock solid. You'll come out ahead. Damn it! Speak!"

He said it just above a whisper. "No. No indictment."

"Of Mickey Chan?"

"Yeah, not yet."

"Are you going for one?"

"Not if it were up to me. But Angela Lamb is the D.A. She calls the shots, God help us."

"Does that mean yes?"

Another pause, then a quieter voice. "What do you think? This could get her some choice headlines. Mr. Liu was a major player in the Chinese community. I'm on my way to the grand jury room soon. Like I told you. We have an eyewitness. Of sorts."

Mr. D. cut in. "Give us the name, Billy. It'll go no further."

"It damn well better not. This is for you, Lex. Ming Tan. She and her husband run a grocery store on Beach Street in Chinatown."

"Mr. Coyne, what do you mean, 'of sorts'?"

"That's for you to find out, kid. Now you tell me. Do you represent this Mickey Chan?"

"Not at the moment."

He laughed, cynically. "Lex, your boy's giving that lawyer crap right back to me. You're training him well. Is that all, kid? Or shall I just send all of our private files over by carrier pigeon?"

"Thank you, Mr. Coyne. No need. But to show you fair's fair, I'll give you back two pieces of information. First, I'd bet my Red Sox tickets on the third base line that you'll be indicting an innocent man."

"Spoken like a true defense counsel. What else?"

"I met with the man I told you about, George, one of the big shots in the Romanian organization."

"Romanian *mafia*."

"As you say. Something's brewing here that's so big it could make the rest of this a sideshow. You have my word. When I have something solid, I'll give it to you."

CHAPTER TWELVE

HARRY AND I needed a secure base for operations in Chinatown. I was still holding a violin for which the tong had already paid a cool million dollars. My failure to deliver it, and soon, would not sit well with that organization. They would likely consider the infliction of substantial pain, followed by an untidy murder—both mine—a mere business transaction.

What we needed specifically was a meeting place in Chinatown far under the eyes of the tong. Not an easy matter. The tong is like a giant spider's web that blankets every shop, street, and alley of Chinatown. Its insatiable fingers reach deeply into the cash box of every restaurant, laundry, medicine shop, poultry shop—every business within its turf. Its constant threat of lethal violence at the hands of its youth gang squeezes total submission from every captive in its clutch.

Evading the eyes of the spider would be a challenge. We needed an ally. Fortunately, we had one in Mr. Wan Leong. Our history with Mr. Leong went back some five years. It sprang from the fact that Mr. Leong was what had been known among Chinese immigrants in years past as a "paper son."

There had been a massive California immigration of Chinese laborers to work on the railroad until it was completed at Promontory

Point on May 10, 1869. When the Civil War ended, the American economy took a dive. White workers visualized the diminishing spate of jobs going to the minimally paid Chinese laborers. The resulting intense hostility to the Chinese led to passage of the federal Chinese Exclusion Acts of 1882. The acts banned immigration of any Chinese capable of taking jobs sought by white workers—virtually all Chinese immigrants. The ban lasted from 1882 through its repeal in 1943, when the bombing of Pearl Harbor shifted white hostility from the Chinese to the Japanese.

The result of the ban was that the mass of male Chinese American citizens had no way of bringing wives to this country. That produced a particular scam called the "slot racket." It became a highly profitable operation for the tongs in this country.

The law permitted a Chinese American citizen to return to China and then reenter the United States. After the destruction of birth records in the 1906 San Francisco earthquake, practically every Chinese male resident could falsely claim American citizenship by birth. If any of these Chinese males returning to the United States from a visit to China claimed that during his stay in China, he had married and sired children, those children were each given a "slot" for immigration into the United States as citizens. The slot was available until the child chose to use it years later.

The racket run by the Chinese tongs was to send Chinese males claiming to be American citizens back to China for a time. On return, they would falsely claim to the Immigration and Naturalization Service—INS—that they had married and sired a specific number of children in China. They would be given a "slot" for immigration for each child. The tong would then sell these "slots" to residents of China desiring entry as citizens into the United States, which was known in China as *Gim Sun*—the Golden Mountain. The going price for a slot was $2,000 to $3,000 each.

Since no birth certificates were being issued in China at that time, there was no way to prove that the person claiming the slot was not the child of the Chinese American citizen. Those people who entered the United States under the false claim of being the child of a Chinese American citizen were called "paper sons."

One disadvantage was that if the INS discovered that an immigrant was a "paper son," deportation was automatic and swift. Since the tong knew which immigrants were "paper sons," they held the threat of deportation over those inhabitants of Chinatown for the rest of their lives.

Harry's friend Mr. Leong was now in his eighties. He had come to this country in 1940 at the age of six as a "paper son." He had supported his family on the income of a small live poultry shop on Tyler Street. Over the years, the tong had bled away most of the profits of his labors with the threat of disclosure to the INS. His business flourished, but Mr. Leong had raised his family in poverty.

He and his wife had a daughter who in turn had a son, Adam. From the time of his birth, Adam was the center of Mr. Leong's every thought, wish, and hope for the future. Adam became the focus of his entire existence.

Adam was equally devoted to Mr. Leong. His success in his studies was motivated by his intense desire to please his grandfather. To his misfortune, Adam was also highly successful in his study of martial arts. He attracted the attention of the tong. When he was fourteen, the tong sank its talons into Adam. The tong demanded that Adam join and serve it as a member of its youth gang under the threat of reporting his grandfather to the INS for deportation. Mr. Leong would have willingly suffered deportation to free Adam from the spider's grasp, but Adam could not live with his grandfather's sacrifice.

Mr. Leong had known Harry since Harry's childhood in Chinatown. He had seen Harry drawn into the youth gang and successfully rebel against it for his own freedom.

On one of Harry's visits as a customer to the poultry shop, Mr. Leong had taken him into his back room. At the serious risk of misplacing his trust, he disclosed to Harry what the tong was holding over him and his grandson. He pleaded for help for the salvation of Adam.

Harry called me. We took the problem behind closed doors to Mr. Devlin. Mr. D. came on board immediately. Mr. D.'s first thought was to take the issue of Mr. Leong's actually acquiring citizenship to his law school classmate whose specialty was citizenship and naturalization. One phone call from Mr. D. got the ball rolling in that direction with the thought of removing the heel of the tong from Mr. Leong's neck on that account.

Harry and I agreed that that was half a solution. The other half would be in Harry's and my bailiwick. It would also require immense courage on the part of this old man who had submitted to demeaning abuse by the tong for his entire adult life.

Harry explained to Mr. Leong what we were suggesting. No one needed to explain to him the dangers at the hands of the tong. He sat quietly, looking down at his hands while Harry spoke in his native language. His expression never changed, but tears began to run down both cheeks. When Harry finished, I was afraid that we were asking too much of this gentle man.

He sat quietly, silently, for a minute. When he looked up, he turned from one of us to the other. The expression on his face never changed, but there was something in his eyes that surprised me, shocked me. The tears were now flowing freely, but there seemed to be a turning back of his age. The beaten-down look of resignation had transformed into—what can I say—an almost youthful look of resolution.

His words were in English for my benefit. "I will do it. Forgive an old man's tears . . . You've given me hope. I have never known hope. I can't thank you . . ."

His head dropped into a low bow. Harry was the first, but I ignored my fear of offending his aged dignity in being a close second to take him into a three-person hug. I could feel in that embrace something that I can only call joyous emancipation.

Now if we could just pull it off.

* * *

Within three days, the agent of the tong was at the poultry shop with his hand out for the weekly gouging of *lomo*—lucky money—paid to the tong to avoid a beating or worse. This time, there was no envelope ready. Harry and I were listening behind the curtain to the back room.

Shock at the rebellion of the old man was instant in the volume and ferocity of the agent's response. It was in Chinese, but I hardly needed Harry's interpretation to gather the threats were of violence. Harry restrained my instinct to burst in to protect Mr. Leong from injury.

Harry whispered, "Not yet. This gangster won't do it himself. He'll send one of the youth gang to rough him up."

As the volume and rage of the threats rose higher, the more they seemed to bounce off the impervious stand of the old man. The stronger the language, the more steel seemed to pour into his resolve. The only word I heard him utter was what Harry told me meant simply "No."

It ended with one last threat and a storming out of the shop. I asked Harry if this meant violence.

He said, "Not yet. He said there would be a visitor, one of the tong big shots, to deal with him tomorrow. The rest of the words you don't have to hear."

The next morning, Harry and I were back behind the curtain with Mr. Leong. We had gone over the plan for the third time, when the shop door was slammed open. I looked through a slit in the curtain. A pockmarked, obese Chinese man of around fifty strode in. He banged his fist on the counter.

I asked Mr. Leong in a whisper if he was sure he was up to it. The tension must have shown in every corner of my face, but to my amazement, there was not a trace of it in his.

He just nodded and walked calmly through the curtain. A blast of Chinese words erupted from the fat man like the flow of lava from Changbai Mountain. It had me clenching my teeth, but as I watched through the slit in the curtain, Mr. Leong's expression never changed.

Once the initial verbal onslaught expended itself with none of the expected effect, the visitor resorted to a more rational delivery. I figured that this was where the rubber met the road. This was where I needed Harry's whispered simultaneous translation.

"Old man, you've lost what little sense you had. You need to be reminded. Do you know who I am?"

Mr. Leong kept his composure. "I know you. Everyone in Chinatown knows you. You are Mr. Tow. Mr. Tow An-Yan. Everyone in Chinatown fears your name."

"Yes, old man. And are you foolish enough not to fear my name?"

I thought I detected the slightest trace of a smile in Mr. Leong's voice, probably the first since childhood. "I am an old man, Mr. Tow. Older than my years because of the pain of your heel on my throat for much of my life. Perhaps I have become forgetful. What can you do to me more than a lifetime of suffering?"

My eyes were glued through the slit in the curtain. The fat man had pushed his sweating face within a foot of Mr. Leong's nose. "Then I shall remind you one last time, old man. You are a 'paper son.' You are an illegal alien. I make one phone call to the immigration. You will be taken out of your home. You will be shipped back to a China that never knew you. That hates you for leaving. You will die in a foreign land. You never see your grandson again. Ever!"

"How can you do this?"

"You watch. I snap my fingers, and you're gone. I'll take your shop. Your wife will have nothing."

I was forcing mental telepathy to get Mr. Leong to press it one more step. I held my breath when he spoke the words.

"But what power do you have to do this to me?"

"I have had power over you since we brought you into this country as an illegal immigrant. You know that well. You've paid us for it all these years. And you will go on paying."

Mr. Leong just dropped his head as if in resignation. "But please, my grandson . . ."

"Your grandson belongs to us now. I'll show you how much. If you refuse to pay, it will be your grandson I'll send with orders to extract it in pain."

Mr. Leong looked up. I read a look of shock on his sad face. This was perhaps beyond what even he thought the tong could do to him.

I looked at Harry. He was on fire. I could read it in his eyes. Not one moment more.

Harry reached out and tore the curtain off the door. The rod clanged to the ground. The noise spun the fat man around in time to see Harry striding across the floor. The fat man froze. Harry grabbed his shirt in both fists. He walked him backwards across the floor and drove him against the wall hard enough to make his head bounce. The fat man just stared at Harry with his mouth open and his eyes flashing something between fire and fear.

The fat man started to scream something in Chinese. Harry cut off the flow with another slam against the wall.

Harry spoke in English with a deliberate calm that only accented the violence of his grasp.

"Mr. Tow, is it? Mr. An-Yan Tow. Do I have your attention?"

The fat man just stared into Harry's eyes in silence. "You're allowed one more word, and that word is 'yes.' Now again, do I have your attention?"

Another bounce of his head against the wall produced a meek "Yes."

"Good. Then you will listen carefully. My friend here is a lawyer. He will now favor you with some legal advice."

I walked to a point where Mr. Tow could look at me while still being held against the wall.

"Mr. Tow. I wish we had had this meeting many years ago, but we must live in the present. Isn't that right?"

The fat man was now staring at me with his mouth open. I tapped Harry on the shoulder. He made a move as if to give Mr. Tow one more slamming. Mr. Tow closed his mouth and nodded his agreement with my last statement.

"Good. We agree on that. Let's move on."

I took a small electronic machine out of my pocket, one without which I never leave home. I hit a couple of buttons and the machine played back a recording of part of the conversation Mr. Tow had just had with Mr. Leong. I turned it off. I walked to within a foot or two of the fat man's perspiration-soaked face.

"Mr. Tow, as a former prosecutor, let me tell you what we have here. In one neat package we have you identifying yourself and confessing to more felonies than I could count on both hands. We could begin with blackmail and move on through extortion, conspiracy, theft, any number of others. Those alone would insure that you will never see the outside of a prison cell for the rest of your life. Am I going too fast here?"

The fire in his eyes was now distilled into fear.

"Am I, Mr. Tow? Are you taking this in?"

I tapped Harry on the shoulder. Tow recognized the signal, and reacted with a shaky "Yes."

"Good. Then let's get to the best part. You also admitted to conspiracy to violate the immigration laws of this country. No need to worry about any statute of limitations, because you are still a party to that conspiracy every day, every time you extort money from Mr. Leong. The wheels of criminal justice might move at a slow pace, but I'll give you my word as a lawyer. If the Immigration people hear this recording, your feet will hardly touch the ground in being expelled from this country you have so dishonored. It will be a race between expelling and imprisoning your pathetic carcass."

I saw panic in his eyes. I pressed on.

"And so, Mr. Tow, let me lay down a few rules for your future conduct. If you, or anyone remotely connected with that scum-pit of an organization—in which you say you are a big shot—touch, approach, speak to, threaten, intimidate, or harm in any conceivable way Mr. Leong or any member of his extended family, copies of this recording will fly to the district attorney, the United States attorney, and hear this particularly, the Immigration Service. Are we totally clear on every bit of that?"

The eyes just stared and the mouth hung open.

"Answer the question, Mr. Tow."

It took a few seconds, but he nodded his head.

"Out loud!"

What came out seemed to be forced through a congested throat. "Yes."

"One more item. It's hands off Mr. Leong's grandson. Permanently. Do we have total agreement there?"

There was a pause, but he said, "Yes."

"Good. There will be no charge for that excellent legal advice."

The humor of that seemed to escape him. I added one last bit of information.

"You may wonder why I don't just turn you in now and be done with you. I'll tell you. As a 'big shot' in the tong, I want you around to give the orders—and enforce them—that everything in connection with Mr. Leong is off limits. You enforce those orders at peril of your freedom and citizenship."

The fire had so clearly gone out of our Mr. Tow that I told Harry he could release his grip and let Mr. Tow be on his way. And he did.

Mr. Leong was speechless. I think he was in shock. I had not clued him in on how far we intended to go, partly because I had no idea. It was mostly ad lib. When he recovered, he could not find enough words in Chinese or English to express what he felt. The tears washing over the smile that was lighting his face were his words.

CHAPTER THIRTEEN

THAT WAS FIVE years ago. It had been five years of peace and unaccustomed prosperity for Mr. Leong. His gratitude remained unabated. So when Harry and I needed an ally for a meeting under the radar of the tong, he was our first choice.

Harry's cryptic text message—"Three. Ten Tyler. Dressed goose"—made sense. I had continued to drop in on Mr. Leong occasionally as a customer, primarily to see that the train had remained on the track with the tong. Harry's message was telling me to meet him at three o'clock at Ten Tyler Street, the address of Mr. Leong's live poultry shop. I was to order a fresh goose, feathered and dressed, which would give me a reason to wait in Mr. Leong's shop.

Ever since the liberation of Mr. Leong from the weekly extortion of the tong, he had put his heart into the business. His shop had blossomed with a steady flow of customers. He had added clerks and poultry dressers. There was, however, no telling which, if any, of the added people in and out of the shop were the eyes and ears of the tong.

Mr. Tow, Mr. Leong's former nemesis, was, as far as I knew, still a high-ranking member of the tong. He might even have been involved in the violin escapade, but I felt certain that final control over a matter that significant would likely be in someone over his head—possibly at the level of the Dragon Head, the very top man, whose identity, according to Harry, was known only to the second in control—whoever that might be. I needed a meeting to sort out the players.

When I came into the shop, Mr. Leong greeted me with his usual smile and sincerely low bow. I returned the bow and gave him an order for one feathered and dressed goose. He knew well that I was as likely to roast a goose as I was to become an astronaut. He took the order with equanimity. He said for the benefit of all present that it would take twenty minutes and that I was welcome to wait with a pot of tea in his office.

I walked back to the office. Harry was already there, having taken, I assumed, the rear entrance from the back alley.

There were a couple of surprises waiting as well. When I closed the door, there were two added starters standing behind the door out of the view of people in the shop.

The first was Mickey Chan himself. It felt like it was the first time I'd seen him when he wasn't somehow pulling my bacon out of the fire. I thought for a moment that he was going to smile, but for stone-face that was not in the offing. Smile or not, I was grateful to Harry for getting us together. Finding Mickey Chan on my own would have been highly unlikely.

The second surprise had me baffled as to why Harry had brought him. I found myself shaking hands with Danny Liu, my seventeen-year-old former client and the son of the man who had enlisted me to pick up that violin in Romania in the first place. A few tumblers clicked in place, and I thought to express condolences to Danny for the death of his father on the swan boat the night before.

There was a lot to pull together, and time was short. I had only until my goose was plucked in the back room. To overstay might raise tong suspicions. My first business was with Mickey Chan.

"Mr. Chan, I had no time to thank you for last night's rescue in the pond—or for that matter, the time in Romania. Without you, I'd be—"

"Mickey."

"I'm sorry?"

"We've been through enough to use first names. It's 'Mickey.'"

That was a bit of social acuity I didn't expect from stone-face. It greased the path for what I was about to say.

"'Mickey' it is. 'Michael' here. Much as I'd like to match my gratitude to your heroics, we have to cut to business. *Tempus fugit.* Whether you know it or not, and you probably don't, you're about to be indicted by the Suffolk County Grand Jury for the murder of Mr. Liu. They have a witness."

That cracked the stoic composure of stone-face. The stunned expression on his face said more than words. I let it sink in.

His first words were, "What witness? Couldn't be. I didn't kill him. Who is it?"

I realized that I was close to the edge in terms of my confidentiality agreement with Billy Coyne. I couldn't go there.

"I can't say, Mickey. I'm already over the line. The point is, you need legal advice, right now. The best kind of gratitude I can give you is to return the favor. Would you like the firm of Devlin & Knight to represent you?"

There was a hesitation.

"It's your choice, Mickey. You can get anyone you want. But I'll give you this much. It better be soon. You need to stay ahead of the prosecution."

He shook his head. "No, no. If you'll do it, I'd like you. I just don't know what it costs."

"It costs two instances of saving one of the partners' lives. You've already paid it. Overpaid it. Are we good?"

He nodded.

"Good. Here's what I want. I want you out of sight, out of reach. Except by me. The time may come when it'll serve our purpose for you to turn yourself in. I want it to be under my conditions, on my terms. Understand?"

He nodded. "How do we stay in contact?"

I looked at Harry. "Okay by you, Harry?"

"Of course."

"Good. Here's the deal, Mickey. I want to be able to reach you quickly. That will be only through Harry. I don't want to know where you are."

"Why not?"

"I may want to be able to tell the deputy district attorney truthfully that I have no idea where to find you."

He nodded again.

"Good. Then let me ask some questions that I couldn't get in at the pond last night. Why were you there?"

"I took orders from Mr. Liu. He told me about your meeting. He wanted me there for protection. I got there about fifteen minutes before you came."

"And?"

"I found Mr. Liu in the swan boat. He was already dead. His throat—"

"Anyone around?"

"No. I waited to see. You came. You saw Mr. Liu and got into the boat. I heard a sound behind the bushes where you'd been sitting. There was a tiny reflection of light on the barrel of a gun. That's why I knocked you out of the way."

"Into the water."

"Yes."

"The man who fired the gun, do you think he killed Mr. Liu?"

I had an opinion on that one, but I needed to ask.

"No."

"Why not?"

"Not his style. He was a Russian assassin. He'd have used a gun with a silencer."

My thought too. I checked my watch. I had about ten minutes before a man with a goose would knock on the door.

"Before you go, Mickey, I need more answers. There are some pieces that don't fit this puzzle. You were in Tesila in Romania the day I went to pick up that violin. Why were you there?"

I could sense hesitation.

"You have to be wide open with me from now on. Both of our lives are on the block. Why were you there?"

"I obey the command of the tong."

I looked at Danny, the son of Mr. Liu whom I defended for car theft when this all began. His head was down in silence.

"Was Mr. Liu high up in the tong? Did he send you, Mickey?"

I knew it was like tearing out his soul to violate the tong oaths he had taken with a sip from a cup of his own blood mixed with the blood of a chicken years ago at his initiation.

"I think the tong is forcing this witness to lie to convict you. They violated their loyalty to you. Loyalty is like a contract. It should run both ways. They broke it first. That should free you of whatever you owed them. If you keep playing on their side, no one can defend you. Will you answer my question?"

I saw Mickey glance over at Danny. Danny's lips barely moved when he spoke to him. "They killed my father. There is no bond left with them."

Mickey looked back at me. He seemed to have crossed a boundary. His voice was stronger than I expected. He simply said, "Yes."

"Are you saying Mr. Liu was a high-ranking member of the tong?"

Again, a glance at Danny, who simply nodded.

"Yes."

"You remember that dinner at the China Pearl Restaurant. Mr. Liu sent me to bring back the violin. Did he send you to Romania too?"

"Yes."

"I assume it was to protect me while I picked up the violin. Because that's what you did. From the Russian assassins. He sent you there to protect me, right?"

"No."

That was jarring. I'd have bet the goose and the whole shop that the answer to that one would be "yes."

"Then why?"

Another glance at Danny. This time he looked directly at Mickey. "It has to come out. It cost my father his life. We have to trust Mr. Knight. You say it. Or I will."

Mickey seemed to brace himself before the words came out. "Mr. Liu ordered me to steal the violin from Mr. Oresciu."

That set my world spinning. "Say what? Why? He had arranged for the payment of a million dollars for it. The money had been transferred to the prior owner by the bank. I was going to pick up the violin to bring it to him anyway. Why would he want to steal it?"

Mickey was still being squeezed by conflicting loyalties. Danny took over.

"My father was playing a dangerous game. You may not know it, Mr. Knight. That violin has great value. More than as a Stradivarius."

"Let's assume I know that. Go on."

"My father was a member of the Boston tong for many years. He had risen to a highly trusted position. He'd spent most of his life faithfully serving the tong."

He stopped. He seemed to be wrestling himself through an impasse. I could sense the moment when he became comfortable with a decision.

"Mr. Knight, you may not know that the tongs in American Chinatowns like Boston were first formed by organized crime gangs in China. Over there they're called "triads." Around the 1900s, they saw the Chinatowns in America as rich communities they could drain by extortion, gambling dens, narcotics, prostitution. In those days, they had tight control over the American tongs. Over the decades, the triads had their own problems in China, especially after the communists took over. Over here, the tongs became free to take over their own control. The triads hardly ever interfered anymore. In fact, almost never, according to my father."

"So what are you saying?"

"I'm saying that this time it was different. This whole business with the violin was directed by a triad in Hong Kong. It was on their orders that my father arranged a loan from our Chinatown bank. They used my father because he knew the bank president, Mr. Chang."

"Yes. I met him. He was at that dinner with us at the China Pearl. Is Mr. Chang a member of the tong?"

"No. He was just arranging a loan from his bank on the security of the Stradivarius violin. I don't think he even knew the hidden value of it."

"What about your father?"

"I'm getting to that. My father's loyalty was to the tong. When the Hong Kong triad suddenly moved in and began giving him orders, he resented it. They treated him like a cooley. No respect for his position in the tong. Then when it became clear to him that the triad in Hong Kong would take most, if not all, the benefit if the violin led to . . ."

"To the treasure. I know about that. Go on."

"My father rebelled. He felt no obligation to the triad. He told me about what he intended to do just in case anything happened to him."

"What was it?"

"It was insane. He pretended to obey the orders of the triad. He made all the arrangements to have the tong buy the violin with the money loaned by the bank. He sent you to pick it up. But it was a complete fraud. Once the money was transferred to the prior owner, my father knew he had nothing to fear from him."

"Do you know who the prior owner was?"

"No."

"Okay. Go on."

"My father sent Mickey Chan to Romania, to Mr. Oresciu's shop. As soon as the money was transferred, he was to steal the violin without being seen before you could pick it up. My father hoped the triad and the tong would believe that the Russian mafia stole it. They were after the violin for the same reason."

"Then what?"

"Then my father would have the violin to himself so he could decipher the code."

"To the treasure of Dracula."

"Yes. I think my father might have had information about how to crack the code. I don't know what it was."

"So what went wrong?"

Mickey broke in. "I got to the shop too late. You came to Mr. Oresciu's shop first. I waited. I saw you leave and walk around the town."

"That's right. Mr. Oresciu needed time to have the payment for the violin transferred from the Chinatown bank here to the prior owner. I came back in about half an hour. Where were you then, Mickey?"

"When you left the shop the first time, I followed you for a while to be sure you'd be out of sight. Then I went back to the shop. I was following Mr. Liu's orders to steal the violin. I thought I was doing it for the tong. I had no idea that Mr. Liu was acting on his own."

"I understand. What then?"

"When I got to Mr. Oresciu's shop, I found him lying on the floor. He'd been beaten. The shop had already been vandalized. I was sure it was the Russians."

"But you stayed there until I came back to the shop. You saw me when I left the shop. Thank God. I ran right into the hands of the Russians. That was the first time you saved my life. One last question. I told you that I had the real violin in that burlap bag. If you were there to steal it, why didn't you take it from me?"

"I knew you were sent there by Mr. Liu. I knew you were following his orders. I thought you'd bring the violin to him yourself."

"I understand. Well, things got a bit complicated after that."

The knock on the door was the signal that my goose was ready to travel. The cover for our meeting had run its course. I needed to put one last question to Danny.

"Danny, I know this is difficult. But it's necessary. I don't know the players the way you do. Do you think the tong had your father killed?"

"I'm sure of it. It's their style."

"And why? Did they find out that your father was betraying them with the violin?"

"Maybe my father, but indirectly."

"Then who directly?"

"You."

"That's crazy."

"Not so much, Mr. Knight. You were my father's emissary to pick up the violin. You were under his orders."

"It was under his request. As a favor."

"It amounts to the same thing. Think about it."

I did. Like a chess match, I put three or four moves together in a flash. I was to deliver the violin to Mr. Liu. He was to deliver it to the tong/triad. I was the one who rerouted it to a secret locker in South Station. Mr. Liu was dead. If the tong/triad wanted to take direct action—and they most certainly did—it had to be against me. That was disquieting.

"One last question. Who would take your father's position in the tong? I'm asking who I need to worry about most for health reasons."

Danny shook his head. "I don't know. My dad didn't talk about the hierarchy."

"Mickey?"

"That's beyond my level."

I looked at Harry. He shook his head. "I've been out of the loop for years. Come on, Mike. Time's up."

Harry and I walked out into the main shop. One of the dressers handed me a package containing one dressed and feathered goose. As I took its limp, lifeless body, I wondered with some angst how much that goose and I might soon have in common.

CHAPTER FOURTEEN

GOOSE IN HAND, I walked out the front door of Mr. Leong's shop. Tyler Street had enough foot traffic at that time of day to give me a sense of safety from whomever the tong might have put on my heels. My optimistic sense also flowed from the fact that I was the only one who had access to the violin. They needed to take me alive. The straw to which I was clutching was the belief that, while a quick knife under the rib cage could be pulled off with anonymity on a crowded sidewalk, a live capture would not be so easy. In essence, I was hiding in plain sight.

When we got to the sidewalk, Harry waited while I made a quick call to my secretary, Julie. I got right to the first order of business.

"How's our pup? How's Piper?"

"He's settled in. So have I, Michael. I don't think I'm going to give him back."

"We'll talk about it. Any calls?"

"You must be kidding. You have cases, remember? These lawyers are driving me daffy. As only lawyers are trained to do. When . . ."

"Tomorrow, Julie. First thing. Any non-lawyer calls?"

"There's a Mr. Chang. He says he's president of a bank. He seems gentlemanly. He wants to see you at your earliest convenience. His words."

"Got it. Anything else?"

"That man who called before. Says his name is 'George.' He seemed nicer this time. He wants a call."

I took down George's number. "Good work, Julie. Will you transfer me to Mr. Devlin?"

"No. Maybe. On one condition."

"Julie, you work for me. Will you transfer the call?"

"First hear my condition."

"I know your condition. I promise. I'll be in tomorrow morning. I'll return the calls."

"Hold for Mr. Devlin."

I brought Mr. D. up to date on everything I'd learned from Danny and Mickey. I also slipped in the fact that we had a new client. I felt I should offer him an explanation. When we formed the law partnership of Devlin & Knight to deal in criminal defense work, we knew that some, if not most, of our clients would be guilty of something, even if not the crime charged. We were comfortable with that, since the only one in the courtroom to balance the totally damning efforts of the prosecuting attorney against our clients would be Mr. D. or me. Somewhere in the middle, justice would result more often than not.

On the other hand, we drew a line. We promised each other that we'd never take on the defense of anyone who made murder a profession. That cut us out of representing anyone associated with an organized crime gang—Italian, Irish, Russian, Albanian, or, relevant here, Chinese. I disclosed up front that Mickey Chan was a lifelong member of the tong.

Mr. D. listened while I drew a fine distinction between the usual business of the tong and Mickey's part in the violin matter, noting that the latter involved the hauling of his junior partner's chestnuts out of the fire on two occasions so far.

That last consideration got Mr. D. on board in short order. He passed on the word that his old pal Billy Coyne had in fact gotten a "true bill," an indictment against Mickey for the murder of Mr. Liu. Only Mr. D. could have pulled the additional information out of his old battle-mate that Mr. Coyne was acting strictly on the orders of his politically ambitious superior, District Attorney Angela Lamb. His discomfort level with the indictment, that he personally would have to try for the prosecution, was around a nine.

I asked Mr. D. the reason for Mr. Coyne's discomfort. His answer was a quote in two words: "Shaky witness."

I postponed returning the call to my new Romanian friend, George, while I cleared an agenda item in Chinatown with Harry. He had misgivings, but he guided our way among the sidewalk traffic down Tyler Street, up Beach Street, and down Hudson to the Chinese Merchants Bank.

We entered the bank and met the graciously smiling loan officer. I felt the first letup of anxiety since we'd walked through the traditional Chinatown entrance arch called *Paifang* in China. It signifies the ancient virtues of loyalty, chastity, and filial piety. I began to think we might finally have found them in this bank, this institutional shelter from the fangs of the tong.

I asked to see the president, Mr. Chang. The usual question about an appointment seemed to be trumped by the mention of my name. That was a pass directly into Mr. Chang's office with an invitation to sit. Tea was offered and refused in light of the fading hour of the afternoon.

"Mr. Knight, nice of you to drop in. You received my call."

"I did."

"If I might come to the point directly?"

"Please."

"Our bank made a loan in the area of a million dollars. You were a party to the transaction after our delightful dinner at the China Pearl."

"I remember it well. I was not actually a party to the loan. I was more of a delivery boy for a violin."

"Yes. A very particular violin. A Stradivarius. That violin was, in fact, the security for our loan to Mr. Liu, as head of the Chinese Merchants Association."

"My understanding, yes. I believe the violin was then to be loaned by the Merchant's Association to the Boston Symphony Orchestra, to be played in concerts by Mr. Tang, the concert master."

"Ah yes. And yet, in my conversation with Mr. Tang this morning, it seems the violin has not been turned over to the orchestra. It seems to have remained in your possession. I find that puzzling, Mr. Knight."

I took that last as a question. My instant assumption, based more on instinct than anything more solid, was that Mr. Chang was not an arm of the tong. I seriously doubted that he was even in the circle of those who knew the real reason why three gangs were scrambling to get their mitts on the instrument. If my assumptions were true, I was on a playing field with Mr. Chang that I could work with. If not true, God help any number of us.

"Mr. Chang, I understand your concerns for the bank's interests. Let me assure you that the violin is in perfect condition, totally secure."

"Ah, Mr. Knight. Your assurance is comforting to the foolish insecurities of an old man. Your reputation is certainly cause for full confidence."

"Thank you."

"And yet, we are both men of experience in an insecure world. My understanding is that regretfully our Mr. Liu is no longer with us.

The source of repayment of the loan is, shall we say, that much more uncertain. We had been content to rely for security on the value that Concert Master Tang assured us resided in that instrument."

"Of course. And—"

"Together with, if I may continue, our confidence in its safekeeping by the Boston Symphony Orchestra. We raise no question whatever of your own integrity, Mr. Knight. You do, however, understand my position."

The hell of it was that I did understand his position. He had approved the loan on the signature of the supposedly honorable, but no longer existent, Mr. Liu. His personal future with the bank could hang on the availability for sale of that fiddle. I knew it was safely, invisibly tucked in a South Station locker. On the other hand, if I didn't give him something to take to his board of directors, he was truly up an undesirable creek without means of propulsion.

On the third hand, the secret of the location of that violin was my only life insurance.

I gave it a few seconds of serious mulling before splitting the difference. I was still assuming Mr. Chang's innocent lack of knowledge of Mr. Liu's tong involvement, a plausible possibility given the anonymity of the higher tong officers.

"Mr. Chang, I'm going to meet you halfway. If you'll meet me in the lobby of the Parker House Hotel tomorrow morning at eleven a.m., I believe I can set your mind at rest."

"Could you be more specific, Mr. Knight?"

"Only to this extent. You have my word that your security interest is fully intact. Tomorrow, I'll back that up with something more concrete."

The tentative smile on Mr. Chang's face said that my words had not given his world the rosy glow of confidence he had hoped. "And they say, Mr. Knight, that we Chinese are inscrutable."

I stood and extended my hand. He did the same. "I believe that if you check any source, Mr. Chang, you'll find that my word is more concrete than any written contract."

He bowed courteously. "I have checked, Mr. Knight. Till tomorrow morning."

* * *

WHEN WE GOT to the sidewalk, Harry gave me a questioning "where to?" look. I made a suggestion. Harry mulled the wisdom of it for a few moments. I could sense his discomfort when he said, "Your call, Mike. Let's go."

We retraced our steps on Beach Street to a small grocery store close to Harrison Avenue. The Chinese symbols on the door, as well as labels on all of the boxed, bagged, and canned items on the shelves, had no English translation. It was no surprise that I was the only non-Asian in the house.

Harry led the way with a whisper over his shoulder. "Walk in here as if you know what you're doing, Mike. Face is everything. Don't look at the Chinese writing. You can't read it anyway. It just makes you look as lost in here as you are. Not a good impression for bargaining."

I whispered back, "Okay. You know what we want. You do the talking."

"Your Chinese isn't too fluent today?"

I gave him a slight punch in the back. He ignored it and walked directly back to an old man who was lifting a thirty-pound bag of rice into a cart for an elderly Chinese woman.

When he straightened up, Harry was beside him. Even before Harry spoke, I saw the grip of tension Harry's presence produced in the old man's face. He turned immediately to the curtain to the back room. Harry caught his arm and said something in a low tone in Chinese. The man seemed frozen. Harry kept speaking in that quiet way of his.

I had no idea what he was saying, but it ended in what sounded like a question. The old man slowly nodded in the affirmative. Harry released his arm. Harry reached back and pulled me by the elbow to stand close to the old man. Harry's next Chinese sentence ended with "Mr. Knight." The old man bowed stiffly. Harry said to me the words, "Luk Tan."

I took it as an introduction, bowed and repeated the name with a "Mister" in front of it. The old man's hands began to quiver. His face expressed either fear or pain. Perhaps both.

Harry continued in Chinese. His tone was soft, but the fear in Mr. Tan's eyes just seemed to deepen. At one point, he shook his head. Chinese words came out in a stream, punctuated by more negative head-shakes.

I started to speak, but Harry squeezed my arm. I took the cue and clammed up. The old man became more effusive. My best guess was that he was pleading. When he finished, Harry looked back at me with a defeated look. "Let's go, Mike." Harry bowed respectfully and led me back out to the street.

On the way out, I became aware of the presence of four Chinese boys in the aisles, probably in their late teens. Their eyes never left us. I needed no coaxing from Harry to take an orderly but direct path to the outside world. We took a left on Beach Street and cut a direct path in the direction of the parking lot. Not feeling on particularly friendly ground, I set a brisk pace. Harry pulled me back. "Slowly, Mike. Don't lose face."

I whispered, "It's not my face I'm worried about. It's the rest of my body."

"Slow down, Mike. Think about it. We were on their turf. They own everyone in that grocery store. If they wanted to take us apart, they'd have done it there."

"Why didn't they?"

"That's what worries me. Actually, more than you and me having to take them on in a hand-to-hand. There were some powerful influences holding them back."

"Such as?"

"I don't know. The tong? Something higher?"

"You mean a triad? Hong Kong?"

"I don't know. I've been out of this world too long."

"So what did we get out of this? What did the old man say?"

"I told him we came to see his wife."

"And?"

"You saw him. He's terrified."

"What about his wife?"

Harry looked over at me. "She's gone. She just disappeared. He said she went with a lawyer to some courthouse yesterday morning. She had to testify about something she saw. She never came back. They made it clear he was not to go to the police."

"Who are 'they'? Did he say the tong?"

"One thing you should know, Mike. These people never say the word, 'tong.' Never."

"What do they call them?"

"They don't. They just go on with life no matter what the tong does to them."

I walked the last block to the car wondering how far we'd advanced the ball, if at all. We shook hands. Harry said, "Call me if you need me. And you will need me before this thing plays out."

I watched my faithful friend walk down the block. About half-way down, he turned around. He yelled back. "We could have, you know."

"We could have what?"

"Taken on all four of those punks, hand-to-hand."

That brought a smile. "You think? Professor Wong? You get into many four-on-two brawls at MIT?" I had to smile. "I admire your self-concept."

"Piece of cake. They'd be no match for the wrestling champions of Harvard Kirkland House."

I said to myself, "Of ten years ago." The words that came out were just, "Good night, Harry."

CHAPTER FIFTEEN

I OWED A return call to my Romanian acquaintance, George. First, I indulged in a luxurious fifteen minutes on the phone with Terry in New Hampshire. It was an injection of pure love and confidence into an otherwise shaky day. I assured her that Piper was enjoying something of a vacation with Julie and that I was cruising at the best speed I could muster to a safe reunion for the three of us. Details about my Chinese and Russian interplay would only have broken our euphoric lift.

My next call was to George. He seemed pleased, if not surprised, that I got back to him. "Michael, you lead a charmed existence. You walk between two of the most vicious gangs that pollute the earth like a mouse between two feral cats. And yet you press on with admirable equanimity. How do you manage it?"

"Remember the song, 'With a Little Help from My Friends?'"

"I do indeed." His tone changed. "And yet, it's a dangerous game."

"Really? I hadn't noticed."

"Hah! You keep your sense of humor. May I be blunt? Your friends can't be everywhere. You wear a brave face, but life is what it is. At any moment, a sniper's bullet, a knife. I'm serious. There is very little reality to back up your admirable bravado."

And thus, in an instant, the juice of euphoria from my call with Terry was drained to the dregs.

"Thank you for the cold shower, George. And do you have a solution? I'm wide open to suggestions here."

"Yes. I like you. I'd prefer that you go on living."

"Two minds with but a single thought."

"Then I have another thought. If that violin fell into the wrong hands and led either of those two scourges to the treasure, the disaster for your country would be immeasurable. It would be even worse for my Romania."

"I know. You've mentioned that. So where does that leave us? You and me?"

"I need to see that violin. Remember, over the centuries it's moved from Odessa through dealers in Guangzhou and Hong Kong, and somehow from there to Mr. Oresciu in Romania. There are a lot of gaps. I need to be sure we're talking about the same violin the ship's doctor wrote about. Otherwise it's a dead end."

"It's a consideration."

"Then also consider this. You're the only one who can produce it. And your life is, as we agree, tenuous."

"Total honesty here, George. Suppose I were to let you see it. Could you tell for sure that this was the one in the ship doctor's journal?"

In a whisper. "Yes."

"How?"

Silence.

"Two-way street, George. How?"

"If I tell you, and you fall into the hands of either mob, they would compel you to disclose it. No question. Their methods are beyond anyone's resistance. It would bring them one serious step closer to the treasure."

"Then we seem to be at an impasse."

"Not necessarily. Shall we bargain, as friends?"

"I'm listening."

"The first step is clear. On whatever terms you like, I need to see the violin."

I knew I had to move the situation off dead center. He gave me a few moments to solidify a decision.

"I'll go this far. I have an appointment to show the violin to a Mr. Chang tomorrow morning. I believe he has no part in the tong. His career is on the line. He's the president of the bank that loaned the million dollars to pay the prior owner for the violin through Mr. Oresciu in Romania. That violin is the bank's only security."

I could feel the tension in his voice rise.

"When and where?"

"Tomorrow, eleven a.m. The Parker House on School Street, opposite old City Hall. We're going to meet in the lobby. If you're there . . ."

I could hear his breath rate increase. "How will you handle it?"

"I know the assistant manager. She'll have a private room for us."

"I'll be there. I could provide security."

"No. Just you. All alone. One more thing, and there is no flexibility here. I'll show it to you, but I keep possession of the violin until this whole calamity is set to rest. Understood?"

"I could provide a safer—"

"No. Here's another condition. If you don't want to tell me how you'll know, you will at least agree to confirm to me that the violin is, or is not, the one. I have the same doubts."

"I promise an honest answer."

"Give me one more truthful answer. If you see the violin, can you interpret the code? Will you know how to find the treasure?"

"No. Not yet. And that's the truth. But we're one step closer. The rest depends on you, Michael."

"Meaning what?"

"The only one I know who can lead us to the deciphering of the code is Mr. Oresciu, the violin maker in Tesila."

"If he can decipher it, why didn't he do it when he had the violin in his shop?"

"I didn't say he could decipher it. He can lead us to someone who can. I have this from his own words."

"Did he mean the prior owner?"

"Unlikely, or the treasure would have been turned up long ago. He didn't say who."

I took a minute to think through the next step.

"Then suppose I show you the violin, perhaps even let you take all the pictures you want—this is just supposing. Why would you need anything further from me? You can get the rest from him."

The conclusion I hoped to jump to was that George could then go on a treasure hunt. Of the three contestants, I was favoring his side anyway. I could turn the violin over to Mr. Chang to secure his bank's loan. I'd somehow get the word to the tong and the Russians that the thing that had them pouncing on me was out of my hands permanently. Terry and Piper could come home, and we'd all live happily ever after.

George's voice lacked the exuberance I was expecting for the solution.

"There's an added complication. As you know, Mr. Oresciu took a terrible beating that day. He's an old man. He's just recently, as the doctors say, come out of the woods. He has no idea which gang did it to him. He trusts no one—except you. You apparently made a deep impression on him."

I was stunned. I knew we formed a bond that day. It apparently ran deeper that I'd imagined.

"Where is he now?"

"He was moved to a small rest home outside of Sinaia. Under a different name for security."

"And he'll talk to me?"

"Only to you. I believe it's his greatest wish."

Two thoughts were wrestling for control. The bond that day with Mr. Oresciu ran both ways. He touched me deeply. I had no time to show it then, but what happened to that gentle man broke my heart. The thought of my being in his company again held a strong attraction.

Pulling in the opposite direction was an eruption of stomach acid at the mere prospect of being back where I had so nearly lost Terry.

I let that decision lie unresolved for a clearer moment.

* * *

When I left Chinatown, I drove a route to the South Station more convoluted than anything even GPS could have conjured. Daniel Boone on his best day could not have followed my tracks.

It was rush hour when I approached the bank of lockers. I opened my two lockers and filled the nondescript shopping bag I had brought with me. I dropped in coins, took back the same keys. Then I blended like one more undifferentiated lemming in the rush-hour crowd back to my rented car.

I made one more tactical stop in Boston before leaving the city. Then I drove north to yet a different hotel on Route 1. I wondered with each mile in my rented Kia if my Corvette, securely tucked into its garage in Winthrop, missed me half as much as I missed it.

* * *

The next morning, I kept a major promise. I drove into the city by a route I hadn't used before through Medford. I used the alley behind 77 Franklin Street, waiting at several points to check for followers. I took the delivery entrance and lift to the seventh floor.

True to my word to Julie, I spent an hour and a half wading through message slips, returning calls, and soothing the savage breasts of lawyers who felt neglected. Lawyers have a fierce intolerance for the inability to reach the lawyer on the other side of a case. As long as their fears of abandonment are soothed by some kind of personal contact, however, postponements are generally handed out like water bottles at the Boston Marathon.

I knew I was on thin ice for the morning's next encounter at the Parker House. I was about to expose the genuine article. That was discomforting. My secreting of that fiddle could have been the only reason two conscienceless mobs had so far foregone the pleasure of dispatching me like an annoying insect.

I parked again in the lot under Boston Common. I took the path across the Common that led toward the Park Street Church, clutching the large package under my arm.

Foot traffic was low enough for me to get a fix on every other walker, mostly tourists, with a sprinkling of suits on the way to offices, courts, or the state house. My antennae were tuned for anyone paying too much, or deliberately too little, attention to my passing. I discounted older people and panhandlers sitting on benches.

By the time I passed the site of the old colonial hanging tree, I felt like a running back of the New England Patriots within easy reach of the goal line. The dense cluster of people pouring in and out of the Park Street subway entrance was the last obstacle. I started bobbing and weaving crosswise through the cluster with an increasing sense of calm, until I felt the presence of a tall man of chunky proportions positioning himself directly ahead of me, close enough to touch clothing. In the next moment, every nerve in my spine reacted to a breath on the back of my neck. A quick glance showed someone equally large, and equally close, directly behind me.

I was in the midst of telling myself that I was overreacting, when the raspy voice behind me with a Russian tinge, said, "Keep moving. Straight ahead."

The final hint that I was in an undesirable position was the dull pain of something steel in my lower spine.

The pace of our little threesome was slowed by the need of the hulk in the lead to find openings through the heavy foot traffic coming up out of the mouth of the MTA station on the right. I could see that we were heading in the direction of a black stretch limo, stopped dead ahead at the curb on Tremont Street. The only certainty I could muster was that if I were forced into that car, it would be the last ride I'd take in this life.

We were just ten feet from the top of the escalator that leads down three stories to the MTA tracks—and moving. I thought of one tenuous possibility. I let myself be swept along slowly between the two muscle-masses without resistance. We were five feet from passing in front of the down escalator on the right. Three feet. One foot. Point zero.

In one move like a muscle spasm, my right arm shot out to the side. The package I was carrying flew out of my hand, careening off the moving steps of the down escalator. It bounced off steps, walls, and riders on a zigzag course toward the distant bottom.

The man at my back jumped. The steel of a gun barrel drove hard into my ribs. The man in front knew something had happened but had no idea what. The man in back reached over my right shoulder. He grabbed the arm of the man in front and jerked him toward the moving stair with a force that knocked several riders off to the side.

I heard a panicked yell in Russian from the mouth behind me. Whatever he said sent the man in front galloping down two steps at a time after the bouncing package, knocking stunned riders into the rails left and right.

The man behind gave his full focus to his partner's scrambling charge. I recalled a move I hadn't used since my last wrestling match at Kirkland House. I spun to the left with a high elbow. It caught the Russian goon in the neck. He was focused on the in-and-out-of-sight package. The blow knocked him off balance into the escalator pit. He tumbled down about ten steps, knocking off riders like ten-pins, and spewing language that would probably have petrified anyone who could speak Russian.

I bolted through the crowd. I darted across Tremont Street with an abandon that would chill the most hardened Boston jaywalker. My pace never slackened up Tremont Street, right on School Street, and up the marble steps of the Parker House.

I caught my breath on the top step while I scanned the sidewalk crowd for anyone who looked like a Russian thug. None in sight. It felt like a safe haven.

*　*　*

The stately lobby of the Parker House, grand old lady that she is, could restore calm to the most agitated soul. I returned the welcoming smile of Neil Albert, the concierge of ten years. He knew why I was there from our conversation the previous evening. I had dropped by the Parker House just before driving north to the hotel. He discreetly nodded in the direction of the chairs just outside of the bar off the lobby.

I spotted Mr. Chang first. Directly across the lobby from Mr. Chang, with his eyes in my direction, I saw George. I made eye contact with George before approaching Mr. Chang. The thought occurred that it might be wise not to mix company at this point. I gave George a very slight shake of the head. He caught it and remained seated behind the morning's *Boston Globe*.

Mr. Chang caught sight of me at ten feet. I could see his eyes scanning me for the package I should have been carrying. I looked for a furrowing of the brow or some sign of deep agitation that I was clearly not carrying the package that brought us there. He held it together well.

Mr. Chang rose, bowed courteously, and bade me a "good morning." I did the same. We both sat.

He led off. "I was believing that you were to bring the item for my inspection. Was that not our understanding?"

I gave him a full play-by-play of my Park Street run-in, including my Tom Brady lateral of "the item" down the MTA escalator.

He listened quietly with an increasing look of concern. He let me finish before commenting quietly. "That is indeed distressing."

I marveled at his reaction to hearing that his bank's entire security for a million-dollar loan had just taken a slam-bang ride to the bottom of Park Street Station. What he termed "distressing" would to me have been a total damn disaster.

"And did the men who attacked you get control of the instrument?"

"I didn't wait to find out. They were certainly making an Olympic attempt. They quite probably did."

"I see. Well, Mr. Knight, then I believe our business here is done."

We rose, exchanged bows and handshakes, and Mr. Chang was on his way down Tremont Street. George had his eye on the scene from across the lobby. He came across at a quick step and slid into the chair beside me. His expression showed what I considered an appropriate level of panic at my obviously empty hands.

His voice was a stage whisper. "Michael, where is it?"

I rose, held up a finger for silence, and beckoned him to follow me to the elevator. We rode in silence to the executive office level. The assistant manager, Marj Dutilly, a friend of many years of exchanged favors, met us at her office door and led us to her inner chamber.

Once the door was closed, I retold my Park Street adventure.

I could see the blood drain from George's face. He simply said in defeat, "Then they got it. The Russians."

I nodded to Marj. She opened her office safe and took out a large cardboard box. She handed it to me and left us alone.

I took the lid off the box to reveal an ancient violin case. George's eyes were like saucers. "Is it . . ."

I nodded. "I left it here in Marj's safe last night."

George gingerly lifted the case out of the box and opened it. He took the violin out of its case as if it were a newborn baby.

He turned his back while he examined it. I found myself holding my breath.

"George, is this it?"

He looked at me with an expression I couldn't read. His voice seemed to catch. What came out was a raspy whisper.

"It is. It is."

"You're certain."

"I am."

He laid it back in the case with extreme care. When he looked back at me, he just asked, "Then what did those Russians chase down the escalator?"

I could not squelch a grin that came from my toes. I looked George right in the eye and milked every word of it.

"I wasn't sure something like that Park Street grab wouldn't happen. I took some precautions last night."

"What did you do?"

He was grinning with me now in anticipation.

"When those Russian thugs turn that package over to their boss, and he opens it, he won't be seeing a million-dollar Stradivarius. I wish I could be there."

"Why?"

"He'll be looking at a $25 ukulele."

CHAPTER SIXTEEN

IT WAS TIME to test the strength of our bargain. George and I walked out of the Parker House together. I was carrying in a cardboard box under my arm what George had just confirmed to be the genuine article. I had kept my part of the bargain in letting George see it. The verbal agreement was that I was to keep possession. If George wanted to break the deal and call in his troops for a grab-and-run, this was his moment.

We crossed School Street and stood talking in front of the original site of the oldest school in the country, Boston Latin School. After about five minutes in the wide open, I was renewing the sense that my trust in him was not misplaced.

I pushed it one step further. "George, now you've seen it. You say it's the McCoy. Would it hurt to tell me how you knew?"

He had a slight grin while he chewed on that for a minute. "I guess not. You held up your end. Maybe we've reached a new level of faith here."

"So?"

He looked over at me. "I didn't always know whose side you were on. So when I gave you the translation of the ship doctor's letter, I left out a line."

"Which said?"

"That he had used a thin blade through one of the holes on the face of the violin to scratch his initials inside. Just shine a light in there when you get it home."

"It's there?"

"It's very faint, as it should be after several centuries. But it's there."

"Interesting."

"More than interesting. Now it's my turn. I caught your signal when you came into the lobby. Why did you want me to stay out of your conversation with the Chinese banker?"

I looked up and down School Street. No sign of any approaching Russian thugs. I nodded in the direction of Washington Street. "Let's walk. No need tempting fate out here. Those Russians are going to open that box sooner or later. They may not appreciate the joke."

I led the way into the Scholars American Bistro on School Street. We took a booth close to the back. We had complete privacy before the lunch crowd arrived. A bowl of their signature buttery Boston clam chowder was perfect comfort food for both of us.

When the waiter left, I leaned close enough to keep it in a low voice. "I'm glad you caught my signal to stay away when I met with Mr. Chang. A few things were coming together. I was getting uncomfortable."

"What things?"

"I was supposed to bring that violin with me. His bank was depending on it to secure a million-dollar loan. Pretty clearly, when I was walking up to him, he could see that I didn't have it. His reaction was mild, to say the least. Almost as if he didn't expect me to still have it. When I told him I'd thrown it down the Park Street escalator and sent two Russian thugs scrambling after it, he found that . . . 'distressing.'"

"It was distressing."

"The hell it was. It was a full-blown calamity from his point of view. When he asked if the Russians got hold of it, I told him it was likely. I can't swear to this, but he seemed almost relieved."

George sat back. Now the creases were on his forehead. "I think I see what you have in mind. Anything else?"

"Yes. Granted, I'm no James Bond. But when I was walking across the Common to the Parker House, I did everything possible to see that I wasn't being spotted. I'd bet my life—actually, I was betting my life, that no one, Russian or Chinese, was on my tail."

"And..."

"And yet the Russians were waiting for me at Park Street Station. That was the most logical path I'd take to the Parker House."

"From which you conclude...?"

"The very upright and honorable Mr. Chang was the only one who knew I'd be coming to the Parker House at eleven o'clock."

His furrows were getting deeper.

I dropped it to a whisper. "I think our innocent banker, Mr. Chang, is up to his ears in the Boston tong. And this next part is insane. I'd bet this has never happened before. I think the Russian mob and the Chinese tong are in bed together on this violin treasure business."

I could see George making the calculations of whether or not I was in fantasyland. And, if I were right, what did that mean for both of us?

The waiter brought the check. I took it and stood up. "This is my turn, George. In fact, the next five are my turn after that lunch at the Wallachia café."

I picked up the cardboard box with the violin. "Let's leave separately. One last thought. You said that Mr. Oresciu wanted to talk to me in Sinaia. Maybe that's the next logical step. This might not be the worst time for me to get out of Dodge for a while."

George stood up beside me. "I'll give you the address of the rest home in Sinaia."

"No, not here. Will you book me a hotel? Something out of the way. I'll give you a call for the address of the hotel and the rest home just before my plane takes off. In case the Russians or Chinese catch up with me before I leave, it's better for Mr. Oresciu that I don't know his address."

He gave me his hand and a very sincere, "Do be careful, Michael."

*   *   *

My highest priority was to get to South Station to secure that hot little item back into the same locker before I attracted unwanted company. When I had left South Station for the Parker House, I had the keys to two lockers. One had been holding the genuine article, and one still held the high-quality, non-Stradivarius violin that I had rented as a "just in case." I wanted to restore that setup.

My previous experience in passing by Park Street Station from the Boston Common Parking Garage convinced me to change course. I walked out of the American Scholars Bistro with the Strad violin in the cardboard box tucked tightly under my arm. I walked at a good clip up School Street to the line of cabs by the curb close to the entrance to the Parker House.

I hopped into the back seat of the first cab in line and told the driver, "South Station." While he pulled into School Street traffic, I glanced at the name on his posted cabbie's ticket. I was struck by the name, Juan Ramos. Ramos is a common name on the island of my mother's ancestry, Puerto Rico. I shot a quick, *"Buenas Tardes, Senor Ramos."*

He looked back at me in the rearview mirror. I tend to have more of the Irish facial features of my father than the Latino features of my mother. He gave a polite response. I'm sure he took me for a Caucasian getting his jollies practicing his high school Spanish.

"*Buenas tardes, Senor.*"

I smiled into his mirror. "*Veo que tu nombre es Juan. Tambien es mi nombre.*" Basically, "I see your name is Juan. That's my name too."

He looked in the mirror again. The name, Juan, might still not have registered with the face, but he was still polite. "*Muy bien, Senor.*"

I caught a trace of the way my mother pronounces words. I asked, "*De donde eres originalmente*—Where are you from originally?"

"*Soy de Puerto Rico*—I'm from Puerto Rico."

"*De Donde en Puerto Rico*—Where in Puerto Rico?"

"*Soy de una pequena ciudad en la costa oeste. Mayajuez*—I'm from a small city on the west coast. Mayajuez."

"*No lo creo. Mi madre es de Mayajuez*—I don't believe it. My mother is from Mayajuez."

By now our eyes were locked in his mirror. Fortunately, we were at a long red light. I pressed on before it changed. "*Todavia tienes familia alli*?—Do you still have family there?"

"*Si, Senor.*"

I interrupted. "*Por favor, llamame 'Juan.' Compartimos el nombre*—Please, call me 'Juan.' We share the name."

"*Bueno, Juan. Mi padre y mis tres hermanos todavia estan alli. Que hay de ti*?—Okay, Juan. My father and three brothers are still there. How about you?"

"*Mas tios y tias y primos ques puedo contar*—More uncles and aunts and cousins than I can count." That brought a larger smile and a laugh.

I was sailing deeper into the comfort zone with this stranger whose family shared with mine a part of that island that holds a piece of both our hearts. Being a believer in small signs from God, I wondered if life's fortune was taking a U-turn to higher ground. I glanced behind us. Another small sign. The license number of the car behind us was 3067—an anagram of our home phone number.

By the time we pulled up to the front entrance to South Station, Juan and I had covered every restaurant, bar, backgammon club, church, and beach in Mayaguez, not to say half of my cousins, a few of whom he had known or heard of. It could have gone on, but I had promises to keep, and miles to go before . . .

I asked about the fare, but he had turned off the meter shortly after we left the Parker House. I appreciated the thought, but I insisted on twice my estimate of what the fare should have been. After all, a *compadre.*

I opened the cab door in a state if intoxicating euphoria, which shattered like crystal when I caught sight of the license plate 3067 pulled in two cars behind us.

I pulled the door closed. It was probably presumptuous, but I outlined a request, a plan that could only come off between two *compadres* from Puerto Rico.

I started to explain that there could be an element of danger. Juan just held up a hand and smiled. "*Amigo,* you're talking to a man who deals with Boston drivers eight hours a day."

Juan moved over to the passenger seat. I passed him my suit jacket. He slipped it on and pulled his Red Sox cap low over his face. I took the real violin case out of the cardboard box and handed the empty box to him.

Juan picked a moment when the foot traffic was heavy. He jumped out of the passenger seat and blended into the crowd going into the station with the box under his arm.

The brief glimpse the men in the car behind us could catch of him must have been convincing. The driver stayed put. Two others jumped out of the car and plunged into the crowd after Juan.

I was able to slip into the driver's seat while the attention of the driver of car 3076 was on the crowd at the station entrance. I drove the cab around to the rear entrance of the station. With traffic and traffic lights, I pulled in just in time to meet Juan coming out empty-handed. I moved over to give the driver's seat back to Juan.

He got in panting for breath—half from running and half from laughing himself almost to tears. When he got his breathing back to normal, he poured out what happened in colorful colloquial Puerto Rican Spanish.

What he said was roughly, "It went just like you said, *amigo*. I made sure they were behind me. I caught a red-cap porter. I gave him your twenty dollars and handed him the box. I told him what to do. He took off down the tunnel to the streetcar line. Those two ran after the red-cap with the box. The red-cap slipped through the turnstile with his pass and started down the platform. Those two saw him running. They had no time to get the tickets, so they jumped the turnstile."

There was another pause while Juan couldn't stifle a laugh. "They jumped the turnstile right into the hands of the MTA police. They're still trying to explain it. I don't think they speak very good English."

He had us both laughing. We gave each other a hug like two life long *compadres*. I rolled up a wad of bills and transferred them in a handshake in spite of his objection.

I took back my suitcoat from Juan and rolled it around the violin. I ran into the back entrance to South Station to finish the business at hand.

Once I had the real Strad tucked into its locker, I walked out the front door. The driver of car 3076 was still parked by the curb waiting for his buddies. The driver was getting nowhere in a debate in broken English with two of Boston's finest over his right to park there.

As I walked by car 3076, I couldn't resist rapping on the front passenger window. His face went from flushed to a lively shade of red when he saw me. I motioned to him to roll down the window. He did. I said, "Your friends want you inside. I think they need bail money. Have a terrific day. *Dosvedanya*."

The afternoon was getting on, and a cool wind was blowing off Boston Harbor. I decided to walk among the afternoon pedestrian crowd to the Boston Common garage for my rental car. I slipped on my suitcoat. When I reached into my pocket for my keys, I found the roll of bills I had tried to give to my new *amigo*, Juan. If I ever needed a long taxi ride, I'd be sure to remember the name Juan Ramos.

CHAPTER SEVENTEEN

IT WAS ABOUT four o'clock when I reached the Boston Common underground garage to pick up my rental car. I sat in the car in the bowels of the garage long enough to make a few calls.

The first was to Julie. She seemed more at ease since I'd spent that morning making peace with all the lawyers who had been making demands she couldn't fulfill.

It was short-lived. I asked her to make an airline reservation for a flight to Bucharest, Romania, that night—and to make it one-way, since I had no idea when I could use a return ticket.

"Michael, are you off on another vacation? Those lawyers will be back taking bites out of my neck if they can't reach you. How about a phone number I can give them?"

I couldn't imagine a worse idea than to let it be generally known that Julie knew where I'd be and how to reach me. I couldn't tell Julie what might be waiting for me in Romania. Her motherly instincts would go into overdrive.

"No need, Julie. I'll be back as soon as I can. Is Mr. Devlin back from court yet?"

"He just went to his office."

"Good. Would you transfer me?"

"Right away. He's even more worried about you than I am. Are you in some kind of danger, Michael?"

"Danger? Julie, I'm a lawyer. We avoid danger like the plague."

* * *

Mr. D. picked up the phone on the first half-ring. I brought him up to date on everything. Once more, I needed to have him and Billy Coyne in the same room with privacy. I asked him to contact Mr. Coyne and invite him to join us for a six-p.m. dinner. I'd make it an offer he couldn't refuse.

I called an old friend who managed a restaurant that is one of the most difficult reservations in Boston. My pal Ed Goodavage came through with a private table at what is now one of Boston's most elite dining spots. It fills the building that was formerly the dour, vermin-infested dungeon known as the Charles Street jail. In its previous life, I'd had the displeasure on many occasions of interviewing clients there while they were waiting to be tried. I always thought that the sweetest sound on God's earth was the sound of that metal door clanging behind me when I walked out of that pit of misery. Now it's almost impossible to get a reservation to get into it. Appropriately enough, the name of the restaurant is "Clink."

On the way to the garage, I had walked up Summer Street for a quick dip into Macy's—formerly Jordan Marsh—across the street from the never-to-be-forgotten Filene's Basement. I needed to re-stock on items from socks to toothpaste and something to carry them in for the trip to Romania. Packing at home in Winthrop would clearly have invited whatever the Chinese and Russians would like to have planned for my evening.

* * *

At 6:00 p.m. on the button, Mr. Devlin, Billy Coyne, and I walked into Clink. I still got the shivers from memories of the old days, but they were short-lived. Manager Ed Goodavage gave us a warm personal greeting and brought us up to what was formerly the third tier of jail cells overlooking the large prisoners' common area of yesteryear. Our table inside one of the original cells set the stage appropriately.

I knew that what I had to share with Mr. Coyne would be likely to derail his digestion, and therefore, probably mine as well. I decided to table the business agenda until Chef Daniel had a full opportunity to perform his *leger-de-main* in the open kitchen below.

I needed to get Mr. Coyne on my side through a few disturbing disclosures. To maximize the odds, I had preordered his and Mr. Devlin's choice of Jameson's Irish Whiskey and my choice of Famous Grouse Scotch, to be at the table when we arrived. I also set up a running flow of Villa Maria Sauvignon Blanc and Pinot Noir through the dinner. The East Coast oysters and lobster chowder, as a prelude to a monkfish osso bucco doused in veal broth, could have braced King Louis XVI for breaking news of the French Revolution.

By the time Mr. Coyne sat back, after the chef's signature desert of blood orange crème brulee, I thought he could handle anything I dropped on him.

I started by laying out the conclusion that even I had trouble accepting. I had his full attention when I said, "I know that the Russian mafia and the Chinese tong are each separately enough to give you and Boston's finest a plateful of trouble, but I can't escape the conclusion that those two have joined forces. I'm certain they're working together in going after that Stradivarius I told you about."

"The hell you say. Could never happen."

"I know. But it did happen. And the treasure it could lead to is so vast that, if they find it, the problems they're creating now in this city will look like inconveniences."

I laid out the chain of events that had led me to that result. I refilled my wine glass in silence to let him digest the facts and come to his own conclusion.

The more he wrestled to reach a different result, the more he settled into a solemn grouch deeper than I'd ever seen, even for Mr. Coyne.

"So where does this leave you in all this, kid?"

"Dead center between the two gangs. That's why I need to be on the same page with the district attorney's office. It's become more complicated."

"Spell it out."

"First of all, that violin that's somehow the key to finding the treasure—I have it. I'm the only one who knows where it is. That makes me the target of both gangs."

"So where is it?"

"I knew you'd ask that. I can't tell you."

He looked at Mr. Devlin. "Why the hell not?"

I answered. "I know it goes against your nature, but you just have to trust me on this. It's best for the both of you if I'm the only one who knows where that damn thing is."

"Not to be morbid, kid, but you don't exactly lead a contemplative life. How many times have they come at you already? God forbid, suppose they get lucky the next time. Might it be wise to share the secret?"

"I've taken care of that. I left a letter with Mr. Devlin. He'll open it only if . . . it becomes necessary."

Mr. D. nodded. I had made that arrangement with him the first time I came back from Romania.

Mr. Coyne just looked at me. At least he was not pressing that argument. I picked it up before he did. "There's another complication. You told us that your office was getting a murder indictment against Mickey Chan."

"Which information was not to leave that table at the Marliave."

"It hasn't. Except for his. I met with Mickey Chan. We've taken on his representation."

His sour expression deepened. He looked somewhere between shocked and angry. "How the hell can you do that? I told you about that indictment in confidence."

Mr. D. stepped in. "You told us there would be an indictment. You told us there was a witness. That's all going to be known by the whole world after the arraignment. No harm, no foul."

"The hell, no harm. That was private information given in trust. You'll get the three of us disbarred."

"Billy, calm down. It's bad for your blood pressure."

"To hell with my blood pressure. I had your word."

"And you still have it. Michael, will you explain it before he self-ignites?"

"Mr. Coyne, I had no intention of breaching our trust. The situation went from a simple problem to a disaster of major proportions in an instant. There was no time to contact you. I did nothing, said nothing, that you wouldn't have authorized if we had had time to talk about it."

He settled a bit. His color went from scarlet to merely deep red. "I'm listening."

"When we talked the last time, you told me—in confidence, I agree—that you were going for an indictment against Mickey Chan. I might add, you were doing it against your professional judgment to satisfy the D. A.'s misguided political ambitions."

"That's beside the point. It was said in confidence."

"Granted. At that time, we were talking about a Chinese tong murder of a member of their own gang. They eliminate one of their own. It happens. Not earth-shaking in terms of the city's big picture. Do you remember that?"

"I remember the whole damn conversation."

"Alright. After our conversation, I had a meeting with Mickey Chan in the poultry shop of Mr. Wan Leong on Tyler Street. Mickey Chan was there and Danny Liu, the son of the murdered man. They added pieces to the puzzle that pushed this thing to a level that could turn into an international crisis."

Mr. Coyne still had doubt in his eyes, but I clearly had his attention. I kept the ball rolling. "I found out that Mr. Liu was more than the head of the Chinese Merchants Association. He was a big shot in the tong. That raised the ante. It went higher. I found out that even the Boston tong is just a puppet. This treasure hunt for the violin is directed by one of the major triads in Hong Kong. Then add this. Mr. Liu, it turns out, was double-crossing both the tong and the triad. He was using me as part of it when he sent me to Romania to pick up the violin. This thing jumped from a little treasure-hunting adventure to a shake-up in the international criminal balance of power—a major shake-up, if we believe what I was told about the extent of the treasure. And I do believe it."

"I still see a violation of trust . . ."

"There's more. The night I was to meet the murdered man, Mr. Liu, at the swan-boat pond in the Public Garden, he and I were the only ones who knew about the meeting. So I thought. All of a sudden, there's a big-time assassin sent by the Russian mafia to blow me away. If Mickey Chan hadn't knocked me out of the way of a bullet, we wouldn't be having this elegant dinner. I didn't put it together completely then, but it was clear when I met with Mickey Chan that this was not just a gang eliminating one of its thugs. This was at least two major international criminal organizations, the Russians and the Chinese, working together—for the first time—to capture a stash of treasure that could double, triple their power to make the world suffer. They could finance their drug trade, human trafficking, illegal arms sales, cyber-crime, all of it on a scale we can't even contemplate."

I could see that he was still having trouble reaching the conclusion he least wanted to accept. I drove in the last nail I had. "There was a repeat performance this morning. I had scheduled a secret meeting with the president of the Chinese Bank of Chinatown. Sure enough, the Russian thugs showed up to make another play for the violin—and possibly me with it. I think I'd be playing loose with my life if I didn't accept the fact that the Russians and the tong are working together."

I let him fit the pieces together while I refilled all three glasses with Villa Maria. The glasses sat there ignored while he wrestled with what seemed to me an inescapable conclusion. He finally looked me in the eye and came back to an issue he could work with more easily.

"What does all this have to do with your representing Mickey Chan?"

"I offered to represent Mickey Chan when we met this morning because I could see he was being framed by the tong. Mr. Devlin agreed. I'm sure now that it's all connected to this scramble for the violin and the treasure. You know yourself you've got a questionable, scared witness in Ming Tan. Here's another piece of breaking news. Ming Tan has currently gone missing, undoubtedly at the hands of the tong."

I could see in his face that that was a jolt. I sensed a shift in his thinking. I fired one more round. "It comes down to this. I think I'm the only one on the side of the good guys who sees most of the total picture here. I may need Mickey Chan alive and free to move to be able to defuse this bombshell before it explodes on all of us."

Mr. Coyne looked as if the stakes in the game were beginning to sink in. He looked over at Mr. D. "This kid gives me a new headache every time I see him, Lex."

"He's no kid, Billy. You should be thanking God that he has the courage to play this game out—for us all. I'd pull him out of this whole business in an instant, but he follows his own conscience. Listen to him."

Mr. Coyne was beginning to settle back to cool rationality, judging by his color. He looked back at me without the fire in his eyes. "What do you want from me?"

"First, I'll tell you what I can do for you. The time will come when I'll walk Mickey Chan right into your office to turn himself in."

"When?"

"When it's safe. If I did it today, you'd run him through an arraignment and lock him up on a murder charge. There'd be no bail. He'd be a sitting duck. There isn't a lockup in this state where the tong or the Russians couldn't get at him to kill him. I need him alive, where I can reach him when I need him."

"Then you do know where he is?"

"No, I don't. I have no idea."

"But you can get word to him."

"When I need to."

He gave it a minute to let the pieces fall further together. "So what do you want from me? I assume this dinner is not totally free of charge."

I leaned in and spoke softly. "Two things. First, let up on the manhunt for Mickey Chan. For the time being. He and I both have enough wolves on our tails. You can stall the madam prosecutor for a few days."

"Maybe. What else?"

"I need you to be fully informed and ready to move in when the time comes. I'll feed you everything I learn."

"And what will you be doing?"

"I leave for Romania tonight. I think the key to this whole thing is unraveling the code to the location of that treasure. And that's tied to that violin. I need to trace it back to whoever owned it before I picked it up. Somewhere up the line, there's someone who can interpret the code."

"If so, why haven't they taken the treasure themselves?"

"Mr. Coyne, you have an instinct for the jugular. That's one of about a hundred questions I need to have answered. I'll be in touch."

* * *

My next to last cell phone call after boarding the 9:00 p.m. Lufthansa flight before taking off for Otopeni International Airport in Bucharest was to Terry. I owed her an honest outline of what I had ahead of me and why. I could practically hear her heart racing at the prospect, but her voice conveyed love and support.

Yet one more time, I vowed to myself that I'd never put her in that situation again. I couldn't speak that vow out loud, because it would echo the vow I'd made before I became ensnared in this mess. How could I promise her that it would never happen again?

My last call was to George. I chalked his cryptic, clipped tone up to a weak cell phone connection. He gave me two addresses on the outskirts of the city of Bucharest. I copied down both.

"What are these, George?"

"The first is the Hotel Cisingiu on Regina Elisabeta Boulevard. You have a reservation."

"In what name?"

"Your own. They'll need to see your passport."

"Okay. What's the second? Is that the rest home? Is that where I find Mr. Oresciu?"

His second answer was more clipped and muted than the first. "No."

"What do you mean, 'No'?"

"Michael, I'm sorry. I have no idea what you'll be walking into. Mr. Oresciu's been taken."

"What does that mean? By whom?"

"I don't know."

"Taken where?"

"Damn it. I don't know. They—whoever *they* are—sent me a message. You're to go to that second address tomorrow night. Ten o'clock. It's about a block from your hotel."

"What is it?"

"It's a club, a nightclub. It's called the Kristal Glam Club. It's near two universities. It'll be crowded, noisy."

"Who do I look for?"

"You don't. Just go there. They'll approach you."

I had to catch my breath. Just once in all this insanity I'd have welcomed a plan that flowed smoothly. For better or worse, clearly this was not going to be it.

"Do we have anyone on our side there?"

"I'll see what I can do. One more time. Be careful."

It struck me that the most careful thing I could do would be to run off that plane at a pace that would leave skid marks before the doors were sealed shut, pick up Terry, and transfer my entire practice to Vermont.

Since that was not in the cards, I settled into seat 5A, buckled my seat belt, and said a deep prayer.

CHAPTER EIGHTEEN

CHECK-IN AT THE four-plus-star Hotel Cisingiu on Boulevard Regina Elisabeta in Bucharest was smooth, warm, welcoming, and decidedly unthreatening. I was tempted to take it as a good omen, but I was becoming leery of misreading omens.

I used the afternoon to scout out the area around the Kristal Glam Club, a few doors down the mid-city boulevard from the hotel. The club was an easy walk from the University of Bucharest and the Academy of Economic Studies. That explained it. I had done enough website research to know that I'd be walking that night into the club with the highest draw of college types in the city.

I found a shop for the kind of clothes that would damp down the suit-and-tie regimen of a Boston trial lawyer. I wanted to be spotted by the people I was there to contact without looking like a duck in a swan pond to everyone else.

I left a wake-up call with the hotel desk-clerk for nine p.m. and caught a few hours of make-up sleep. By ten that night, I was up, dressed, and ready to pass as a grad student, Bucharest style.

Before cruising into a foreign club for a rendezvous with people I only knew as the thugs who would brutally beat and kidnap an elderly violin maker, I needed some down-home fortification for both body and spirit. Two Big Macs and a super-sized order of fries at the McDonald's across from the hotel filled the bill nicely.

* * *

The Kristal Glam Club was precisely the magnet it was reputed to be. There was a line of late-teens to mid-twenties waiting to be cleared for entry by one gargantuan sentry at the door. Except for the particular language of the chatter, the entire line could have been cast from any urban college in America.

It took me about twenty minutes in line to reach the checkpoint. I could feel the eyes of the sentry giving this American a scan like an MRI. I was also scanning him for any sign that I was expected. None whatsoever.

Passing through that door was a jolting reminder of how many years it had been since criminal defense work had left time to check into the fads and fashions of club life in Boston. My first broad scan of the elbow-to-elbow expanse of humanity, grinding and bouncing in synch with the numbing pulsations of electronic sound waves, was like watching a wheat field in a hurricane. Half a football field across the span of heads was a platform on which a slim gent in his own world of gyrations was engrossed in fingering the knobs of a rack of electronic amplification that could equal the studio of Boston's WBZ.

Finding an entry point into the wheat field was only the first problem. Once in, where in hell should I head to maximize discoverability by the one person in all of that morass I needed to contact?

For lack of a plan, I followed my first inclination. When in doubt, start where they serve the drinks. I slid into the first crack in the crowd and ducked elbows and knees in an erratic path toward the wall-length bar to the right. My evasive, defensive movements must have given the impression of dancing, because except for the occasional vague smile, there was not one glimmer of notice, much less recognition or contact. And contact was the sole object of the game.

I managed to find a stationary landing spot a couple of rows from the bar. Within about ten minutes, I was actually leaning on solid wood and willing eye contact with any of the three flying bartenders. Bottles of unfamiliar brands were being juggled *ala* the fifteen-year-old American film *Coyote Ugly*. Orders from my sardine-packed bar-mates were being hurled above the pulsing din of the music. They were somehow being heard and filled by the performing bartenders.

It took less than thirty seconds to realize two things. First, even if I caught the fleeting glance of a bartender, I would have no notion of what the options were to order. Every bottle I could make out was labeled in Romanian. Secondly, and infinitely larger on the scale of concerns, anyone trying to make actual contact with me in that human boom-box would likely be whistling in the wind.

I came to a conclusion. I'd give it ten more minutes before gyrating my way back though the wheat maze to the fresh, still, silent air on the other side of that door. I'd call George, whatever the hell time it was in Boston, and tell him to come up with a plan that would touch base with reality—and do it before I executed part three of my plan, which was to book the next thing flying back to Boston.

My countdown got as far as seven minutes. It finally penetrated my awareness that one aspect of the endless pounding pulsations was a rapping on my shoulder from behind. I twisted around, expecting to see the ice-cold eyes of some Russian mob contact man. I was both disappointed and, truth be told, relieved when I followed the tapping hand, down the arm to a face. It was lit with a smile as warm as an outbreak of spring sunshine. The girl, about nineteen, cute and perky as a commercial for Pepsi, was mouthing something—probably in Romanian—that I couldn't catch. I smiled back and tapped my ear to signal "*No comprendo.*"

The boy holding her hand beside her smiled and made eye contact. He leaned forward close to my ear. "You look American. First time in club here?"

"It's that obvious?"

His grin broadened. He yelled back, "Yes. Pretty much."

The girl tapped my shoulder again and motioned to me to bend down. I did. She yelled close to my ear, "It won't work that way. You'll never get a drink."

I raised my hands in my best, "Then how?" gesture.

She gave me a signal I finally interpreted as "push to the side." I did. It opened a tiny path to the bar. The boy beside her, who obviously understood the plan, took her by the waist and propped her up to be sitting on the bar. That caught the eye of the nearest bartender. Within seconds she was yelling something in his direction. The bartender nodded. The boy lifted her back down beside me.

She had me laughing now. "I'll be sure to try that next time."

The boy leaned over, laughing too. "It won't work so well for you. It only works for Irina. She's prettier than both of us."

Within a few seconds, the bartender was handing me a glass with a good four fingers of amber liquid over ice.

My two interpreters were each grinning with the light of good-deed doers. They both nodded and said with gusto, "*Sanatate buna*!"

I gave a questioning look. The girl, Irina, cupped her hand to her mouth and said, "It means 'Good health.'"

That brought a warm smile on my part. I replied with a grateful nod to them both and a hearty Irish, "*Slante*!"

The emptiness I had felt at the obvious failure of my primary mission was suddenly all but drowned in a warm feeling of actual contact with two friendly members of the human race at the opposite side of the earth. I toasted the commonality between us with a deep sip of the amber liquid.

In that one instant, the warmth of the moment turned as cold as the ice in my glass. It was replaced by the jolting realization that, like it or not, my mission was about to be accomplished. Unlikely as it seemed, that first taste told me that those two warm, smiling young faces were my contact with the world of Russian thugs. The liquid in my glass was unmistakably a message—my personal favorite—Famous Grouse Scotch.

I let the familiar slight burn of the Grouse work its way into every corner of my throat. When I looked back at my teenage benefactors, the warm smiles were gone. Only the direct eye contact remained. Irina spoke first in words I could read on her lips. "Follow me."

She took the path of least resistance around the three layers of students in front of the bar and then walked close to the wall. We were moving away from the entrance door and around the hall toward the music platform. I could feel myself being sucked further and further away from an escape route and deeper into God only knew what. At least the mission was back on track.

There was a door behind the stage. The boy was gone, but Irina led me through it. As soon as I passed to the outside, I felt the grip of powerful arms around my chest. The hands moved over every inch of my upper body. I felt a shoe kick out on the inside of my left foot. I nearly toppled, but I caught myself in a spread position that allowed the search to be completed.

There was a black automobile in the alleyway in front of me. Its back door stood open. When the hands finished the full tour of my body, there was a solid nudge in my back to start me toward the open door. With little choice, I started to walk. Just before I got into the car, Irina ran up beside me. She looked very young and vulnerable. Her voice was soft.

"I'm sorry. I had to. I hope you'll be alright."

I had no anger. I had no answer either. She gave me a brief hug. The goon behind us grabbed her arm and flung her like a twig back against the wall. In almost the same motion he gave me a stabbing jolt in the back that sent me moving quickly into the open door of the car.

I was alone in the back seat. I heard the click of the lock on the doors. The car picked up speed down the alley.

The darkened glass of the back-seat windows together with the black of night made it impossible to see anything but random lights flying by. When the lights diminished, we picked up more speed. I knew we were out of city limits. Another half hour and we made a sharp turn to the right onto a long gravel road.

Then the car stopped in a skid. The door was yanked open. A hand like a bear claw reached in to grab me by the arm. I figured I had two choices: surrender myself up to whatever these clowns had in mind, or fight the whole process.

I chose a middle ground. I smacked the back of the hand with every ounce of leverage I could muster. The hand pulled back out of instinct. I used the moment of surprise to get myself out of the car as if it were my choice. I reacted to the brief moment of shock on the face of the goon in front of me. "Keep your damn hands off of me!"

We were standing in front of the front door of what looked like an old farmhouse. There were lights inside. I chose to act as if I had been the beneficiary of an invitation—crude as it was. I started to march up to the front door.

Then the charade ended. I felt a smack on the back of my head that erased any notion that I was in charge of my fate. The bear claw grabbed my shoulder with a grip that repaid the smack I'd given his hand. My feet hardly touched the ground as I was marched up to the front door.

I was frozen in the pain of the goon's grip, when the door opened. We were caught in the light from the inside. A voice from a figure in the doorway in front of me cut through the pain.

"Leonid! Gently! This man is our guest."

The grip fell away. Anger and residual pain brought the words out of me. "Yeah, Leonid. Get your damn hands off of me! You touch me one more time, and I'll take you apart."

I actually said that, just that way. Of course, it was with the sincere prayer that Leonid did not speak that much English.

In the presence of the rather short man at the door, probably in his fifties, Leonid backed off. The man smiled benignly and reached out a hand as if to welcome me in. As I passed him, he said in a whisper, "A word of caution, Mr. Knight. I wouldn't push Leonid any further. He has a certain flash temper. Occasionally he does something rash in spite of my orders."

My host was putting a velvet glove on a clear threat. The decision to follow his advice seemed wise.

He led me into what would be called a parlor in that setting. I noticed that the furniture and pieces of rustic art in the room were probably of the same vintage as the farmhouse, but well kept, and possibly, to my untrained eye, the kind that pop eyes on *Antiques Roadshow*. For some reason I made note of that. I also noted that three more goons out of the same mold as Leonid were stationed around the room.

"Please sit down, Mr. Knight. I hope you'll forgive the . . . drama with which Leonid . . . invited you here. He's impetuous. And we have serious business here, you and I."

"Leonid is a goon, Mr. . . . ?"

"I think names don't matter for our business."

"And yet you know mine."

He smiled and nodded. "You may call me 'Boris.' You were saying . . . Michael, if I may be familiar."

"You may. And if I may, your Leonid is a goon. I was basically kidnapped. I'd like to be clear. Am I here to do business? You know, I do for you, you do for me. Or am I your prisoner?"

He shrugged. "Does it matter?"

"It does to me. You'll find I react differently to the two situations."

He smiled again, which meant nothing. "Let me explain why you're here. No pretenses. Cards on the table, as you like to say."

That was the second subtle hint that forced me to wonder how much they actually knew about me, and of more concern, about Terry. The Famous Grouse at the Kristal Glam was the first eye-opener. He was also right about a phrase I tend to use. I tried not to react.

"Definitely . . . Boris. Cards on the table."

He indicated a seat in front of the crackling fireplace. I sat while he walked to a small wagon of bottles. "Would you prefer vodka, or perhaps *tuica*. I believe you've tried it." Another jab of familiarity to make it clear that he knew about my meetings with George. "Perhaps your Famous Grouse?"

"I'll settle for an honest discussion. Let's talk about why I'm here?"

He sat opposite me. His tone became less casual. "I think you know why you're here. I won't underestimate your understanding of these matters. You'd do well not to underestimate mine. To be brief. You have an object. You've so far eluded our efforts to relieve you of it. Never mind. There's yet another piece to the puzzle. Yes?"

"And that would be?"

He smiled without warmth. "Is there a need to be coy, Mr. Knight? There is very little that you've said or done in the last week that I couldn't relate to you. Shall we not waste each other's time?"

Again, the first stab of concern was whether his knowledge included Terry's relocation. I needed to gain some foothold of control.

"Agreed. But let me be clear about something you may not know. Cards on the table, right? We're talking about some treasure that goes back five or six hundred years, that may not even exist. I was sent blind on a goose chase for a violin that may or may not have some kind of code. This business has consumed my life since I was sucked into it. Hear this. I want just one thing. I want out. Frankly, I don't give a damn which of you three blights on the earth go after it, or get it."

He ignored my reference to "blights."

"Yes. It would seem so simple. You give us the violin and walk away. And yet, it's not quite that simple, is it? When you first came to Romania, you met a violin maker, Mr. Oresciu. He holds the key to the code in the violin. Or he knows who does."

"And he, like me, is your prisoner. Correct?"

"Mmm. I dislike the word 'prisoner.'"

"So do I. But if I headed for that door, I assume I'd be reacquainted with Leonid."

"Let's not quibble over semantics. Mr. Oresciu is proving to be an obstacle. He refuses to discuss the matter with anyone—except you."

"You amaze me, Boris. I've heard that your methods of torture are irresistible. Don't tell me you've grown a conscience."

His voice became low and tense. "Don't misunderstand me, Michael. Your Mr. Oresciu is in frail health. It's unlikely that he would survive the methods you refer to. You, however, seem in excellent health."

"What do you want me to do?"

He leaned closer. "You'll speak with him. You know what we need to know. You'll tell us what he tells you about the code. Then you'll hand over the violin. No more tricks. No more games."

"And then I'll walk away from this whole business and resume a long happy life."

"Of course."

I could only smile. "You seem to know more about me than my mother. What in my background makes you conclude that I'm simple-minded enough to imagine you'd let me live ten seconds after I give you the violin?"

He returned my smile. "We would never consider you simple-minded. Who knows? Perhaps you can resign yourself to . . . such a final conclusion. On the other hand, you might be less dismissive of what might happen to your wife, Terry. There might be room for bargaining on her behalf."

He touched the one nerve that controlled all of my thinking. I could simply nod. "Alright."

CHAPTER NINETEEN

BORIS SMILED AT my apparent surrender. "Very wise. Then you'll come this way."

He led me to a door at the far side of the room. He used a key to open a dead-bolt lock and shoved open the door. I waited for him to lead the way in, but he just stood back beside the door. "In there, now. You'll ask the right questions. You'll get what we need from him. He's a stupid old man. Old men can be stubborn. Especially Romanians."

I nodded. "Yep, not like you smart, honorable, easygoing Russians. Right, Boris?"

He forced a smile. "Have your little joke now. But remember this when you go into that room. The continued health . . . pretty face . . . perhaps life of someone very close to you will depend on your treating serious business seriously. Do you fully understand that?"

I went into a silent struggle to suppress a raging anger at what he was suggesting.

"I'll have an answer. This may be the last chance to get the information from that crazy old man. He won't last long. I want you focused. Do you understand clearly what will happen if you disappoint us?"

I tamped my emotions down from the verge of an eruption to a controlled boil. I turned to get a dead-on look into his eyes. "Boris, you are the lowest, filthiest piece of scum I've ever met. I don't think there's an ounce of your ignominious being that deserves to be called human. There's nothing I can do to change that. But before I walk into that room, by damn, you will give that man the dignity he deserves. You will refer to him as 'Mr. Oresciu.'"

He was stunned for a moment before he quickly remembered that he still had the upper hand. That brought a sardonic smile back to his puffed-out lips. He held a hand out to the open door. "As you wish, Michael. You will now go in there and speak with . . . Mr. Oresciu. You will not come out of that room without the information we need."

He stood back. I walked into the room with a dread that ran down to my toes. I had a clear vision of the sweet gentleness of that man whose entire life had been consumed with giving the joy of music to the world. I could visualize that warm smile when his eyes had looked into my heart. Then I recalled the broken, abused body that I held in my arms on the floor of his violin shop, and my heart constricted all over again.

I walked in slowly, silently. There was a heavy wooden bed at the far end of the room. The size of it exaggerated the diminutive size of the fragile body lying in the center of it.

When I walked up to the edge of the bed and touched the pillow, that serene face turned toward me. There was a recognition that brought an instant light to those tired eyes. He licked dry lips and found the strength to say, "Michael. You found me again. Just like before."

How I wished it were "just like before." I could relive in my mind, just for an instant, that long conversation about music over coffee that we would never again savor in this life. The emptiness it brought was hard to bear.

"My dear friend, how I wish I could have gotten here sooner."

I could see a tiny waving off of a small, calloused hand. "No, Michael. No regrets. We should thank God for these minutes together." His smile brightened. "I will thank Him. I'll be seeing Him soon. I'll thank Him for the blessing of having you come into my life. It was brief perhaps. But not to be missed."

I wanted to tell him that the blessing was most certainly mine, but the only parts of my face that seemed to be working were the tear ducts.

His hand rose above the covers and rested on mine. It was still the strongest hand I'd felt since shaking hands with a jockey.

His expression became serious. "Michael, I'm afraid we've fallen into the hands of people not like us. They want information. I'm sorry to place this burden on you. If you wish, I can just take it with me."

"My dear friend, if you trust me with whatever it is, I'll do my best to see that it does as little harm, and as much good as possible. I'm afraid that if I leave here without something, other people will suffer deeply."

He nodded his understanding. The weight of it seemed to take him to a new level of weakness. His breathing was becoming shallow. I could see his hand beckoning me to bring my ear closer to his mouth.

"How sad that that miracle at the hands of Mr. Stradivari is being so misused. I think you know, that violin carries a code that could lead to a wealth these men will use for . . . terrible . . ."

I tried to tell him to rest, but he shook his head feebly. "No time, Michael. They think I can give them the code. I can't. I never heard it. I'm afraid they will be angry with you."

The look in his eyes was purely concern for me. He took a few shallow breaths to gain the strength to say, "But this may help. The one to ask . . . The person who may have it . . . is . . . the person who translated . . . the ship doctor's journal."

"I read the translation. There's nothing there. Nothing about a code. I read it all."

His hand gripped mine. "Not all, Michael . . . It's . . . not all there. The translator . . . She held back . . ."

I could feel the pressure of his hand slowly release. The deep concern in his face slowly melted into a pure peace. I knew that he was at last in the hands of the One who had given all music to the world. And I knew he was home.

*   *   *

I sat there, holding that hand that had brought nothing but musical beauty into the world. I was alone with my prayers.

I had a decision to make, and quickly. My friend had given me the key to the next step in this satanic quest. It was on my shoulders now. Do I give Boris and his cutthroats the name of the woman at the university who translated the journal, and most surely bring into her life whatever hell these Russian gangsters could devise? Or do I shield her—at the expense of whatever horrors they had planned for Terry?

I struggled for an answer, but the time was up. The door burst open. Boris stomped his overstuffed carcass across the floor to the side of the bed.

"He's dead?"

I stood up. "Yes. There's nothing more you vultures can do to him. He's out of your grasp."

Boris looked into my eyes. "But you're not. And may I remind you there's another who's not beyond our reach. Tell me. What did he say? I advise you to be truthful."

I needed time. "You don't know? Don't tell me your technical geniuses didn't have the room bugged."

"I'm growing tired of your humor, Knight. Yes, of course we did. I heard enough to know he gave you information. He spoke too softly to hear it clearly. You will now tell me exactly what he said. And understand. I heard enough to know if you choose to lie."

I was still wrestling with the decision. I had nothing to offer at that moment but silence. Boris' eyes bored into mine for the few seconds I could salvage.

It was short-lived. He took a cell phone out of his pocket. He dialed a number. "I'm a patient man—when patience is called for. But no more."

He hit the speaker button on the phone. I could hear a ring tone and the click of the connection on the other end. My heart froze. The voice repeating "Hello" was Terry's.

I erupted. With a closed fist, I smashed my knuckles into the hand that held the phone. I could hear the bones in his wrist snap like twigs. Absolute hell consumed the minutes that followed.

The cacophony of the clattering of the phone against wall, bedpost, and floor was punctuated by the raucous curses and squeals of the writhing Boris. It nearly drowned out another sound I could not understand. I could swear that I heard the explosive splintering of the front door in the other room. It was followed by the stomping of heavy boots charging into that first room where three of Boris' thugs were waiting. More Russian curses from that outer room drowned out Boris' tantrum, but only for an instant. Rapid, deafening bursts of automatic weapon-fire filled the air for what seemed like ten seconds. Then sudden silence, filled only by the sound of heavy bodies hitting the floor.

Even Boris was stunned to silence. Our eyes were fixed on the bedroom door. I was beyond astonishment to see the small figure of Irina, the girl from the Glam Club, appear in the doorway.

In an instant, she pointed at Boris and screamed, "Michael!" I turned to see Boris struggling with his good hand to pull a gun out of his pocket. He jerked it free and leveled it at my head. Once more I heard, "Michael, here!" I looked just in time to see Irina tossing me a handgun. Without thought, I caught the gun and dove to the floor. I fired two rapid shots toward Boris' bulbous torso. Both shots struck home. His eyes were the size of fried eggs. He teetered backwards in stunned silence and crumbled in a heap on the floor.

My eyes were snapped back to the door when I heard Irina's voice at top pitch, "Michael! Back!" Her hand was out. She was focused on something in the other room that had her frozen to the side of the door.

"Now, Michael! Gun!"

I rolled on my side. I gave the gun a toss like a quarterback's lateral. She caught it, spun, and fired every shell left in the clip. The thud that followed shook the floor. I could see the top half of the hulking Leonid spread across the doorway, arms outstretched within half a foot of Irina.

I got to my feet. My first instinct was to run to her. To my surprise, that young, vulnerable girl from the Glam Club was quietly leaning against the doorframe, looking with cool, expressionless eyes at the fallen figure of Leonid.

"Are you alright, Irina? Was he coming for you?"

She answered in a voice that was alarming for its composure. "Yes. I'm alright. It's not the first time he's tried to put his hands on me. But it's the last."

I took the time to catch my breath and check the outer room. The three thugs who had been in the room with Boris were strewn around the floor in positions that suggested they had fought their last fight. There were also three men, dressed in black with black hoods, holding automatic weapons and searching the fallen bodies. They seemed to be taking anything that would identify the bodies.

I looked back in the bedroom. Boris was on the floor, rocking back and forth. His previous shrieks and curses had fallen to a droning whimpering. Based on the location of two spreading circles of red, my shots had caught him in the left shoulder and right thigh.

In spite of his threats, I thanked God that I hadn't taken his life.

The sight of Boris brought back a flash that needed immediate action. I found my cell phone. I dialed a number and said a prayer at the same time. It took only one ring to hear the shaken, but alive, voice of my Terry.

"Michael, what's happening? I got a call . . ."

"Terry, thank God. Are you alright?"

"Yes. I'm fine. But what . . ."

"Just listen, Terry. I'll explain later. I want you to do something right now. I want you to go out the front door of the cottage. Walk down the beach to the fifth house. Knock on the door. Their names are Armand and Michelle Roy. I'll call them. They'll be expecting you. Stay there until a man comes to pick you up. He'll mention the name Tom Burns. You'll be safe in his hands. Do you understand?"

"No. I mean I understand what you said. I don't understand what's happening."

"There's so much I'd like to say, Terry. But not now. Move fast. Don't try to take anything with you. Just go. I'll be in touch."

"Are you alright, Michael?"

"Yes. No more talk now, Terry. Except I love you. And I promise—never again. Go."

I hung up and speed-dialed Tom Burns. He caught it on the second ring. "Mikey. Do I assume you have another disaster for me?"

"Of course. No time to explain. Can you get a man to my cottage in Milton, New Hampshire? You've been there. You know where it is."

"As fast as possible, Mike."

"No. Faster, Tom. Have him pick up Terry at the Roy house, five houses to the right. Get her to a safe house. I'll contact you later. Can you get on it?"

"I already am. I have a man on an assignment about ten miles away. He's breaking the speed limits from Farmington right now. What should he expect?"

"Depends on how fast he gets there. Possibility of Russian mafia. I don't know how many."

"I'll let him know. Should I call you?"

"Hell yes, Tom. Soon as you have Terry safe."

I hung up and dialed the number of the Roy family at the lake. They were friends since childhood. In the calmest voice I could muster, I prepped them for the knock on their door by Terry, followed by a pickup by Tom Burns' man. I added the promise of a full explanation later.

I took a few moments to get back some equilibrium. Irina was standing beside me. The questioning look on my face almost made it unnecessary to ask, "How did you find this place? There was no car following us out here."

"You can thank your friend George. You know him from America, yes?"

Her words brought back what George had said when I asked him if I'd have anyone on my side when I walked into the Glam Club. He simply said, "I'll see what I can do."

"I know him well. But how did you find me?"

"I should tell you first, I'm Russian, but I was born in Romania. I speak both languages. The Russian mob recruited me to work for them, but Romania is really my home. Someone you don't need to know on the Romanian side asked me to go with the Russians, but report back to him."

"So you were a double agent. I still don't know how you found me."

"Do you remember I gave you a hug when you got into the car to leave the Glam Club?"

"Yes."

"Look in your pocket."

I took out a strange object that I was seeing for the first time. I looked up at her.

"It's a tracking device. We could follow you far enough back so you wouldn't see our car lights."

"I can't believe it. How do I thank you?"

"Did you get the information you came for?"

"To some extent, yes."

"Then you can thank me by sharing it with George. He wants to hear from you."

Through all of the clutter, one thought was coming foremost in my mind. Both Terry and I would likely have been casualties but for George's calling out the marines. I could feel myself crossing a line. I was now permanently on his side.

"I'll call him."

I looked over at the now glaring figure of Boris on the floor. "I'm afraid your cover is pretty well blown, Irina."

She smiled and shrugged. "It would have happened eventually. There are other ways to serve my people. Meanwhile, remember that you owe George a call."

CHAPTER TWENTY

IRINA MADE A call to the local authorities to alert them to the accumulation of bodies we were leaving at the farmhouse. She did it anonymously, as nearly as I could tell, it all being in Romanian. Then she and the three other members of my rescuing contingent gave me a ride back to Bucharest.

At my request, and on her recommendation, they dropped me at the Vila Toparceanu, a neat little eight-room hotel within ten minutes of the Coanda Airport in Otopeni outside Bucharest. I booked a flight for the following morning through Atlanta to Manchester, New Hampshire. The primary goal was to leave Bucharest and arrive home, unscathed by Russian mobsters at either end.

My first call from the hotel was going to be to Tom Burns, but he beat me to it.

"Hey, Mikey."

"Tom, before another word, tell me it all went well with Terry."

"Alright, I will. It all went well with Terry."

"A few details."

"That girl is a trooper, Mike. Why the hell don't you stop playing James Bond and give her a decent life?"

"Excellent advice, Tom. This is the last quagmire I'm going to get us into. I promise both of you."

"Excellent. That promise and five bucks will get you a cup of coffee at any Starbucks."

"No. Not this time. I mean it more every hour. Tell me about Terry. How is she?"

"My man got there and picked her up. Just to let you know, when they were driving the road away from the cottage, they passed a black Lincoln with four bozos who weren't your typical New Hampshire campers. It was that close."

"Thank God for Tom Burns."

"I think you're working both me and God overtime. I might add, I'm on Terry's side in this."

"It's hard to believe, but so am I. Someday I'll step back and try to explain to all three of us how I got sucked into this morass. Where is she now? How do I reach her?"

"My man took her to Rochester. She's at the Governor's Inn. I figured you'd want her at a five-star hotel."

"Right on that. How do I reach her?"

"I had my man register them both as husband and wife so she could go under the name of Mrs. Edward Barrett. It's a better cover. Just call the hotel. They'll connect you. Do it on a prepaid phone. You can't be too careful."

"Agreed. How's she doing?"

"Other than being worried sick about your imperiled hide, she is, as I said, a trooper."

"Thanks, Tom. If I need you . . ."

"Don't worry, Mikey. My man'll keep an eye on the hotel. You take care of yourself. For both of you."

* * *

My plane landed at the Manchester-Boston Regional Airport around four in the afternoon. I made the hour drive by rented car from the airport to the Governor's Inn in Rochester in less than forty minutes.

My reunion with Terry was like a "happily ever after" scene from a fairy tale. "Ever after" was one day, but it was a welcome oasis in a very arid desert.

I had decided in advance, with no objection from Terry, to eliminate that next day from the calendar. It didn't exist in the real world. For twenty-four hours, there were no gangsters, no treasure, no world beyond the Governor's Inn.

For the first time since what was billed as a "second honeymoon" began in Sinaia, Terry and I could feel together, alone, and in real communication. We were at lunch at Benedict's Grille when it happened—one of those moments that puts your life on a totally different plane.

I began to tell Terry that as soon as I could see this debacle to a conclusion, I'd see to it that we'd have peace and permanent safety for the rest of our lives. My professional life would take a serious reversal. Whatever might come along, I was ready to promise her the life together that we both wanted more than anything on earth.

I got as far as the word "promise."

Terry stopped me. "No. No promise. No matter how deeply you mean it. Are you listening to me?"

I most certainly was.

"This time, Michael, it has to be more than a promise. This time it has to be a fact . . . for the three of us."

Those last three words shifted gears in my mind with an instant resolute finality. From that moment, I knew that my life—our lives—would belong not only to each other, but to someone we could both hardly wait to meet.

The joy of that moment could only be expressed in a hug that lasted for what must have been minutes. When I could find my voice again, I whispered, "No promise this time. I'll make it a fact. For the three of us."

* * *

On the day after that, as Mr. Kipling once wrote, "The dawn came up like thunder." The world's entanglements came back into our lives like gangbusters. But we were recharged to face it.

What had happened in the farmhouse outside of Bucharest had undoubtedly been a severe poking of the Russian hornet's nest. I had also had a flash course on how closely they had been able to monitor my Boston doings in spite of evasive tactics. I began to realize that sticking to populated public places was my best, if not only, protection.

I got back in action in Boston that first day with one hell of a to-do list. It began with phone calls to Mr. Devlin, George, and Harry Wong to set up an agenda.

I dialed Mr. Devlin on his direct line to avoid explaining to my secretary, Julie, why I didn't have her book the flight home from my "vacation" in Bucharest. Mr. D. settled for a brief synopsis, with the promise of details at lunch at the Marliave, hopefully with Deputy D.A. Coyne in attendance. I knew that the Marliave was probably under the ubiquitous surveillance of the Russian mob, but to hell with them. They'd be unlikely to pull a grab-and-run on me in such a populated place at noon.

The second call was to George. He picked up on the first ring.

"Michael, are you alright? Are you back?"

"Yes and yes."

"I heard you had a bit of an adventure."

"Before we talk, can you pick up a prepaid, untapped phone in the next ten minutes?"

There was a brief hesitation. "I can. Do I assume I should not ask why?"

"Good idea. Call me back when you're in a safe place, alone."

George was quick on the pickup. He simply hung up.

My third call was to Harry Wong.

"Mike. I was wondering when I'd hear from you. You staying out of trouble?"

"Of course, Harry. Just a poor boy tryin' to make his way in the world."

"Uh-huh. That sounds ominous. What's up?"

"How does your morning look?"

"Well, I could research an article on photo plastic solvents. I could attend a lecture on metallic stress in alloys. Or I could join you and probably put my skinny yellow neck in a guillotine. Pick one."

"Let's go with the guillotine. Chinatown? Back room of Mr. Leong's poultry shop? Ten o'clock this morning? You ready to saddle up?"

"Hi-yo, Silver."

Only my trusty Harry could joke about it. What I had in mind could well fit his "guillotine" metaphor.

I had just hung up with Harry, when George called back.

"Good timing. You're on a safe phone?"

"As requested. Why so?"

"I have reason to believe that our Russian friends have more access to my personal life than I find comfortable. It may be an excess of caution, but . . ."

"There's no such thing for people in our business."

"*Your* business, George. It's strictly a one-shot freelance for me. The more one-shot, the better."

"Understood. Tell me about Bucharest."

"You could say that Romanian hospitality fell short of its reputation. I take it Irina gave you the details. Probably better than I could."

"It was a close call. I had no idea what you were walking into."

"Your young lady is quite a surprise. I owe the rest of my life to her."

"Irina is one of a kind. Probably not quite as young as you thought she was at the Glam Club. But amazing."

"I'm afraid her undercover work is cut short. The head of that mob of Russian thugs at the farmhouse, Boris, he could be a problem. I shot him twice, but not fatally. He could break her cover."

"Don't worry about Boris. My people cleaned up. Her identity is safe."

Without asking, I assumed that that meant Boris was no longer on the active player roster of the Russian team. Perhaps selfishly, I was still glad that it was neither of the bullets I fired that had permanently dispatched him to his final accounting.

"You and I have to meet, George. We have things to talk about."

"I was hoping so. Dinner at the Wallachia Café?"

"No. I hate to tell you this, but I'm afraid your boat has a leak. Boris and his pals seemed to know about everything we discussed during our lunch at the Wallachia."

That seemed to trigger more tension than anything else I'd ever said to him. I was becoming more convinced with each contact that in spite of his outlaw pursuits, George and I shared a mutual respect for loyalty. Betrayal by someone in whom we placed trust had a personal sting that went beyond the danger it presented.

There was a heavy pause. "We'll talk about this further. Where shall we meet?"

"What do you know about sea dragons?"

"Probably a lot less than you."

"I doubt it. Maybe it's time we both learned. I'm thinking this afternoon. Three p.m. The sea dragon exhibit at the New England Aquarium. It's on the second floor. Are you game?"

"You're a never-ending surprise—one of your greatest charms. Sea dragons it is. I might be a few minutes late. No worries. I'll be there."

*　*　*

At ten o'clock on the button, I walked among the sidewalk population on Tyler Street to Mr. Leong's poultry shop. I could sense both Russian and Chinese eyes watching my every step. It could have been an overactive imagination, but no matter. I felt free to move as long as I was wrapped in the protection of a public crowd.

Mr. Leong greeted me with a smile and a gracious bow, both of which I returned. I asked for his well-being, which he rightly took to mean freedom from the tong's fist in his cash register, and more critically, their talons on his grandson. His smile broadened. He simply nodded twice. That said it all.

Still the master of coded speech, he said within hearing of his customers, "Your package has arrived. It is in my office. You may pick it up while I attend to my customers."

I nodded, grateful that my purpose in being there was undisclosed without having to find a way to dispose of another goose.

I walked back into Mr. Leong's office. I closed the door. Harry was there, as expected. I was relieved that without my asking, he had brought Mickey Chan with him. I assumed correctly that they had again used the back-alley entrance. I indulged the belief that neither the Russians nor the tong had their eyes on Harry or Mickey.

By now, I had some notion of a plan for dealing with the Chinese team of treasure-hunters. It required face-to-face dealing with the top dog on their side. And that required learning who he might be. I laid out the problem for Harry and Mickey.

Harry explained the first hurdle. The tong thrives on secrecy— particularly in the matter of the upper levels of the chain of command. The second in command, the *Fu Shan Chu*, is known to only a few at the top. The dragon head, the very top man, the *Shan Chu*, is known only to the *Fu Shan Chu*.

Mickey chimed in to remind us that there was another layer. At our last meeting, Danny had mentioned that, because of the size of the prize involved, the parent triad in Hong Kong had taken over the running of the hunt for the violin.

"Then that's the man I need to meet. The man with power to make a deal. How do I find him?"

Harry answered. "You don't. Not directly. Too much secrecy. You have to jump in at some level and work your way up."

"So where do I jump in?"

Harry and Mickey looked at each other. I knew they were thinking alike. Mickey said it. "How about the fat man you scared the crap out of for Mr. Leong. His name is Tow An-Yan. You already have some leverage on him."

"Good thought. Maybe we can get some more mileage out of the deportation threat. How do I make contact?"

Mickey had the idea. "I know the route of the collection of *lo mo*, lucky money—extortion from the shops in Chinatown. I used to be part of it. On Thursday, the youth gang will collect from six shops on Tyler Street. They'll bring the collection to the fat man."

"Where?"

"That's the problem. It's called the 'large-stakes gambling den.' It's open twenty-four hours. It's also the banking operation that funds all of the tong's other criminal activities like drugs, bringing girls from China for prostitution, money laundering, murder for hire. Every Chinatown has one."

"Do you know where it is?"

"Yes."

"Can you take me there?"

"No."

"No? Why not?"

"It's strictly guarded by the tong's *boo how doy*, the youth gang enforcers. You'd have a better chance of getting into Fort Knox, alive."

"Then what? I just need to plant a message that'll get to the man from the triad."

It was Harry's turn. "I can try. I'll go there. I speak the language."

"I'll go with you."

"Not a good idea, Mike. Not a healthy one anyway. You're a *gweilo*—non-Chinese. The welcome mat is not out for you. In a big way."

"On the other hand, I'm the only one who has access to what they want. The violin. The only lead to the code."

"And with that you want to walk into their den?"

"'Want' may not be the word, but yes. You handle the introductions. If you can get them to listen, I'm going to make them an offer they can't refuse."

"And if they shoot first and listen later?"

"Then we'll know the plan isn't working."

Harry just looked at me.

Mickey offered to come with us. I jumped in. "No. As your lawyer, I want you under wraps. You're still under indictment. Go back to wherever you were. I don't want to know where. Keep in touch with Harry."

Harry still looked unconvinced. "Are you sure about going with me, Mike? I could deliver the offer myself. You stay out of sight."

"Doesn't work that way, Harry. It only has leverage because I'm the only one with the information. If I can pull it off, it might solve two problems. You ready?"

It took a second, but Harry gave me the nod.

CHAPTER TWENTY-ONE

HARRY LED THE way down Tyler Street at a brisk, self-confident, man-on-a-mission pace. I followed suit, according to instructions.

"'Face' is everything, Mike. The message we exude is 'We're in control. No fear.' Like the old joke—walk this way."

And I did. It's a funny thing about putting on "face." No matter how shallow it runs, it can give you a totally unfounded sense of confidence.

We turned left at the end of Tyler Street and crossed Beach Street. While we walked, an idea began to congeal. I had just one card to play and very little time to make the most of it. I pulled Harry to the side of a building out of foot traffic. I needed one phrase in Chinese. I said it to Harry.

Harry shook his head. "You can't say that, Michael. You're playing with dynamite. No one says these words in public, not even a Chinese."

"That's what I was hoping. Say it slowly in Chinese."

Harry was obviously uncomfortable, but he said the Chinese words four or five times while I repeated them. I worked them over until I had the sounds, the pitch, and the inflection as close as a *weilu* could get to Harry's phrase.

"Good enough to be understood, Harry?"

"Close enough to get your head taken off in one swipe."

"That's close enough. Let's do it."

"God help us."

Harry put us back in motion. He led us half a block to the ancient door of an unexceptional building. His pace never slackened. He walked straight up to the stone-cold eyes of two late-teens in leather jackets, one by each side of the door. They caught sight of me behind him and moved together like a brick wall in front of the door. Harry's voice descended half an octave and took on a serious bite.

Whatever he said to them in Chinese would have moved me aside just from the tone. If it had any effect whatever on the two terra-cotta soldiers in front of us, they hid it well. One of them never took his eyes off of mine. The other one matched Harry's commanding tone and raised it a level.

I kept eye contact with my staring partner until I heard rapid footsteps coming down the sidewalk from two directions. I broke contact just long enough to confirm with a glance that two more well-muscled teenage terra-cottas were boxing us in from behind. At this point, the face of confidence I was putting on had no substance behind it whatsoever.

About a minute into the confrontation, Harry suddenly put his fists on his hips for five seconds in silence. His features radiated a glaring message of impatience. His expression suddenly melted into one I can only describe as formalized respect. He turned to me. He gave a slight bow in what looked like a conveyance of deep deference. To my total befuddlement, he spoke to me softly but firmly in Chinese. The befuddlement was apparently contagious. Whatever he said stemmed the raucous flow of words from the soldier to the left.

To my surprise, all eyes were on me in silence. The stage was set for my cadenza. I drew myself up, slowly inhaling oxygen and false courage. With full Shakespearian projection, I delivered the words Harry had coached as if they were in my native tongue.

Miraculously, while Harry's previous Academy Award performance had no impact that I could detect, my rehearsed opus seemed to crack the stone. I caught what I could only call a shocked freeze on the two faces.

Harry picked it up like a fullback driving through an opening off-tackle. The intensity of what sounded like his demands rose to a peak. His last two words were the first I'd understood in ten minutes— "Michael Knight."

The terra-cotta soldier in front of Harry still looked a bit stunned. He turned to the one in front of me and barked an order. My soldier quickly opened the door and disappeared inside. In less than twenty seconds, the door reopened. A man well fitted in a suit of excellent silk bowed to each of us—me first, I noticed.

His hand gesture invited us to enter. Again, me first. I accepted the invitation, relieved that Harry was on my heels.

If the outside of the building was mundane brick, the inside could only be described as unstinted opulence. From the crystal chandelier that could have opened a performance of *Phantom of the Opera* to the flocked, hand-painted, silk wall-covering, and everything in between, I felt as if we'd been transported into the entry hall of the palace of an emperor of the Ming dynasty.

We were graciously escorted by the silk suit to a private room to the left of a grand staircase. If the entrance hall was palatial, this room could pass for the domain of the royal harem, absent the ladies. The silk suit made a gentile gesture that invited seating on a silk-brocade sofa that would have had any museum guard shooing visitors away like flies.

The silk suit said something in Chinese that went over my head, but it sounded unthreatening. Harry waved it off. The silk suit bowed, left, and closed the door.

I was next to Harry with a low whisper in a flash. "What the hell was that?"

Harry's whisper was even lower. "That last? I passed up the offer of tea. Did you want tea?"

"To hell with the tea. What's happening?"

"Listen to me. We only have a minute. This is a miracle. You're probably the first *weilu* to ever make it through that door."

"I'm honored."

"Yeah, well, the real miracle will be getting our breathing bodies out that door."

"What exactly did I say in Chinese?"

"There wasn't time to explain on the way. You wanted the Chinese words to ask to see the man here from the Hong Kong triad. They could have gotten you killed. No *weilu* should even know he's in the country."

"So what did I say?"

"These people thrive on secret codes. You demanded to see the man from Hong Kong by a number code name that no white man on earth could know. Thank God, I heard it years ago. Those goons at the door were so stunned when you said it—with great 'face,' I might add—they were afraid not to relay the message inside."

"If this man from Hong Kong does come in here, do we do this in English? My Chinese is not what they seem to think it is."

"Don't worry. He'll be well educated. He'll speak English."

"Do you know him?"

"No, of course not. I only heard his code name by accident years ago. Remember, I've been out of this gang for a lot of years. One more thing. Since it will be in English, you're really on your own. I have no clout here. In fact, I'm a pariah to them. Remember, I broke the sacred oath of the tong when I left the youth gang. Above all, no matter what, keep face."

The latch on the door clicked. We both stood. A man of about sixty years in a very fine, conservative light wool suit came into the room. The one deviation from an impression of typical corporate ascendency was a scar of old vintage from his eyebrow down the length of his right cheek. He bowed to me. I bowed to him. He smiled to me. I smiled to him.

He said in impeccable English, "Mr. Knight, may I say, you show exemplary courage in coming here. I respect courage. Please be seated."

Harry warned me, but I was still taken aback. This man whose word could mean life or death was being gracious to me and visibly snubbing his countryman. Harry very apparently was a pariah to the tong. I clung to the hope that the deal I had in mind would carry Harry as well as me to greener pastures.

Before I sat, I noticed an older man in more traditional Chinese dress enter quietly and take a seat by the wall.

I sat facing our host. I did my best to focus on his eyes and not the scar. I made the first move blindly. "You have my name, sir. If I may have yours?"

"Ah yes. You may call me 'Mr. Chin.'"

Even I knew that that was like a Caucasian saying, "Call me 'Mr. Smith.' Nonetheless, I felt as if I'd made it to first base.

"Thank you, Mr. Chin. I believe we—"

"If you'll pardon the interruption, Mr. Knight. There is one more necessary preliminary before we speak freely."

He summoned one of the boy soldiers from his position at the door. With a head gesture toward Harry that reeked of disdain, he ordered his soldier to "remove this person from the building."

That was a stunner. I looked at Harry. He stood, seemingly willing to comply with the demand. I stood as well.

Harry held a calming hand out toward me. "It's alright, Mike. You have important things to discuss."

I faced Mr. Chin directly. The tone was low, but I gave it as much bite as I could and still remain civil.

"With respect, Mr. Chin, it is not alright. We came together in good faith. There's serious business to be done here. We remain, or we leave, together."

Mr. Chin rose slowly. The message I received from his eyes made me thankful that I did not know in detail what happened to anyone who crossed him. "You are an outsider here, Mr. Knight. There are matters beyond your understanding. This . . ." Again, he gave a withering head gesture to Harry. ". . . will be ejected immediately, as I ordered."

"Then we walk out that door together. Mr. Wong's presence is an essential part of my offer."

"You will not dictate terms in this house."

I could sense all of the chords in Harry's neck tightening. I could almost hear him conveying the thought, "'Face' can be overdone. Back off!"

At that instant, I caught sight of the most fleeting look in Mr. Chin's eyes. It put steel back in my posture and tone.

I nodded to Harry, who seemed to have aged ten years. I took two steps toward the door, stopped, and faced Mr. Chin straight on.

"It's your decision, Mr. Chin. I had hoped that your sense of business would prevail. I would not be here if I could not provide you with something your organization desires very deeply. You must also realize that I have taken precautions against it being taken from me against my will. That said, I require few conditions. One of them is that this man remain in the conversation. That is not negotiable. Again, your decision."

I glanced at Harry. If his bulging eyes were a clue, he was half-an-inch from a heart seizure. He looked as if he saw his life in the hands of a demented child—me. I remembered hearing from Danny Liu that the big boys in the Hong Kong triad had taken control of the violin quest out of the hands of the leaders of the Boston tong. I was betting our two lives that that was what caused Scarface to flinch at some signal from the old man at the side.

I saw it again. It was a flicker of expression in the eyes, but it seemed to take the venom out of Mr. Chin's fangs. He simply sat down. I could practically smell the smoke of his smoldering temper. He was barely holding it in check.

From across the room, I saw the elderly man in a traditional Chinese robe rise from his chair. He walked slowly toward Mr. Chin. Without a word, Mr. Chin stepped away from his chair. He left the room in a cloud of shattered face. The old man sat in the vacated chair. There was clearly a new hierarchy in place.

The old man smiled. He gave me an inviting gesture toward my seat. Before accepting, I asked, "And Mr. Wong?"

The old man waved a dismissive hand. "His coming or going is of no matter. There are no children in the room now. Shall we speak as businessmen?"

"It's my every wish."

I nodded to Harry. He sat gingerly, as if he thought the chair might suddenly burst into flames.

The old man smiled again. "You have my full attention, Mr. Knight."

Out of respect, I did not ask him to manufacture a false name. I simply entered on what felt like a summation to a jury that had both of our lives in its hands.

CHAPTER TWENTY-TWO

I SAT FACING the old man eye-to-eye. On nothing but intuition, I thought I saw a depth there that I could speak to.

"I could begin by assuring you that every word I'll speak will be the truth as I know it . . . But I won't do that."

I noticed a narrowing of his eyes. "I won't do it because it would be insulting to both of us. Neither of us would waste time with the other if that were not to be expected without words."

His smile slightly broadened. He simply nodded assent.

"I will, however, begin at ground zero. There's a treasure that may or may not exist. History, legend, myth say it does. It has the attention of three major competitors. Russian, Romanian, and Chinese. Do we agree so far?"

"Of course."

"There are two necessary elements to finding the location of the treasure. A certain violin that somehow holds the key to the location. And secondly, a code for interpreting that key. Neither is of any use for finding the treasure without the other. Still agreed?"

"It would seem so."

"Good. Then let's be completely open. I have possession of the violin. It is completely secure in my hands. So much for the obvious. Of more interest, there have been repeated threats, attacks, ambushes, all in the attempt to take the violin out of my hands. They've all failed."

The old man leaned forward. The gentle smile remained, but it would take a fool not to see in his eyes a calculating intelligence that could seriously raise the level of the competition.

He interjected, "May I call to mind, Mr. Knight, that none of these attacks you mention were at the hands of Chinese."

I wondered without asking if he was implying that the Chinese were above such tactics or that, if they had been behind them, they would have succeeded. I dropped it with a simple, "Noted."

"Please. Continue."

"The second half of the puzzle—the code, and how to apply it to this particular violin—that's another matter. Without it, we simply have an expensive musical instrument."

"And do you have an idea that may lead to the discovering of this code?"

"I do."

"And would you be willing to discuss this idea?"

"No. Not at this time."

"Very interesting, Mr. Knight. May I pose a question? Purely hypothetical. Just to satisfy the curiosity of an old man."

"I wish you would. I don't want to leave this room without complete understanding between us."

"In that spirit. Suppose, purely hypothetically, you were to fall into the hands of one who might, shall we say, possess methods of ancient origin that have never failed to open the lips of the most stoic person, even one honor-bound to secrecy. Might not that captor acquire both the violin and your path to the code?"

The smile was ingenuous, but his eyes bore into mine like lasers. He held his hands open in anticipation of an answer. His word, "hypothetical," hid nothing. It was three balls, two strikes, and he was delivering a fast ball right over the plate. I thanked God for it. This was the moment that brought me here.

"No. Not possible."

"And that because?"

"The violin is secreted in a place to which I and only one other have access. If I don't contact that other person with a certain frequency and pass on a certain word that changes by the hour, the violin will be placed beyond the reach of either of us."

"I see."

"Not entirely. As a further precaution, if I were to convey a different code word, shall we say, if I were under compulsion, the alert would be given. The violin would simply be destroyed. The treasure would remain a legend, a myth for all time."

The smile faded. "You would destroy such an instrument?"

"The plan is securely in place. If your hypothetical someone were to compel me to convey the code word, he would have no way of knowing if I called for the preservation or the destruction of the only means of finding the treasure."

"You have an interesting mind, Mr. Knight. I might have thought you had Chinese ancestry."

"Who knows? But why dwell on these dark thoughts. That's not why I'm here. I have a more positive proposal."

"Now you truly have my interest. No more hypotheticals."

"My proposal is simply this . . . Leave me alone. Just leave me alone."

He thought for a moment. "That sounds like half a proposal."

"It is. I said I have a path that might well lead me to the code and its application to the violin. I plan to follow that path, wherever it leads. I believe it holds the clearest possible promise of finding the treasure. I'm speaking plainly."

"Plainly, yes. But of what interest to me?"

"I make this pledge. Whatever the end result of my search—I promise to pass my findings on to you before touching the treasure myself."

I could see his eyes narrowing as he sat back in the chair. His mental calculator was operating at full throttle.

Before he could speak, I added, "Understand why I make the request that you, whether tong or triad, simply leave me alone. The chance of success of my search will be greatly increased if I don't need constant eyes in the back of my head for an attack by the Chinese. Tong, triad, whatever."

I could see him carefully framing his next question. "You ask me to place extraordinary trust in what you call your pledge. Why would I be inclined to do that?"

"Two reasons. The first and most important is this. You and I are, in a sense, extraordinary people. You wouldn't be wasting your time listening to me here unless you'd investigated, unless you found that the honor of keeping my word once given is as important to me as what you call 'face' is to you. I may not be Chinese, but I suspect that in that, we're two of a kind. I can think of no more important reason for trust than that. On both sides."

Again, he was smiling. "And the other reason?"

"Pure logic. As I suggested, any other course would risk loss of the treasure forever. For us all."

The old man rose slowly and walked to the window. He reminded me of what my partner, Lex Devlin, would do when I'd given him an eye-crossing conundrum.

He turned and looked in my eyes. "You mentioned two other suiters for this treasure. The Russians and the Romanians. What of them?"

Here I knew I was on a tightrope. "Shall we be completely open with each other? My recent experience tells me that there is some sort of pact between the tong—and possibly your triad—and the Russians. I would leave it to you to present the proposal that they too stop throwing up roadblocks. It would be in the interests of all of us. My pledge is to report any success to you personally. Whatever you commit yourself to share with the Russians, that's in your bailiwick. I only ask that you do whatever is necessary to neutralize any further threat to me or my family."

"This gang of Russians. That's another matter. You might have found that in matters of honor, respect for a word given does not run quite so deeply with them. However, one can do one's best. And the Romanians?"

"I have no such commitment to them, as I would have to you."

The next few moments hung like a suspended sword. The old man gazed out the window. I knew that there was nothing to be seen out there that was churning in his mind.

When he turned back, I could read absolutely nothing in his expression. He walked back close to me. His voice was firm and steady. "What your people seal with a handshake, we seal with a bow. I give you my word now. You will suffer no harm from my organization—either tong or triad."

I returned his solemn bow, and he extended his hand, which I accepted.

I took the first full breath since Harry and I walked down Beach Street. I had even forgotten that Harry was there, until I heard a deep exhaling coming from his direction.

The old man walked us to the door. Before opening it, he said, "I mean this not as interference, as you say. Is there any assistance I might offer? I'm not without . . . connections. Internationally."

"I'll take your offer with me." I turned back. "There is one thing. In a way it's connected. I represent a young Chinese man. His name is Mickey Chan. He's actually saved my life several times in relation to what we've been discussing. He's being framed for the murder of the man who brought me into this affair, Mr. Han Liu. I believe the president of the Boston Chinese bank, Mr. Chang, is behind it. Some kind of tong politics."

"And how can I help?"

"The only witness is a Mrs. Ming Tan. She's clearly been threatened to lie under oath."

"I still don't see . . ."

"She's been abducted by the tong. They'll keep her until she appears in court to falsely convict Mickey Chan."

"I see your dilemma. Now you must see mine. Control over the Boston tong by our triad in Hong Kong is a matter of delicate limitation. We've stepped in on the matter you and I have been discussing. But there are boundaries to be observed."

"I understand."

"Perhaps not entirely, Mr. Knight. But certain matters I'm not free to explain. Let me give it some thought."

He opened the door. He raised his hand slightly, and the silk suit who let us in appeared. The old man introduced him. "This is Mr. Lao. If you need to contact me, do it through him. He can always be found here."

He bowed, as did I. "Until we meet again, Mr. Knight. Go in safety."

*   *   *

Harry and I left in silence. I'm sure in our thoughts we were both replaying the scene we had just lived through. We stopped on the sidewalk. Harry leaned close to be heard. "Michael."

When Harry calls me "Michael" and not "Mike," I know it's not to discuss baseball scores.

"Do you have any idea . . . No, I'll put it this way. You have absolutely no idea of the power of that man you just dealt with. If we were not under many eyes here, I'd bow to you in humble admiration. Incidentally, that was one hell of a promise you made. Was it off the cuff?"

"No. No, Harry. Some things are finally coming together. I'm getting a better picture of how I might be able to see this thing work out. What I said to him was part of the plan."

"Could you share the plan?"

I touched his shoulder and looked at him. "No. Much as I'd like to. It's better that I carry this thing alone for now. I want you to be able to say convincingly that you have no idea what I'm up to. Someday it could save your life."

He just nodded.

We began to walk down Beach Street, when I felt Harry's elbow in my side. I caught his whisper, "Three o'clock. Doorway."

One quick glance to my right brought the chills back to my spinal cord. The fat man with the scar, who had been reduced to faceless indignity by the old man, was standing in the shadow of a doorway across Beach Street. It was just a glance, but enough to catch with a certainty that his malevolent glare was directly at us.

Harry picked it up first and tapped me again. The two well-muscled late-teens who had first stopped us at the doorway were half a block in front of us. They were marching our way. I hardly had to look back to know that the other two were closing in from behind.

I kept it to a whisper. "Any ideas?"

"Yes."

I was a bit stunned at the force of his answer.

"I'm wide open to suggestion."

Harry sounded almost pleased. "I said this the last time, Mike. I'll say it again. We can do this."

"Harry. It's four to two. And those are not cream puffs."

"It's four punks against two members of the Harvard House League championship wrestling team. I'm actually sorry for the four punks, but they chose the odds."

Given the lack of any obvious alternative, I whispered, "When you put it that way, how can I disagree? Choose your ground."

"In here."

Harry turned left. He walked at a steady pace into a narrow alley between buildings. I followed. We got about twenty feet inside of the alley. The footsteps behind told us that two of them had us boxed in from behind. We continued to walk straight ahead until the other two showed up at the alley entrance ahead of us. Each of the four was manipulating a set of nunchucks that could break a bone with every strike.

We stopped when both pairs were about fifteen feet away from us and coming on. I faced the two in front. Harry faced the two behind. There was no point in whispering now.

"And the plan is?"

"Do you remember Professor Kamuki's lecture on defensive tactics?"

"Like it was yesterday."

"Good enough. Just like he taught us. Do you remember the poem he used?"

"Every word."

"Then let the games begin."

Harry's apparent comfort with the situation was contagious. I was lost in the moment with him. It was like ten years ago. We were next up in a simulated class exercise. This time it was not simulated, but to hell with it. Damn the torpedoes. Full speed ahead.

All four were ritually swinging the nunchucks like black belts.

We let them come to within three feet. Harry suddenly barked it out like a Marine drill-instructor.

"Mary had a little lamb!"

For that instant, the incongruity stopped them short.

I picked up the bark. "Its fleece was white as snow!"

Now they stared at me. Harry's turn. "And everywhere that Mary went!"

My line, at a volume that shook the windows. "The lamb was SURE . . . TO . . . GO!"

Like a drill we'd rehearsed, in perfect synch, we both dropped to the ground. We were flat on our backs. With all of the leverage and power I could muster, I drove the heel of my left shoe into the knee of the man on my left. The crunch of bone and squeal of pain he let out matched the sounds I heard from Harry's man behind me.

A bare split second later, my right heel flew like a battering ram into the crotch of the man to my right. Again, shrieks of pain ahead and behind were timed like a synchronized machine.

Within a second, Harry and I were on our feet, looking down at four squirming, squealing bodies. Four sets of nunchucks were still clattering on the hard pavement.

Harry tapped me on the shoulder. "I told you, Mike. The odds were in our favor."

"This time. Let's get out of here before the odds change."

We walked back out of the alley to Beach Street. I still had the words of the old man ringing in my mind: "You will suffer no harm from my organization—tong or triad."

I led Harry back to the door of the gambling den. I was about to knock when the old man opened the door.

"Mr. Knight, I can only apologize from the heart. Mister . . . Chin . . . apparently did not suffer loss of face without revenge. He acted before I could give the order. I can now assure you. He will be of no further concern to me or to you."

I looked across the street. Scarface was nowhere to be seen. I thought it wise not to press for details. One more bow cleared the air.

CHAPTER TWENTY-THREE

OUR LITTLE BAND of three were becoming regulars at the Marliave. I arrived five minutes early. As usual, I could reset my watch to high noon by the arrival of Mr. Devlin and Billy Coyne.

Tony seated us in our usual private chamber. He suggested three irresistible courses off-menu. On the way out, he quietly closed the door. Something about the click of that particular door had a calming effect on my heart rate—perhaps, at that moment, more than anywhere else in the city.

Mr. Coyne cut straight to business. "Listen, kid. I can't stall this thing much longer. This Mickey Chan, this client of yours, he's been indicted. I should be pushing the warrant for his arrest. The D. A.'s started riding my backside for results."

Mr. D. broke in. "Your boss was born with a nose for a headline."

Mr. Coyne shrugged. He focused on me. "So kid, give me a good reason for continuing to take the heat here."

"I'll do better than that, Mr. Coyne. I'll turn off the heat. You can start the police search for Mickey Chan anytime you want. It won't be a problem."

He looked surprised. "What do you mean? I thought I was doing you one hell of a favor here to stall off the arrest."

"You were. And I thank you for it. I owe you. But it's not necessary now. You can give it your best shot."

"Why? What's changed?"

"I've learned more about Mickey. And about Chinatown. It's a different world. I realized that it doesn't matter what you or the police do. You'll never be able to find him anyway. I'm more concerned about the tong running him down. They have techniques and connections your people can't use."

That stunned him for a few seconds. "But I suppose you can find him, right, kid? You could flush him out."

Mr. D. leaned in. "Billy . . . attorney-client privilege. Remember?"

"Then why the hell are we here? You could have said that much over the phone."

Secure as I felt, I instinctively dropped my voice. "Because this whole thing is beginning to come together. Not just Mickey Chan. This whole Russian, Chinese, Romanian chase for the treasure. I don't think I have to tell you again what's at stake for this city and beyond."

"I know. Keep talking."

"There's a necessary piece to this thing. You're the only one who can bring it. We need your help to put this puzzle together."

"I'm listening."

"Good. Because this is not defense counsel hype. This is God's truth. Your witness, Ming Tan, is being forced by the tong to lie about who killed Mr. Liu. It's tied up in tong politics. Someday I'll tell you the whole story. For now, I can just give you my word. I know it for a fact. Mickey Chan had no part in the murder of Mr. Liu."

I'd said it before, but this time he was listening with a neutral expression.

"Right now Ming Tan is being held captive by the tong. They'll produce her as a witness against Mickey when it comes to trial. Not before. She'll say what they tell her to."

"You told me that. There's still no police report of a kidnapping."

"And there won't be. No one in all of Chinatown would inform on the tong."

"So we're at a stalemate."

"You are. I'm not. A crack in the armor might have opened up. For me. You can't go there."

"So what am I doing here?"

"As I said, I need your help. Without it, all I can do is get people killed."

Mr. Coyne looked over at Mr. D. who was giving nothing but confirming looks, in spite of the fact that I hadn't had a chance to brief him on any of it.

I pulled in closer. "If—and it's one hell of an 'if'—I can break Ming Tan loose from the tong, we'll be running for our lives. I need you to set her up in the witness protection program. I need it in advance for both her and her husband. And for their kids, if they have any. I'll let you know about that."

That put creases in Mr. Coyne's brow. "I hear what you're saying. You know it as well as I do. Witness protection is federal, not state. It's not mine to give."

"I know. But you have connections with the U.S. Attorney that I don't have. You two have worked together before. I have to know it's firmly set to take those people into protection immediately before I can make a move. If I can do what I have in mind, there'll be no time for decisions or paperwork. Any delay could leave a number of dead bodies around Chinatown."

Mr. Coyne looked at Mr. D. "What is it with this kid, a death wish?"

"It's commitment, Billy. Like you're not likely to find around those corridors of City Hall. What can you do for him?"

Billy went into a few seconds of thought. "The U.S. Attorney's office doesn't hand out witness protection without something back."

"I thought of that, Mr. Coyne. How's this for something back? If we can get Ming Tan and her family clear of the tong's threats, there's a good chance she'll give evidence on members of the gang. That could help the U. S. Attorney bring down tong members like dominoes with federal RICO prosecutions. Heaven knows, the tong is a 'Racketeering Influenced Corrupt Organization.' What the federal prosecutors always lacked is a witness who isn't terrified into silence."

That had him thinking. "It doesn't end there, Mr. Coyne. Ming Tan's testimony could also give our crusading district attorney some high-level state prosecutions of her own. The *Globe* would eat it up. Front-page stuff every day."

Mr. Coyne's mind was jumping three moves ahead. "When do you have to know about witness protection?"

"As soon as you can get a commitment. I'll be out of town for a while. If you let Mr. Devlin know, he'll get the word to me."

"And what are you going to be doing?"

That was the killer question. "I wish I could tell you. Hopefully some dominoes will fall for me too. Someday maybe I'll write a book about it. I could call it *High Stakes*. I'll send you the first signed copy."

* * *

It was finally beginning to feel like I was putting together pieces of a jigsaw puzzle, rather than just finding new ones. I timed the walk across town to the New England Aquarium on Boston Harbor to arrive a few minutes before three. I was on the elevator to the second-level Temperate Gallery in time to be in front of the sea dragon exhibit at exactly three o'clock. The idea was to avoid standing still in any one place long enough to be a target. Based on past meetings, I was counting on my Romanian meeting partner, George, to match Billy Coyne and Mr. D. for split-second punctuality.

I was wrong. I spent fifteen minutes exchanging eye contact with a couple of weedy and leafy, sea-horse looking, sea dragons. No George.

I was getting increasing sensations of confusion, discomfort, and concern. My impression of George was that every move he made was calculated to avoid any misstep that, in his profession, could shorten his life span. Casual lateness was out of synch with the pattern.

Another five minutes and I was doubting the healthfulness of my own staying in one place too long. There had been other tourist fish-gapers there when I'd arrived, but they had all moved on.

I gave it another three minutes and decided to abort the mission. I turned to make a rapid exit and almost collided with the late George. His apologies were sincere and accepted, but I was still curious.

"You're never late without a reason, George. Little as I know about you, I'd bet my Corvette on that. I won't push it, but I'm curious. Could you tell me why?"

"In this case, yes, Michael. Since you were the cause of it, perhaps I should."

"My curiosity just doubled."

He rechecked our surroundings for additional ears. There were none. "You gave me reason to believe that, as you put it, there was a leak in my operation. I appreciate that information more than you know. Disloyalty can't be tolerated. Fortunately, you also gave me a method of, shall we say, sealing the leak."

"How?"

"Our meeting here at this multi-level aquarium. There were just three people in my organization who could have known the information you believed was leaked to the Russians. I've put complete trust in all three of them for many years."

"I understand. What did you do?"

"I told each of them separately about our meeting at three o'clock here at the aquarium. Fortunately, it's large enough so I could tell each of them that we were meeting at a different exhibit. If you were right about the leak, one of them would tip off the Russians. I figured you were their target. There'd be Russian agents at that exhibit to do whatever they had in mind for you."

"So I was the staked goat."

"Not as bad as it sounds. My people would be here to see that the Russians, if any, would be . . . neutralized before you could come to harm."

"That's comforting. Sort of. What did you tell the three men?"

"I told one of them we were meeting at the seal exhibit. I told the second one it was the jellyfish exhibit. I told the third one it was the scorpion-fish gallery. I knew you'd be up here at the sea dragon exhibit. You'd be out of harm's way."

"By one flight of stairs. Suppose the Russians came to the wrong exhibit or just started looking around?"

"The chances were good that my men would have located them. The danger was within controllable limits."

I gave him a dubious look.

"My dear Michael, in our business, some calculated risks are inevitable."

"My dear George, how the hell do I convince you once and for all—I'm not in your business."

He returned my dubious look. "Think of your past week, my young friend. Is there really a difference?"

He had me. I moved on. "This trap of yours, any results?"

I saw a bit of sincere emotion. "I'm afraid so. I thank you that you were right. The 'leak,' as you say, was a man I've known since we were children in Romania. We were like brothers. He was closer to me than any relative. I'd never have suspected."

"Did you see him here?"

"I did. It's why I was late. I had to see him face-to-face before I could take any action. My people let me know the Russians were waiting for you at the seal exhibit downstairs. He was there with them."

"What did you do?"

"My men removed the Russians first."

"How?"

He waved the question aside. "You needn't concern yourself with that."

"And your man?"

The darkness deepened in his expression. "I asked him, 'Why? After all of our years. Why?'"

He stopped.

"Did he answer?"

"Yes. But not in words. He simply wept. As did I. You won't understand. We embraced each other like the brothers we'd been."

"And then?"

He straightened up. "He knew. There was no going back. He asked my forgiveness."

"Did you?"

"Did I forgive him? Yes. From the heart. We made peace, so we won't meet in anger in the next life."

"Is he still . . ."

"On this earth?" He shook his head and looked in my eyes. "No. He understood. As I said, there's no going back. It's simply the way things are. We know that, all of us, when we make our choices."

I have to admit it. I was a bit stunned by the unrelenting reality of George's life. He could see it in my eyes.

"Perhaps our worlds are different after all, Michael."

I had no words. I could only nod my agreement.

He gave a quick check for other ears in the room. There were none. "You wanted to see me. You have news?"

"I have a decision. I also have the beginning of a plan. You might approve. First let me fill in some gaps."

I told him everything that had happened in my meeting with Scarface and the old man from the Hong Kong triad in the large-stakes gambling den and in the alley off Beach Street in Chinatown. I told him in great detail. It seemed important that he understand the full background of the decision I'd reached.

"And where does all of this lead you?"

"To a conclusion. Let me put it this way. There are three compet- ing forces, all after the treasure they think is tied up in that violin. The Russians, the Chinese, and your Romanians. That's obvious."

"True."

"You once pointed out to me that the only one of the three that wouldn't happily chop me into molecules if it would get them the violin, let alone the treasure, was your Romanians."

"I'm glad you remembered."

"I remembered because you've had several opportunities. And yet here I am, still breathing fresh air."

He just smiled.

"You also told me that the treasure, if there is one . . ."

"There is."

"That the treasure was amassed by the Impaler, Dracula, by extracting heavy burdens of tribute from the Romanian people. It would seem after some five and a half centuries that if anyone has a legitimate claim to it, it's the Romanian people. Perhaps it could do them some long overdue good. Heaven knows, that treasure would bring disaster around the world if the Chinese or the Russians got their hands on it."

"I like where this is going, Michael."

"So do I. Because for the first time I have some clarity of purpose. My conclusion is that from this point on, I'm in your corner. I think we should work together as partners. Maybe we can see some justice come out of this thing after all."

He put his hand on my shoulder. "Before you make a commitment, I want you to be sure. What happened earlier today in this building must convince you that I don't take a pledge of partnership, of loyalty, lightly. Be very certain of the extent of your commitment before you make it. At this moment, we can both walk away. It's your decision."

"Perhaps you've noticed. I don't give my word lightly either."

I held out my hand. He saw my hand, but he hesitated. He looked for something more in my eyes. Apparently, he saw it, because a partnership was sealed with a handshake.

CHAPTER TWENTY-FOUR

GEORGE AND I took the escalator to the aquarium ground level. We had unfinished business, and there was no better place to put it in order than the Harbor Walk off Atlantic Avenue. I could sense as we strolled beside the open ocean that there was a new openness on both sides of our relationship.

"You mentioned a plan," he said.

"The outline of a plan. I'll have to see where it takes us."

"Fair enough. What is it?"

I let my eyes wander out to the islands in the harbor. The question was where to begin. The answer became clear. Right at the heart of it.

"It's time we stopped nibbling around the edges. Let's go after the treasure. I have the violin. The violin has the code, let's hope. Someone must have the key to interpreting the code. My guess is you have some sense of how to find that someone. Let's make use of the trust we have in each other to combine resources. We'll find it, or we won't. We'll live to tell it, or . . ."

"Or we won't. I'm in."

There was a new fire in his words. "Where do you propose we begin, Michael?"

"We have limited choices. Most of the people involved in the his-tory of this thing have been dead for centuries. The last words Mr.

Oresciu spoke to me gave me the clue. I'll start with the interpreter of the ship doctor's journal. The Turkish professor. If he's still alive."

"She. Professor Sakim. She's in the Linguistics Department of Koc University. It's in Istanbul. I can make a call."

"Good. Will you see if she'll see me? I can be there in a day or two."

"Shall I go with you?"

"Not this time. Maybe later. Let me do the ground work. Let's see if it leads us anywhere. For now, I'd like to have you here to coordinate. I can always reach you by phone."

"Alright. Is there anything else I can do?"

"There's one loose end here. Let's talk about it. I think I reached an understanding with the old Chinese man from the Hong Kong triad. He seems to have taken over control from the Boston tong leader, whoever that is. He actually agreed to call off the dogs. No more threats from the Chinese gang while I followed the leads to the treasure."

"In exchange for what?"

"In exchange for my promise to let him in on whatever information I turn up, and to do it before I actually lay my hands on any of the treasure."

That brought a scowl. "I think you've given away the store."

"Not a bit of it. I chose the words very carefully. I had to go that far to get the Chinese threat off my back so I could focus on the search. It all fits into what I see as the end game. I'll tell you about that in a minute."

The scowl softened, but did not disappear.

"There's another piece here, George. The real pains in the butt so far have been the Russians. It seems every time I turn around, I'm barely squeaking out of some new threat from them. That's got to cease. If I go to Istanbul, right on the Black Sea, I'll be practically in their backyard. I need a truce at a high level."

"How do you plan to pull that off?"

"The old Chinese man. You and I have suspected that there's some kind of working agreement between the Chinese and the Russians. The old man didn't deny it. I think both gangs would slit the other's throats for one gold coin. In fact, I'm counting on it. But for the moment, they're allies. More or less."

"So how does that help?"

"I asked the old Chinese man to use whatever leverage he had with the Russians to get them to make the same agreement. Just leave me alone. I told him he could pass along to them the same commitment I made to him."

"To tell them anything you discover?"

"Yes. Before I touch the treasure myself."

"And knowing how you honor your word, that would mean telling them everything you find out. In detail. No false leads."

"Yes."

"Including, perhaps, the exact location of the treasure."

"Yes."

Now the scowl really deepened. "Michael . . ."

"It's alright. You have to trust me. When this thing ends, I want it over completely. No loose ends. No loose cannons. For either of us. Let me tell you how I hope this thing will finally play out."

We walked all the way to the end of the wharf. The only sound over the waves lapping the pylons, the occasional horn of a ferry or fishing trawler, and the angry screeching of seagulls competing for a shiner was my low voice spelling out for the first time in words what had been congealing in my mind as a plan. It was full of contingencies. There were parts where the question, "What could go wrong?" could only be answered, "Everything." But I could see the scowl on George's face slowly morph into a grin.

"So? What do you think?"

"I think it's absolute insanity. I think we'd be ready for a padded room if we even consider it. It has more holes than a Swiss cheese."

"In other words, you're ready to commit to it one hundred percent."

"Yes. Completely." The grin now covered his face. "I once mentioned to you that we have very little fun in our business."

"Shall we have some fun?"

"Let the games begin."

For the second time that afternoon, we shook hands.

Before George and I parted company, I revisited what seemed to me the weakest link in my proposal.

"One thing. I trust those Russians as far as I could throw this wharf. The old Chinese man seemed to have the same impression. The fact that the Russians were here looking for me today tells me that either the old man hadn't gotten word to them, or that it made no difference. Before I start this trip to Istanbul, I'd like to be more comfortable on that score. I'd be totally exposed to another Russian attack over there."

"I agree. What can we do about it?"

"I'd like to try something. Who is the head of the Russian gang in Boston? Do you know?"

"Yes. He came over from Moscow to take over about five years ago. His name is Vasily Laskovitch."

"Do you know where I can find him?"

"I do. But I wouldn't go near there with less than a division of Marines."

"Any chance he'd meet me on neutral ground?"

"There is no neutral ground. He could have his gunmen anywhere in the city."

"Then one place is as good as another. Actually, one place is better. Where're his headquarters?"

"This is not a good—"

"Where is it? This is not as crazy as it sounds. If I meet him where he thinks I'd never dare to go, it might make my proposal more believable. It may be the only way it'd work. Where is it?"

Concern was written all over his face. "I can't provide you with protection there. This is totally enemy territory."

"I don't expect protection. I have to do this alone to make it believable. I need to get their curiosity first. Then, if I can sell it, their belief in what I'm proposing. That's the best protection I can hope for."

"I don't agree."

"You will when you think about it. Believe me, there's no other way. So where is it?"

George looked at me for a few seconds. Then he looked out to sea. "It's a bar-café on Commonwealth Ave. in Brighton. The sign on the window is in Russian. *Za Vashe Zdorovie*. The words are a Russian drinking toast."

"If it's just in Russian, how does the non-Russian public know it's a café?"

"It doesn't matter. They're not looking for drop-in customers. That would include you."

"Can you get a message to him?"

"We're not pen pals, but I think I could get word to him. What would you want me to say?"

"He should know my name by now. He's tried to kill me often enough. Tell him I want to see him. Face-to-face. I'll come there. Alone. Unarmed. As soon as possible. Maybe this evening. I want to make him the offer about Dracula's treasure personally. That should get his attention."

"This is insanity. And we were just becoming friends. I'll miss you so much."

"Don't pick out a suit for the funeral just yet. I wouldn't try this if I didn't think I could pull it off. Let me know what he says."

* * *

I spent the afternoon keeping to public places and touching the essential bases. I dropped by the office to bring Mr. Devlin up to speed. I could see in his eyes how strongly he was against my continuing on a course that could deprive him of a junior partner—and more to the point, an unofficially adopted son. He would have ended my involvement in a heartbeat, even if he had to take my place to do it. But he understood and honored my commitment— even to the point of personally covering the trial of any of my cases that couldn't be postponed.

I also checked in with my secretary, Julie. This time I had to be honest with her, even at the risk of taxing her motherly concern. She had taken in our Sheltie, Piper, without question. It was time to let her know why it was necessary, leaving out some of the more worrisome details. Like Mr. D., she reluctantly accepted the uncertain future to give me the freedom to do what I had to do.

* * *

I stole the major portion of the evening from everything else to spend it with Terry. I had a different rental car delivered to the alley behind my office building. I took minor streets that my father had shown me as a kid to hit Route 1 above Danvers for a straight shot to the Governor's Inn in Rochester, New Hampshire. The time Terry and I would have together might be only hours. Given what I could see ahead, not one of those hours was to be missed.

We were in our own world, halfway into the bourbon pecan salmon in the Spaulding Steak and Ale Restaurant of the Inn when my phone buzzed. My first impulse was to drop my cell phone into the tall glass of Brother Thelonius brew I was sipping. I followed my second impulse and answered it.

I could hear the hesitation in George's voice. "One last time. There must be a better way."

"There isn't. Tell me."

"I got your message to him. He actually got back to me. He will share a bottle of his best vodka with you tomorrow at noon."

"That sounds inviting."

"Very inviting. Like the spider to the fly. For better or worse, you have an entrée. Do you want my advice?"

"No. I already have it. I'll follow it next time. This time it has to be my show. I assume he speaks English."

"He speaks Russian, English, and violence. And not in that order."

I was glad we were not on speaker-phone for what was left of Terry's peace of mind.

"Thank you, George. I'll give him your regards. What's the address?"

*   *   *

I left Rochester early enough to find the café on Commonwealth Avenue a little before noon. I figured that to be on time shows a collected mind, focused on business. To be early would signal the weakness of overanxiousness. To be late, disrespect. I arrived on the button of noon.

I sucked up every ounce of false courage I could pretend. I put it all into an ice-cold, emotionless projection of attitude for my entrance. My dark blue suit, white shirt, and conservative red striped tie said, "Don't mess with me. I'm here on business." I hoped.

Once in the door, I took a deliberately unhurried stride between the line of well-bulked, Eastern European looking loungers at the long bar and those strewn among the scattered tables. If the eyes I passed could burn holes, I'd have been a walking Swiss cheese.

When I passed by, I caught a side view of a couple of the bar-loungers starting to rise with a purpose. Others next to them, who apparently had been alerted to my "invitation," reached for their shoulders or elbows to settle them back down.

There wasn't a man in that room who didn't know that I was responsible, one way or another, for the deaths of some of their fellow thugs. The trick was to keep walking, unflustered, through an atmosphere of barely restrained violence you could slice with a cleaver. Focus was the key. Prayer and focus.

My legs carried me on a direct, deliberate path to the bartender halfway down the bar. Two thugs with at least fifty pounds of muscle and one scarcely concealed weapon more than I had under my dark blue suit stood between me and the bar.

I made no eye contact. I looked straight between them. I could only hope they understood the words, because I had no second opening line. I kept it in the mid-baritone range. "A word with the bartender."

They indulged in several more seconds of glaring hostility before slowly separating. I was now facing the bartender, who was closer to my proportions. He was the only one in the room I could address without looking up.

His attitude could hardly be confused with hospitality, but at least he nodded. I took it as a cue to speak. "Mr. Laskovitch is expecting me."

I put the name out front in case anyone in the house thought I'd dropped in for a bowl of borscht. No words passed his lips, but the bartender picked up a phone from under the bar.

Whatever he said in Russian produced, a few seconds later, the sound of a door opening at the far end of the room. In the dim back-lighting, I saw a figure that could have been a cutout of Nikita Khrushchev.

He took a few steps closer into the light. I caught a better look at his slightly grinning face. My first thought was that he could have had wolf blood in his ancestry.

A man of the same cut as those surrounding me came from behind him. He walked up to me and signaled an arms-up order for a hand-frisk. I expected it, so I raised my arms and opened my legs without debate.

The grinning wolf in the doorway barked out an order, in English for my benefit. "No. No. No. This man is our guest. We treat him with dignity."

He slowly walked in my direction. He waved off the goon who was about to give me the frisking of a lifetime. He addressed the goon. "Alexei, would you walk into the den of our enemies alone, unarmed? I don't think so. Yet here he is. This man has the soul of a Cossack. We respect such courage."

He waved two men off of the chairs at a table in the center of the room. The grin persisted. "You are Michael Knight, undoubtedly."

I completed the introductions. "And you could only be Vasily Laskovitch."

The grin broadened. "You've heard my name. Good. I'll say this, Mr. Knight. This place where you are is like being on Russian soil. We are not barbarians. We know how to treat a guest. Please."

I followed his gesture and sat in one of the two seats. My host took the other chair. He called to the bartender. "Ivan. Vodka."

The bartender took a bottle from the shelf. My host barked, "*Nyet*. Not that. My very best."

The bartender replaced the bottle and took one from under the bar. He brought the bottle with two large shot glasses to the table. My host took the bottle out of his hands. He filled the two glasses to the brim.

"We have traditions. We never take vodka without a toast. Will you join me?"

The only answer that occurred to me was "Yes."

"There are three traditional toasts. First, we drink to the one who provides us with the vodka."

He raised his glass. I followed suit. He downed his glass in one swallow. I could do no less. I expected to feel fire from my lips to my stomach. I was stunned. No burn. Just velvet smoothness.

By the time I put my glass back on the table, he had refilled his own. He tilted the bottle toward mine.

"And now we toast the good fortune of the one who receives this gift of vodka."

Another full glass down in one gulp. Again, I could do no less. This time it was even smoother. My glass no sooner touched the table, but again my host was refilling it to the brim.

"And we drink the third toast to the hope that this acquaintance will ripen into a friendship. Yes?"

"Yes." As I raised the third glass, I could begin to feel the first two taking a grip on my mental state. There was, however, no safe way to stop. In for a penny was in for a pound. We downed the third full glass in synchronized motion.

He settled back in the chair. I thought, "Thank God there is no fourth toast. I have to find the door on the way out."

"So you have a message for me, Mr. Knight. Is that not what brings you here?"

This was it—the second most desperate closing argument of my life. This was where I could win the freedom to walk back out onto Commonwealth Avenue with all of my parts attached and functioning.

Or not.

CHAPTER TWENTY-FIVE

I HAD EVERY eye and ear in the house. Even those at the bar who spoke only Russian had eyes focused on the alien in the blue suit. I kept saying to myself what the Christians in Rome must have said—ignore the lions on the periphery—deal with the one in front of you. In my case, it was Vasily Laskovitch.

The grin had faded. The toasts had ended. It was finally show-time. We sat at the table directly across from each other. His eyes were narrowed and searching mine for any hint of trickery. There was no question of how to open. Nothing short of blatant truth would get his attention.

"Cards on the table, Mr. Laskovitch. You want Dracula's treasure. I have the violin with the code to where it's hidden. I'm ready to go after it. I have every reason to believe I can find it."

That caught his interest. His silence said he was waiting for more.

"You want to know what good that will do you. Then hear this. I'll give you my word. When I break the code, when I learn where the treasure is, I'll promise you that I'll give you all the information I have, including the exact location of the treasure. And I'll do it before I ever put my own hands on the treasure. That will be my promise."

He began to smile—until I added, "Perhaps."

The smile was gone. There was a brief flash of temper. "Do you come here to play games?"

"No. No games. Hear me out. We get to have this conversation just once. I'll say it clearly so there'll be no misunderstanding. I'm being smothered by your gunmen waiting to attack me around every corner. If I'm going to follow this thing through to the treasure, I need to be free to do it without looking over my shoulder. It's the only way I can bring it off. And when I do, I'll tell you everything I learn. All of it."

The temper was gone, but the intensity of eye contact multiplied. "And why would you suddenly become so generous?"

I returned the intensity of eye contact. I knew this was the hardest point to sell.

"Because there are things in this world I value more than money. If I can buy them back for the price of that treasure, no matter how much it is, it'll be a small price to pay."

I could see doubt in his eyes. "And just what are these things you say are so valuable?"

"The safety of my wife. Being with her without fear. The life we had before this insanity began. No, that's wrong. The life we *will* have. For a year I've let work take too much of my life away from her. Never again. Thank God this insanity has taught me something."

He was still listening without comment. I dropped my voice for his ears only. "Can you understand that, Mr. Laskovitch? Isn't there anything in your life that you wouldn't give up even for that treasure?"

He stood up. He seemed to need to look down on me. "We make choices in this life, Mr. Knight. Some of those choices can't be unmade. Does that answer your question?"

I looked up at him. However he might take it, I said it from the heart. "If you mean what I think, I'm sorry for you."

He waved it aside. The chill in his eyes told me we were back to business.

"Exactly what do you want from me?"

"There's only one thing I want. And it's not that treasure. That damn thing's covered with centuries of blood, and it keeps demanding more. You can have it with my blessings."

I could still hear doubt in his voice. "Then what?"

"I want my life back, with you and all of your people out of it. I'm willing to give you the secret to the treasure to get my freedom in exchange. It's that simple."

He sat back. He had Mr. Devlin's habit of putting his hand to his jaw when he was playing verbal chess. The idea of anyone not willing to sell his soul for anything that could be turned into money was straining his comprehension. I knew he'd have to poke it on all sides to see if it could be real.

"If it's that simple, why not just hand over the violin? Right now. We'll follow the lead ourselves. You'll be out of it."

"You asked me to speak plainly. Is that still your wish?"

"Of course."

I pulled my chair closer and dropped my voice again for his hearing only.

"Then here's how it is. The truth is, you would not be able to accomplish what I believe I can. Your methods would not work. Your threats of violence won't work on the kind of people who have the information we need. Then you'd be back in my life to get me to unscramble the pieces for you. By then, the trail would be trampled out of existence. This is the plain truth. Your best chance of getting the treasure—my best chance of getting my life back permanently—is for me to find the treasure and just tell you where it is."

I said it with passion. I realized that I was gambling that he'd see enough logic behind my blunt words to douse the anger I could see rising. I could only pray that his greed for the treasure would trump his urge to squash the demeaning bug in the blue suit.

He was silent. I could sense him holding his anger in check for at least half a minute. The heat seemed to dissipate slowly, but I had no idea what would take its place.

At last, he simply took a deep breath. He slowly looked around that room. If I could read him, he was breathing in the sense of power he felt in being surrounded by an army of killers who would commit any act at his command. I could almost see it healing any effect my words could have had on his sense of total control.

It was time to play my last trump card. This time I did it in a voice they all could hear. "Mr. Laskovitch, this is the deal. If you give me your word, just your word, that you'll call off the guns as of right now, you'll have my trust. I believe you'll act as a man of honor in front of these men you lead. On that basis, I'll give you my promise. The next time you'll hear from me will be to give you the location of the treasure. We'll shake hands, and the deal will be done."

I could see him slowly tasting it in his mind. A radical new way of controlling his world. Trust, in place of raw violence. I prayed that it could take root.

"Those are fine words, Mr. Knight. Well said here in this room while we're face-to-face. But what assurance do I have when you walk out that door?"

"Two things. You'll have my word. Ask around. That's the best assurance you'll ever have."

"And the second thing?"

"If you ever find that I haven't kept the promise I make to you here today—you know how vulnerable I'll be to your vengeance for the rest of my life. This city is my home. I'll be easy to find. If you know me as I think you do, you know I'll never let it come to that."

That was my last card. I looked down at the table. The game and my life were in his hands. If I'd had anything left in this life to wager, which I didn't, I'd have had no idea in the world what outcome to bet it on.

He sat back down. Our eyes met again. He seemed to be trying to draw some unspoken message out of mine. I sensed that he was on the tilting edge of a decision, but needed one more push to take the plunge. I had no more to give.

I noticed his glance for a fraction of a second to one of the goons standing behind me. Before I could move, I felt an arm clamp like a steel band around my chest. It held me paralyzed. The band tightened until my lungs could only take in air in quick gasps. I thought I was about to be suffocated, until a hand came around my shoulder. It held the point of a blade directly on top of my jugular vein.

I was frozen still. The only thing running through my consciousness was a prayer. I became vaguely aware that Laskovitch was standing, looking down at me. Whatever he was saying I couldn't make out.

He leaned across the table. He was still speaking. There was a roaring in my ears that garbled his words. It didn't matter. I couldn't have responded anyway.

I thought I saw him look up and nod to whatever thug had me in his grip. I felt the tip of the blade dig into the skin. A trickle of moisture started running down my neck.

I closed my eyes and concentrated on a prayer for the people to whom I'd never have a chance to say goodbye.

Somewhere in that fog, I became aware that Laskovitch was shouting. He was barking out the word "*Stoy!*" I felt the blade slip a quarter of an inch deeper. Laskovitch yelled it one more time. Louder. "*Stoy!*"

This time it was punctuated by the crack of his fist slamming the table.

What little consciousness I had left began telling me that the tip of the blade was moving back out of my skin. A second later, the steel band on my chest was gone. I took three deep breaths to make up for lost air. When I could look up, I saw Laskovitch glaring at me.

"Now, Mr. Knight. Now we'll talk about an agreement. You have a taste of what will happen if you should be less than faithful to your promise. Your talk of trust in your word is good in a room of your fine lawyers. In this room, I want the consequences of betrayal clearly understood. You made your point. Now I've made mine. Do we agree?"

I wasn't sure I could get out words, but the agreement I needed was on the table. I nodded assent.

"Good. Then we have a bargain. I'll not be the first to break it."

My voice sounded hoarse, but it came out. "Nor will I."

He pounded his fist on the table. He looked around at the thugs surrounding us. "Hear me, all of you. I've given my word. It goes for all of us. I'll deal with any man who betrays that word."

He grabbed the bottle of vodka. The grin was back. He was filling both glasses with the remains of the bottle. He raised his glass. In the last minute, I'd become totally sober. I picked up my glass.

"Mr. Knight, a toast. Very traditional Russian. 'May there be as much trouble in each of our lives . . . as there shall remain drops of vodka in these glasses.'" We both swallowed every drop.

We stood. My last words to Mr. Laskovitch were from the heart. "I thank God that your man with the knife finally obeyed your command. I assume you were telling him to stop. I had serious doubts that he would."

Mr. Laskovitch came close enough to whisper. "I had serious doubts myself, Mr. Knight. The man you shot in Romania. The man who died. The one you called 'Boris.' He was this man's brother."

CHAPTER TWENTY-SIX

Since this lunacy began, I'd been walking with each foot in a different pool of quicksand—one Chinese and one Russian. For the first time in what seemed like a year, I let myself feel freedom. I drove to the Wallachia Café in Roslindale without once looking back or even pushing the speed limit. I still aggressively contested the right of way at all of the intersections, because to do otherwise would only confuse the other Boston drivers.

On the way, I called George. This time I was inviting him to lunch. It was a late lunch, because I had one important milestone to reach first. I returned both rental cars. I asked the second rental company to meet me to pick up its car at our home in Winthrop. My confidence in getting the two bands of gorillas off my back ran so deep that for the first time since that dinner at the China Pearl Restaurant at the start of this odyssey, I drove to the café in my very own Corvette.

George and I sat at the table in the same private room where we'd first had an open discussion. He offered a toast with a new bottle of *tuica*. I sipped enough to cover the bounds of courtesy, but then switched to straight Coca Cola. My system was still recovering from its earlier immersion in Russian vodka. George understood.

He sat back and just shook his head with a broad smile. "Michael, you're a damned fool. I did not expect to see you again. How the hell did you do it with the Russians? I want every detail."

It took ten minutes in the telling without interruption. It seemed like a release for me to relive it out loud. The last thing I described was my agreement with Laskovitch.

George looked at me for about five seconds and then just nodded. "You were there, Michael. As far as it's possible to read that mobster, you seem satisfied. I knew you were when you drove up. You were in your Corvette."

"I have no choice. I have to trust both the Russians and the Chinese to keep their end of the bargain. It's the best I can get." I leaned a bit closer. "You do know, it also means I have to keep my word to them. As I told you, it's all part of the plan. Are you still on board?"

"I'm in all the way. But you have the heavy oar. Remember, I'm here to do anything you need. When do you want to leave for Istanbul?"

"Tonight. Do we still agree that the first contact has to be the woman who translated the journal of the ship's doctor? Professor Sakim?"

"Yes. I called her after I talked to you. She has an office in the classical languages department of Koc University. I'm afraid you'll have to sell your story all over again."

"Is she willing to talk to me?"

"She's willing to see you. Whether she'll talk to you about the treasure? That's another hurdle. She did admit that she kept a part of the ship doctor's journal out of the translation. She's the only one who knows what it says."

"Do you know why she did that?"

"I'm not sure. She wasn't about to pour it all out to me over the phone. We've never met. Remember, she's an academic, not a gangster. My guess is that she held back the key to locating the treasure for the right reason. She knew that if the wrong people got to it, it could be disastrous."

"I'll give it my best shot, but I'm wondering. If you're right about her reason, why should she trust me?"

This time he was grinning. "I don't know. Why did I trust you? You have that boyish innocence."

I forced an innocent smile, and he laughed. "Then I'd better get this boyish innocence over there while it lasts. I'll fly out tonight."

"What can I do?"

"How well do you know Istanbul? Around the university?"

"I've been there."

"Good. Can you book me a reservation at a hotel near the university? And can you get me an appointment with her tomorrow? Let's make it in the afternoon? I better get a few hours' sleep before this one. I know I won't sleep on the plane."

"Of course. Anything else?"

"I'll need the location of her office. And her full name."

"I'll get it. I'll call you this evening. Anything else?"

I sat back and looked him in the eye. "As a matter of fact, there is. If I'm going into this thing with a partner, I'd better know his full name. Might we even say his *real* full name?"

That brought a smile. "It would seem that for some reason, I've trusted you from the start. George is my real name. George Calinescu."

I held out my hand. "Pleasure to meet you, Mr. Calinescu."

He took my hand. "The pleasure is mine, Mr. Knight."

*　*　*

In my newfound freedom, I went home to Winthrop to pack for the flight instead of sneaking into Macy's to restock. After packing, I settled into my favorite chair on our front porch with a few fingers of Famous Grouse Scotch over ice cubes made of good Boston water. I set aside fifteen solid minutes for just mindlessly looking out to sea. Graves Light was the anchor of my random focus. My attention floated gently from sails on the horizon to the occasional lobster boat fisherman pulling up traps between the near shore and Nahant.

My fifteen minutes were cut to ten by a call from George. "Where are you?"

"In the Garden of Eden."

"My biblical history's a bit rusty. Where might that be?"

"Right here on the shore of Winthrop Beach. I'm home. What's up?"

"I have everything arranged. Can you take notes?"

I grabbed a pen and notebook. "Shoot."

"I just spoke with Professor Sakim. Elena. She's in her office at the university."

"What'd she say?"

"I wish I could say it'll be an easy sell. She's willing to see you, but I wouldn't count on her opening the store on information about the treasure."

"Did you get a sense of why?"

"I think I was right. I believe she has strong fears about what would happen if the wrong people got hold of that treasure. I'm sure that was why she held back on translating that part of the doctor's journal. Nothing's changed in that respect."

"Has anyone else asked her about it?"

"My guess is no. Both the Chinese and the Russians have been focused on getting their grubby little hands on the violin first. You know that story."

"I do indeed. Well, that's good. I like the idea that I'll be the first one to talk to her. At least the ground won't already be poisoned."

"True. I still think you'll need every ounce of that boyish innocence."

"Uh-huh. Where do I meet her? And when?"

"Tomorrow afternoon. Four o'clock. She'll meet you after her last class. She'll be in the small outdoor amphitheater at the base of the tall clock tower. You can see the tower from anywhere on the campus. It's a beautiful university. It's on a sixty-acre estate. About sixty-some buildings with connecting courtyards. You can walk across the whole campus in about fifteen minutes."

"Good. And where am I staying?"

"You have a reservation tomorrow night at the Yuva Hotel. It's right on the shore of the Black Sea. You'll feel at home by the water. I set you up with a rental car at the airport. It's an easy drive to the hotel, and from there to the university."

"That covers it. Thank you, George. I'll keep in touch."

"*Mult noroc*, my friend."

"If that means 'Good luck,' I accept the wish."

* * *

I spent what was left of the afternoon making the familiar loop with updates on my immediate plans. It was the first chance I'd had to bring Mr. Devlin in on the long-term plan I had for ending this entire adventure. Like George, he probably thought it was like shooting at the moon with a slingshot. Fortunately for me, he had been on enough improbable rides with his junior partner to suppress conveying his doubts. He just came on board with an open offer of help.

The most important assist I needed from Mr. D. was an unrelenting riding of the backside of the combative deputy district attorney, Billy Coyne, to solidify arrangements with the U.S. Attorney for witness protection for Ming Tan and her family. Mickey Chan's case was going to get my full attention as soon as I landed back on American soil.

After the call to Mr. D., I made another to Julie to have her book me an evening flight to Istanbul.

Then I filled the rest of the afternoon with a call to Terry. Her honest trust seemed to call for a full explanation of how I hoped, planned, and prayed to tie up all the loose ends. Her support for this last inescapable venture was clearly hinged on more than a promise from me to stop playing Indiana Jones in the future. We were completely in sync, especially since both of us clearly had in mind the life that was going to make our duo a trio.

* * *

I landed at the Ataturk Airport in Istanbul early the next morning. The rental car was waiting for me for the drive along the Bosporus Strait to the Yuva Hotel. True to George's word, it was right on the coast of the Black Sea. The temptation to explore the area was overcome by the need for a few hours' sleep before my appointment with Professor Sakim.

* * *

I rehearsed my pitch as I drove through the forested hill country that surrounds Koc University. I was parked in the university's periphery parking area by three thirty. Oddly, as I walked through the campus, I felt a resonance that I could only attribute to the fact that the entire university was designed by the Iranian-American architect Mozhan Khadem who's headquarters are in Boston.

I found the small outdoor amphitheater at the base of the clock tower. I'd sat for about five minutes when I saw a woman I'd place in her mid-fifties in professorial slacks and jacket coming toward me. She approached with her hand out and a genuine smile.

"Mr. Knight, I presume."

"I appreciate your meeting me, Professor Sakim. I know you're busy."

"As I assume are you. And yet you took the time to fly all this way for our chat."

"I wish I were here strictly as a tourist. I love universities. This one is exquisite."

Her smile broadened. If there was any tension, it seemed not to be on her part. "Thank you. Let's walk. I can treat you to a cup of Turkish coffee. Perhaps some of our pastry?"

That brought instant recall of the homemade pastry I shared with Mr. Oresciu at our first meeting. There was no possibility of refusing.

Our walk through interlocking courtyards between crisply designed academic buildings was an unexpected delight. My guide illuminated the identity and significance of each building and statue with an understated but obvious pride. By the time we reached what at Harvard would be called the faculty dining hall, we were on a first name basis.

The conversation was easy. We talked of many things, but the pleasurable encounter went over the top when a student waitress brought to our table a Turkish desert called *kaymakli kayisi*—sweet golden dried apricots grown in Malatya, simmered in red wine, stuffed with *kaymak*—buffalo milk clotted cream—and coated with fragmented pistachios. To combine it with Turkish coffee, hot and strong, in the warm afternoon sun on a patio in the heart of a truly top-drawer European university is to define a setting that could only set one's mind at peace.

Elena seemed to be in no hurry. I was happy to let the conversation drift from one unthreatening subject to another for the better part of an hour. When the chime in the clock tower announced the hour of five, I was brought back to my reason for being there.

"Elena, I've enjoyed this time so much. You're a most gracious hostess." I left a slight pause. "I think George mentioned why I asked to meet with you."

I expected a cloud of tension to immediately fill the atmosphere between us. Whether for better or worse for my purpose, her gentle smile never wavered. I saw no physical signs of tension whatever.

"Mr. Calinescu said you wanted to discuss my translation of Doctor Demir's voyage journal. Have you seen it?"

"Yes. George Calinescu showed me a copy. He found it in the professional journal where it was published."

"And you have a question."

I hesitated, partly out of fear of failing in my purpose, and partly out of reluctance to diminish the incipient friendship that had blossomed in only an hour.

"Michael, let me help you broach your point. I'm sure you found the ship doctor's telling of the episode with the pirates, and with the dying Turkish soldier somewhat gripping. But that's not why you're here, is it? Shall we just put it on the table openly? You want to discuss the soldier's discovery of Vlad the Impaler's supposed treasure." She smiled. "Is that correct? Yes, I'm sure it is. There now. That was not so difficult. Please tell me what you want to know. Then we'll see if I can help you."

The air was clear. The anticipated infusion of tension was dispelled before it ever settled in by her gentle directness. I owed her the same openness.

"Elena, may I tell you a story?"

She settled back, coffee in hand. "I'd be delighted."

Where to begin. I remembered the simple advice of the king in *Alice in Wonderland*: "Begin at the beginning, go on till you come to the end, then stop." I did exactly that. I began with the dinner at the China Pearl Restaurant and gave her a flowing discourse of the events that led finally to the visit I was enjoying with her over coffee and pastry.

It was truncated, somewhat, but I was sure to include all of the details that would lead her to an understanding of which of the characters were scurrilous villains, and which not. She never interrupted, even with a question. More to the point, her interest never seemed to flag.

She set her coffee cup down on the table. This time I could see her carefully choosing a starting point.

"You've had quite an adventure. It tells me a number of things. I guess the first is that I find you quite open and honest. I understand why George Calinescu trusts you implicitly. I'd be inclined to do the same."

I started to thank her, but she continued. Her smile had faded. I could see lines forming in her forehead. "It also tells me that my intuition years ago was correct. This supposed treasure of Vlad, Dracula. Whether it exists or not, the mere possibility of it is enough to drive certain men to inflict pain, death without discrimination, without limit."

It was my turn to listen without interruption.

"And that's just to get their bloodied hands on it. What unimaginable evil would they bring about once they have it?"

She had been looking toward the clock tower across the campus. Now she looked directly at me. "I believe you have a good heart. Can you put yourself in the quandary I faced when I was translating the doctor's journal? There was the telling of a Turkish soldier who claimed to have actually seen this treasure. He said he knew where it was located. He put a code to that location somewhere in a violin he kept close to him until his death. But I knew the code would be unbreakable without other information—first how to find the code in the violin, and then how to interpret it."

She moved her chair closer to mine and spoke more softly, but more intensely. "What would you have done? Suppose that the only way to find the key to the code was actually included in the ship doctor's journal. Suppose you were the only one who could translate it. Would you put that information out there, publicly, knowing that by doing so you might be unleashing an avalanche of death, pain, untold suffering? And all of that evil just for the enrichment of whoever is strong enough to take that treasure by violence? I repeat—what would you have done?"

Her eyes were looking for an answer. I could only be truthful. "Under the circumstances, exactly what you did. Leave it out of the translation."

She sat back with a deep breath. "I know why you're here, Michael. You're going to put me back into that same quandary after all these years. You're going to make me decide that question all over again. You want me to give you the information I've kept hidden since I first translated that journal."

Her eyes were looking into mine for some suggestion of an answer. In a way, they were transferring the quandary from her shoulders to mine.

"Elena, with the exception of George, I've been dealing in this business with thugs, gangsters, men with the morals of alley cats. In a way, it's more difficult explaining my proposal to you. We've known each other for maybe an hour. But I have the very highest respect for your integrity. I'm going to make a suggestion. More importantly, I'll give you the reason for it. Then I'll leave it completely in your hands. I'll put complete trust in the rightness of your decision. It will be final. I'll never put you to that decision again. Is that fair?"

"I guess I knew it would come back to me someday. At least I thank God that it's coming from you and not one of the gangsters. I'm ready to listen."

CHAPTER TWENTY-SEVEN

THIS WAS THE third time I was about to put into words my sketchy plan for ending this episode. I laid it out for Elena with as much optimism as I could legitimately pour into it. I was bolstered by reminding myself that any other resolution I could imagine could bring disaster on a major scale.

She took in every word in stone silence. The dark cloud in her expression seemed almost to plead for a solution to her personal quandary. The ball, for the moment, was in my court, but the weight of a major decision was still on her shoulders. George had bought into the idea because it provided some slight hope of a positive outcome for his own interests. Mr. Devlin was just faithfully backing the proposal of his junior partner. With Elena, it ran deeper. If she were to tie into the plan, it meant exposing information that she had determined to keep buried from the world for the best of reasons.

When I finished laying out my idea, Elena sat quietly in her own thoughts. I left her to them. When she looked back at me, I could still see indecision in her eyes.

"Michael, it's a bold idea. I'll ask you this because you'll be the one on the front line. Tell me from your heart. Can you make it work?"

I returned her direct eye contact. "I wish I could say it's a sure thing. I can't. I can only paraphrase what someone once said about democracy. It's the worst idea I could possibly imagine—except for every other idea."

The cloud remained, but she smiled.

"I might add one thing. I say this not to persuade you by fear. I just see it coming. The Chinese and Russian gangs are both standing back. They're letting me take the lead here. If I can't convince you to give me something to bring back to them, it won't be me sipping coffee with you next time around. It will quite likely be one or both of them at your door. I don't want that to happen."

She sat quietly for ten more seconds. When she stood up, the cloud of indecision was gone.

"Will you come with me?"

"Certainly. Where?"

"My office."

We walked across a courtyard to an adjoining building. Stairs to the second floor and a long corridor led us to a corner office. She led the way in.

Stacks of books stood like pillars on the floor. Foot-high columns of journals and documents, some new, some yellow and curled with age, were mounded on tables, chairs, and a central desk. The whole scene screamed of intense academic research.

Elena pointed to a chair. It had books on the seat and an academic robe slung over the back.

"Sit down. Just put those anywhere."

Easier said than done. "Where?"

"Doesn't matter. Give me a minute."

By the time I'd gathered the books from the chair, Elena had cleared herself a path to a small safe in a corner. She was down on her knees, working the combination. The thought occurred that in that hodgepodge, why the safe? You could hide a small elephant in plain view.

My thought must have been obvious. She said, "It's not what it seems. There's an order to this chaos. I can find any document in this room."

"Good. Because unless you speak, I can hardly find you."

I didn't say it. I just looked for a place to stack the books from the chair. I wound up saying, to hell with it. I just sat on the books.

She came back to her desk with an ancient-looking volume bound in yellowed cloth. "This is the ship doctor's journal. I have to return it to the ancient documents department someday. Meanwhile, no one'll find it in the safe."

"For that matter, no one'll find the safe."

I didn't say that either.

She sat at the desk and opened the journal. She turned some pages and looked up. "I'm going to read to you the lines of the journal that I left out of the translation I had published. I'll translate as I go. Do you want to make notes?"

She threw me a blank pad. I took out a pen and listened. I could hardly believe what was about to happen at that moment. I was thinking of how many people had already been killed over several centuries just to hear those words.

Elena found reading glasses under a sheaf of papers on her desk and began. "These are the words written by Doctor Demir in his journal aboard the Turkish ship. This is the part where he's writing what he heard from the Turkish army captain about the violin. Remember, this goes back to 1699. The captain had been retreating with the Turkish troops ahead of the Christian forces. At this point, he was nearly dead from his wounds. Are you ready?"

I nodded.

"Alright. You've heard this part. It reads, 'He put every ounce of the last drop of strength Allah gave him into his final words: *The key . . . to locate the treasure . . . it's . . . the violin.*'"

She looked up. I could see hesitation creeping back into her eyes. I said, "It's still your decision. If you wish, I'll simply leave."

That seemed to make a difference. She smiled. "No. I have to pass this on before it takes more lives. I'll give it to you. And God help you. Are you ready to take it?"

"Yes."

"This is the part I left out. 'Luthier . . . Karasu . . . Abbas Ataman . . . He made the code . . . He knows . . .'"

She looked up. "That's all of it. Did you get it?"

"Yes and no. I wrote down the words. I'm not sure what they mean."

"Let's start at the top. A *luthier* is someone who makes or repairs stringed instruments. In particular, violins."

"And what does *Karasu* mean?"

"It's the name of a town. Again, this was written in 1699."

"Is there still a town by that name?"

"No."

I felt a drop in the pit of my stomach. She went on. "But the town of Karasu was rebuilt by Ottomans in 1856. The new name is Medgidia. It's about thirty-nine kilometers west of the Black Sea port of Constanta. And it's still a center for violin makers."

"And *Abbas Ataman*. I take it he was the luthier the soldier meant. He was the one who somehow put the code into the violin. Is that right?"

"It would seem so."

I sat back. "But that was 1699. Where does that leave us?"

"I was curious about that. I traced the shop of Abbas Ataman to see if it still exists. The fortunate thing is that the violin-making trade is one that's typically passed down through generations."

"And what did you find?"

"On the western outskirts of Medgidia, there's a little family lu-thier shop that advertises that it's been in existence for over 350 years. I called it. I found that the man who runs it is named Ataman."

"Could be a hit."

"Could be. But Ataman is not an uncommon Turkish name."

"Did you ask them about Abbas Ataman?"

"No. That was as far as I wanted to go. I didn't want to stir up curiosity."

I finished making a note and sat back. "Then that's my next stop."

"Do you want to phone them?"

"No. I want to see them in person. I need to judge if they're tell-ing me the truth. That's best done eye-to-eye."

Elena put the journal back in the safe. "I guess I wish you luck. I'm not sure that finding this treasure is the best thing for you or any of us."

"Whatever comes of it, I want you to know that today was well worth the trip. I enjoyed the afternoon."

"As did I. Will you let me know what you find?"

I was about to say, "Of course." Something kept the words from leaving my mouth. I was halfway to the door. I turned around.

"Elena. I'm going to ask an absurd question. Just chalk it up to American impetuosity."

"What?"

"Will you come with me?" Before she could answer, I added, "I don't know your schedule. We could do the whole trip there and back by car in a couple of days. I have a car. You must be curious."

She didn't say "No."

"To be honest, I have an ulterior motive. If the original Abbas Ataman left any writing about it, it would be in three-hundred-year-old Turkish or Romanian. In either case, it would be Greek to me."

"Probably Turkish. The Ottomans ruled Romania in 1699."

"There you go. That's your specialty."

She looked at me with a growing smile, and shook her finger. "Michael, you're pulling me back into this."

I held up my hands. "No. I won't do that. You've given me more help than I could possibly ask. I'll let you know what I find."

I got as far as the door when I heard her voice. "I'll call you tonight at your hotel. Don't leave without me."

* * *

I got a five a.m. start the next day. I picked up Elena as she requested at the university. It was an eight-hour drive to Medgidia. I had reserved rooms at the Luxor Hotel on Strada Republicii. We checked in and decided to have dinner and get a fresh start in the morning.

When the sun came up, we were both hustling through breakfast. The day ahead could produce a dead end that would bring the entire adventure to a dull thud. The opposite possibility had us searching out the address of the luthier shop in Medgidia that bore the name "Ataman."

We found it on the outskirts of the city. The ancient wooden building reminded me of the violin shop of Mr. Oresciu where the whole search began.

My pulse was elevated and rising when we entered the shop to the tinkle of a bell similar to Mr. Oresciu's.

The walls and counter were covered with suspended violins that showed violin workmanship that was clearly not mass-produced. A dark, bearded man in his thirties bade us welcome. I introduced myself and Elena. When he said that his name was "Ataman," my pulse rate shot a degree higher.

I looked at Elena. She nodded at me, which I took to mean that I should take the reins in stating our reason for being there.

I began. "Mr. Ataman, I have a very unusual request."

Without mentioning the words "Vlad Dracula" or "treasure," I told him the story of an Ottoman army captain who came to the shop of a luthier named Ataman sometime in 1699. "It was a turbulent time. The captain was retreating from the conquering Christian troops. At his request, a luthier by the name of Abbas Ataman did something special to a violin the captain had with him."

From the expression on the man's face, I could have been reciting a nursery rhyme. The words clearly meant nothing to him. I decided to give a bit more.

"What Abbas Ataman did to the violin was to create some kind of code. A very significant code. Again, this goes back to 1699. Is it possible that there is any written record of that?"

In just asking the question, the absurdity of expecting any record after three centuries drove my pulse back down to normal.

There was still no light of recognition in his eyes, but the man gave us a glimmer of hope. "I think you should talk to my grandfather. Give me a minute."

He went behind a curtain in the rear of the shop. I don't know about Elena, but I was holding my breath. In about two minutes, the man was back. He was holding the curtain open. "My grandfather will see you. Will you come back here?"

We stepped through the curtain into a workroom filled with the scent of freshly worked wood. A portly man with a beard over most of his dark-complected face turned from a well-worn bench. He had Mr. Oresciu's smile—which made me wonder if it's inbred in violin makers.

He held his hands open to us. *"Hosgeldiniz."*

Elena walked past me to accept his handshake. As she passed me, she whispered, "He welcomes us." As they shook hands, she said, "*Cok Tesekkur ederim,*" which I assumed meant "thank you". She followed that with, "*Ingilizce konusabiliyor musum?*" My guess was that she was asking if he spoke English. He smiled more broadly. "Very badly, I fear."

Elena called me over to him. He took the hand I offered in his two hands. Again, I felt the strength of a jockey's grip. He gestured toward a table in the corner with chairs. We both followed the invitation to be seated.

I was not surprised when he said something in Turkish to Elena and immediately said to me, "Please, accept coffee. Perhaps tea? You would do an old man honor."

Elena gave me a firm nod that said, "Accept it."

I said slowly, "That's very kind. We'd both be delighted. Perhaps coffee."

Mr. Ataman seemed very pleased. He called something in Turkish to his grandson in the next room. For the next five minutes, Elena engaged him in conversation in Turkish. He was kind enough to include me by smiling and nodding to me every minute or so.

When the curtain parted, I must admit to being very happy to see his grandson carrying a tray with a metal coffeepot, three small cups, and a plate of some kind of cookies that were dripping in honey. Mr. Ataman poured the coffee. It was strong enough to walk on and thick enough to chew. I realized why the cups were small. A full coffee mug of that wonderful brew would have had me wired tighter than his violins.

We ate. They talked. And the cookies disappeared from the plate. Mr. Ataman refilled our cups twice. When the last drop had been drained, it was crunch time. This time, the laboring oar clearly had to be in Elena's hand. I quietly suggested that she explain our visit to Mr. Ataman.

Elena spoke slowly and softly for about five minutes. I studied the expression on the face of Mr. Ataman, searching for any hint that what she was saying registered. None.

When she finished, there was just silence. She looked at me with a defeated look. "I tried Michael. I told him the whole story. Whatever record was left must have been lost. I'm sorry."

Mr. Ataman turned to look at me. "Mr. Knight, you've come a long way. May I ask whom you represent?"

My mind jumped to another level. It was suddenly clear that Mr. Ataman was considerably more fluent in English than he'd led us to believe.

"It's complicated, Mr. Ataman. I'm not sure what Professor Sakim has told you. Your English is certainly better than my nonexistent Turkish. If I repeat something, please forgive my ignorance of your language. I will, however, be perfectly honest."

"As I would expect, Mr. Knight."

The subtle force behind those words indicated that I was speaking to a man of firm principle. That made it easier.

"I've made promises to representatives of two criminal gangs, one Chinese and one Russian. If you have time, I can explain why and to what extent."

He raised his hands. "I have whatever remaining time Allah allows me. I'd like to hear it from your lips."

I filled him in on the promises to convey whatever information I gained to the two gangster leaders. That brought lines of concern in his face. I took the time to add, however, the fact that I had no intention of allowing the treasure to fall into either of their hands. The lines disappeared. I thought I saw a smile creep in as I laid out the plan I had in mind to prevent it.

He looked at Elena and said something in Turkish. She laughed. She turned to me. "Mr. Ataman finds you interesting. He says you are young enough and innocent enough to think like one of those 'superheroes,' his words, his grandson watches on the television." We all laughed.

When his smile faded, he asked me, "Then if you have not sided with either of the criminal groups, may I ask again, whom do you represent? Do you have ambitions of your own for this supposed treasure?"

We looked eye-to-eye. "Yes, I do."

His eyebrows raised. "You're very honest, Mr. Knight. What might those ambitions be? Do you wish to be one of the wealthiest men in the world?"

"No. I'm wealthy enough. My involvement in this hunt was far from deliberate. I've simply followed one moral obligation after another until I reached this point."

"I see."

"I don't think you do, Mr. Ataman. You asked about my ambitions. They're these. I want to put the pieces of my life back together. I want to live in peace and safety with my wife. I want to practice law with a certain man of your age who means more to me than all of the treasures in the world. That's ambition enough for any three men."

His eyes shown with intensity. He asked, "And if you were to find this treasure you ask about, what would you do with it?"

I could read into his question the same weight of responsibility that had been on Elena's shoulders. I laid out the rest of my plan for ending this entire chapter of my life.

He poured one last refill of coffee into Elena's and my cup, but not his own. He looked at Elena. "Perhaps you and I have reached the same conclusion about this unusual young man."

Elena nodded. He stood up. "You'll please do me the kindness to enjoy your coffee in my absence. I'll not be long."

When he returned, he was carrying a small wooden box that had clearly seen many decades. He set it on the table between us.

"This box has come down through our family, those of us who followed this trade, for over three centuries. As it passed through each generation, it remained sealed shut. I think perhaps this is the time it should see the light of day."

He took a sharp instrument from his workbench. He used it to cut through the crusted wax seal on the box. His hand was on the freed lid of the box. He said it quietly, reverently. "May Allah guide whoever receives the contents of this box."

He opened the lid. The wood inside showed the cracked veins of aging. The only thing it contained was a document as aged and faded as the box itself. Mr. Ataman removed the document as carefully as if it could crumble under his touch. He handed it to Elena. She unfolded it as softly as if it were the original parchment of the Gospel of John.

I watched her scan the faded ink figures on the paper. She looked up at me. "It's in ancient Turkish. I'll need materials in my office to be sure of the translation. I believe it was written by Mr. Ataman's own ancestor. Probably in the presence of the only man ever to discover Vlad Dracula's treasure. I think . . . I feel certain. This is the key to the violin code."

CHAPTER TWENTY-EIGHT

Eight hours later we were in Elena's office. She gently lifted the fragile document out of the centuries-old box. She unraveled it in slow motion on the flat surface of the cleared table. Her delicacy indicated a career of dealing with papers and parchments that could disintegrate with a sneeze.

She placed soft padded weights on the four corners and focused the beam of a strong light clamped on the side of the table. Given the cracks in the paper and the fading of whatever substance was used to write the words, I probably couldn't have read it if it were in English.

"What do you think?"

The lack of an answer told me that her concentration was not subject to interruption. She moved with surprising agility, leaning over the document with a magnifier from the front, the back, and each of the sides.

I felt like an extraneous piece of furniture. I tapped her shoulder. "Elena, I'll leave you alone. I'll be back in an hour."

For the first time since we came into the room, she recognized my existence. "Two hours."

"Good. Done. What do you think about it?"

"I think you should have some supper in the faculty dining room where we ate. Two hours."

"I mean, do you think you can read it?"

Silence. She continued to buzz around the document like a bumble bee on steroids.

"Can I bring something back for you? You should eat."

"I have all the nourishment I need right here on this table. Two hours, Michael. Go."

I went. I used one hour to call Terry; Mr. Devlin; my secretary, Julie; and finally, George. Terry was ecstatic to hear that what I was doing was so far not life-threatening. In answer to my question, our prospective third family member was not affecting her vigorous health. Mr. D. told me that Billy Coyne was, as he put it, making positive progress on witness protection for the Tan family. Julie seemed happy to be asked to make a home-bound plane reservation for the next day from the airport in Constanta. And George was trying unsuccessfully to restrain his excitement over the discovery of the document.

The second hour, I spent in nervous distraction over an excellent *tava*, Turkish stew. Before I left, I asked the waitress in the faculty dining room to put up another order of *tava* to take out.

When I walked back into Elena's office, she was standing at the base of the document writing notes.

I was surprised that she knew I was there. "Come on in, Michael. Sit. Give me another minute."

I set the stew down on a pile of bound documents and took my seat on the books still on the chair. Even better than the stew, I knew the best thing I could give her was silence.

Five minutes later, she stiffly straightened up. She took a quick scan of her notes and looked back over the faded, crackled document. "Michael, this is incredible."

"Does it talk about the code?"

"The man, the luthier, who wrote this had much more education than most people in that trade did in those days. Without his putting it in words, his writing tells so much about his thoughts, his trade, the times he was living in. Just in these ten sentences. It's a piece of history."

"That's all interesting. But does it speak about the code?"

I doubt that she even heard my question. She had the exhausted look of a runner who's just completed a marathon. She walked to her desk and just collapsed into the desk chair. Her body seemed drained, but her thoughts were spinning.

I gave her time. In about a minute, she looked over at me as if she was just re-recognizing my presence. "It's right here."

I was praying that she meant a key to the code. "Could you be more specific?"

She bounced forward at the desk as if something infused her body with resurging energy. "It's the code. It's right here. Amazing. It's brilliant. It's so simple. Only a luthier could have dreamed it up. No wonder people have been scanning that violin for centuries and never saw it."

"Now you've got me on the edge of this seat. Tell me!"

She wiped beads of sweat from her forehead. "Damn. I wish we had that violin here. We could solve the code in a minute."

"I'll get out the violin as soon as I get home. I promise. I'll call you as soon as I do. But can you tell me about it right now?"

"I'll do better than that. I'll read you the direct translation."

* * *

The flight back to Logan Airport in Boston the next day seemed as long as a trip to Mars. Elena's handwritten translation of the document was burning a hole in my mind and my pocket.

I picked up my Corvette in long-term parking. I forced myself to go lighter on the gas pedal than my nerves were demanding.

I was still enjoying a euphoric confidence that neither clutch of gangsters was on my tail. It allowed me to cruise through the tunnel and take a direct route to South Station.

For the first time, I opened the locker that held the Stradivarius without looking over both shoulders. I also took the decoy violin out of the adjoining locker. It had been like a security blanket if either gang had put me in a tight squeeze. It no longer seemed necessary.

With both violins snuggled up on the seat beside me, I took another direct route, this time to the Broken Neck Guitar Repair Shop on Boylston Street. I returned the expensive decoy violin Lanny McLaughlin had loaned to me with thanks.

"Anytime. You taking up the violin? I have something a little lower on the price scale if you're interested."

"Not at the moment, Lanny. On the other hand, I think this'll be an afternoon you'll remember. Let's go back to your workroom."

With a nondescript bag under my arm, I followed Lanny through the door in the back to his workroom. It had a wood-like aroma that reminded me of the shops of Mr. Oresciu and Mr. Ataman.

I set the bag gently on his workbench. I had his full attention. "What have we here?"

I took the old violin case out of the bag. His eyes were glued to it. "Go ahead. Open it."

He unclicked the snaps and slowly raised the top. He had it halfway open when I saw his lower jaw drop to half-mast. By the time it was fully open, his jaw was working again. "Holy crap! What the hell *do* we have here?"

I'd never heard Lanny use a word you wouldn't say in nursery school. He stared for about fifteen seconds. He gave me a blank look. "If this is . . ."

"It is. Go ahead. Take it out."

He used two hands to lift the violin out of the case as if it were a vial of nitroglycerin. He looked at it from every angle. He looked at the faded label on the inside which could still be read: *"Antonius Stradivarius Cremonensis Faciebat Anno 1 . . ."* The last three digits of the date, 1690, were handwritten, as was Stradivari's custom.

"Michael! This is the real thing! It's the first one I've ever actually touched."

"Enjoy the moment, Lanny. When you come back to Earth, I want you to do more than look at it."

"Sure, anything. Just give me a minute."

When he finally set it down, all he could say was, "It's as fine as every word I've ever heard about it."

"Try the sound."

"Really?" He picked up a bow from the shelf and played a part of Tchaikovsky's violin concerto. The tone rang through the studio as clearly and brilliantly as new snow. When he set it down, neither of us could find a voice for a few seconds.

I thought I heard him whisper, "I may never play another violin again." He looked at me, and then he looked up. "Saint Peter, I'm ready to go."

"Not quite yet. I want you to do something for me."

I recalled the words of Elena's translation of the luthier's message from 1699. This was crunch time. I said every word as slowly and clearly as I could.

"This is what I want you to do, Lanny. Look at each of the four pegs at the end of the neck of the violin. Those things you use to tune the strings."

"The tuning pegs."

"Probably. There should be a thin, tiny, almost invisible scratch mark on the long part of each of the pegs where it goes into the end of the violin."

"The pegbox."

"Right. Can you see them? Those little scratches were made over three hundred years ago. They could be difficult to see. Probably impossible if you don't know what you're looking for."

Lanny brought the violin delicately under a bright lamp on his bench. He turned the violin slowly while he scanned each peg.

"Can you see them?"

"I don't know. Wait a minute."

He reached in a drawer for a magnifying glass and scanned the pegs again. "If I can see it on one peg, it'll tell me what to look for on the others . . . Hah! There it is. Give me a minute. Yes . . . I can see all four. Now what?"

"Now I want you to look at the place where each peg goes into the hole at the top of the neck."

"Right. The pegbox."

"Okay. Somewhere on the pegbox where each peg is inserted there should be another barely visible scratch line. A thin scratch beside each peg. Can you find them?"

This time he knew what to look for. It took a minute, but he found all four. By that time, I could feel my shirt sticking to my back with sweat.

"Okay. This is the hard part. First, I want you to tune the violin the usual way. To the usual notes. G, D, A, and the highest note, E. Just the way you usually tune a violin."

While he did it with painstaking delicacy, I reread Elena's translation to be sure we were on course. He looked back at me when he finished.

"This is the critical part, Lanny. Now I want you to tune each of the strings to a higher pitch. Turn each tuning peg until the scratch on the peg is exactly lined up with the scratch next to it on the pegbox."

I could see sweat coming out on his forehead. He carefully tightened each peg for a perfect matchup of scratches.

"That's it. That should be right on."

"Good. Now, my man. This is the crux of it all. I want you to play each string and tell me what note it sounds."

"Starting with the high string or the low one?"

There was no indication in the translation. I made an intuitive guess. "Start with the low string."

While he played each of the notes, I was trying to get my mind around what was about to happen. If we'd gotten the process right, I was about to be the first person in three hundred years—actually six hundred years—to hear the sole clue to where the infamous Vlad Dracula chose to stash one of the world's greatest collections of wealth. It was numbing.

I knew Lanny had the gift of perfect pitch. That meant that he would be dead-on when he named the notes he was hearing.

"Here they are. Beginning with the lowest pitch string, the four notes are A, B, E, and C."

I wrote them down as a backstop for my memory. "Good. You can reset the violin back to the usual tuning."

In a bit of over-caution, I wanted the code notes to be removed from the tuning of the violin as soon as possible, just in case.

As Lanny retuned it and laid it gently to rest in the case, I was recalling Elena's words. That old luthier back in 1699 was damned clever. Whoever got their hands on that violin through the centuries could scan every inch of it for the rest of their lives, as undoubtedly some had, and never find the clue to the treasure.

Appropriately, the code was not visual. It was in the sound of that unique instrument.

*   *   *

Within three minutes, I was back in the Corvette, driving from Lanny's violin shop to the Wallachia Café. I felt like Tom Brady of the Patriots after winning a division championship. It was a half victory, not to be given short shrift. But it was still a long way from the total prize—winning the Super Bowl. I had a string of four letters, which was more than anyone else had had since that Turkish captain happened on Vlad's treasure. But the puzzle remained. How do those letters get us to the one exact location in all of Romania?

On the way to the Wallachia Café, I phoned George. I could tell he was on pins and needles from the exuberance of his "Hello, Michael. What?"

I asked George to meet me on the sidewalk of the café. I popped the inauspicious-looking bag with the Strad into the trunk. When I pulled into the curb with the convertible top down, George practically jumped into the passenger seat. "Where are we going?"

"I thought we'd just go for a nice little drive. Get away from it all. Enjoy the warm sun on our arms, our faces."

"Michael, I'm fond of you, but you can be a pain in the butt. This is the Jamaicaway. You're doing nearly twice the speed limit. Where the hell are we going?"

I looked over at him and smiled. "I hope we're going to make your dreams come true."

I parked in Copley Square. George was getting more antsy as we marched double-time into the classic building of the Boston Public Library. It was time to take George off the bed of nails I had him on.

We rode the elevator in the McKim Building to the Norman B. Leventhal Map Center. I found us two chairs in a quiet corner. We settled in.

George was practically panting when I took out Elena's hand-written translation of the violin code. He read it twice and looked up. The question mark was written on his face.

"Here's the good news—as far as it goes. I had a violin expert apply the code to the Stradivarius. He found the scratch lines and he matched them up. I have the code in four letters."

"Excellent. What are they?"

"I think the letters refer to a place. It has to be somewhere it would make sense to hide something as large as a treasure. I think it's also someplace that had a serious personal connection for Vlad Tepes, Dracula, back around the 1460s. You know the country and the history. So here it is. Please tell me this rings a bell."

I put a slip of paper in front of him. It had just the four letters: A B E C.

My breathing stopped. I watched his eyes for any sign of elation. No sign. I gave him thirty more seconds to let the letters take shape and hit home. Still nothing. Instead of elation there was an emptiness.

"It's alright, George. It's not a dead end."

I stepped outside into the hallway. I used my cell phone to call Elena's office. It was still before noon. Given the seven-hour time difference between Boston and Istanbul, I figured I could still catch her at work. I let out the breath I was holding when she answered.

I gave her the four violin letters—A, B, E, C. Again, there was no instant jubilation on the line. But instead of emptiness, she told me to stay where I was. She'd call back in ten minutes.

I paced the corridor for fifteen minutes. I caught the call on the first half ring.

"Michael, you darling. I think you found it, but . . ."

"Please, don't give me a *but*. Not after all of this."

"The *but* is that you started from the wrong violin string. I'm sure of it. The code starts from the top string, not the bottom. It's not ABEC. The name is CEBA. The 'C' should have a little pronunciation mark below it, but you can't put that into a violin string. It should be pronounced *Cheba*."

"Is it a place? Where is it?"

"Is George there?"

"He's inside. We're at the map room of the Boston Public Library."

"Excellent. Get him. Put it on speaker."

I did. I held the phone on low speaker close to the ears of both of us. Elena had the floor. "You boys are in the right place in that map room. That name, Ceba, I've come across it somewhere. I'm going through some papers. Michael, I told you I could find anything in this office. Hold the line."

George and I were frozen in position over my cell phone in the corridor. In less than two minutes, we heard a loud "Aha! Eureka!" from away from her phone. She was back in an instant. "Gentlemen!"

"Go, Elena."

"This came up in a paper I did for my degree. See if the library has a map of the area around Ploiesti going back to the 15th century. It's around sixty-five kilometers north of Bucharest. That luthier must have been a student of Romanian history. Look for 'Ceba' on the old map. It was a fair-sized market town at the intersection of three trade routes. One of them linked Vlad's capital, Tirgoviste, to Braila. Ceba was a port on the Danube. I don't know what Ceba's called today. George, if you find it on the ancient map, you may recognize the area."

"We're on it."

"Call me."

Thanks to the Boston Public Library and one particularly acute staff member, within ten minutes, George was pouring over a map of the Ploiesti area of Romania dating back to the fifteenth century. Sure enough, there was a town named Ceba within ten miles of Ploiesti.

George spotted it first. He started thumping it with his finger. His face was beginning to turn crimson.

"Dammit, Michael! This is it."

"Before you melt down, what is *it*?"

He kept thumping the spot with his finger. "It's exactly where it should be."

"Could you be specific?"

"That luthier doubled the code. He encrypted the name in the violin, and then he used a place name that's no longer in existence. Ceba. It's exactly there."

"So what's there now?"

"It all fits perfectly. It's where Vlad Tepes, our Dracula, built the Monastery of Targsor."

CHAPTER TWENTY-NINE

GEORGE WAS ON his feet, pacing. "This has to be it. Just what you said. The location has to be someplace that had special meaning to Vlad. Yet not too obvious."

"So why is this place special?"

George pulled out the chair next to mine and sat close. "Dracula's father, Vlad Dracul, was the ruler, the *voivode*, of the province of Wallachia. It's just south of Transylvania. The word is that he was killed by Vladislav II in 1448. Vladislav took his place as ruler for the next twelve years."

"So?"

"So, on August 20, 1456, our Dracula, Vlad the Impaler, got even for his father's death. He killed Vladislav II. He did it personally in a hand-to-hand battle. That's how our Dracula came to power. He ruled Wallachia as the *voivode* for the next six years."

"Again, so?"

"Whether Dracula had pangs of conscience over the murder of Vladislav, which I doubt, or he was just worried about where he'd spend eternity, which is more likely, he wanted to do something major to atone for the sin of murder. Christians in those days believed that doing good works, like building and endowing a monastery, would help eradicate sins."

"And?"

"His act of atonement was to build a monastery at the exact location of the murder. It's right there on this old fifteenth-century map. Look at the name of the location. 'Ceba.'"

"Is it still there?"

"The town? Yes. But not by that name. The name was later changed to Targsor. It means Little Market. There's not much left of the town. It was attacked by Stefan IV of Moldavia in 1526. It slowly died after that."

"Do you know how to find it?"

Now he had a grin to match his enthusiasm. "Look here on this modern map. There it is under the new name. Targsor. Just a little south of Ploiesti."

"How about the monastery? Is it still there?"

"The building stands, but it's just a ruin. It's long since been closed as a monastery."

He sat back. The look on his face broadcast assurance. "Michael, this is it. I feel it in my bones."

"I have the same feeling. But where in the monastery? If it's a ruin, the treasure can't be inside the building. Someone would have seen it."

The assured look persisted. "So what does that tell you?"

"It could be underground. Buried somewhere around the monastery."

"And where would it be buried?"

"What the hell is this? Twenty questions?"

"Yes. Remember, that this area of Christianity was always under the threat of attack by the Muslim Turks. They could have invaded at any time. In fact, it was the Turks who actually drove Vlad north to the mountains in 1462. So, under that constant threat, what do you suppose the Christians in the monastery would have done for their own safety?"

"They went underground."

"When Christians went underground, what did they build?"

"You're becoming annoying. What?"

"You say it. You'll believe it more if you think of it yourself."

"Catacombs. A web of tunnels under the monastery."

"You are so clever."

"Were there catacombs?"

"Yes. There's a high hill just next to the monastery. The catacombs were dug under that hill."

"How do you know?"

"I was there two years ago. I wasn't looking for treasure. I was visiting friends. I actually stayed in the town. I'd heard about the tunnels under the hill that were the catacombs in Targsor. A guide from the town showed me where they were. This brings it all back."

"But if the treasure is there, and people can go into the catacombs, why wasn't the treasure discovered before now?"

"Two reasons. First, until ten minutes ago, nobody had any idea that the treasure might be buried in those catacombs. Secondly, well before Dracula fled north in retreat to his castle on the Arges, he had the entrances sealed with piles of stones, He concealed the stones by planting bushes and trees. The entrances are well hidden. Unless you know where they are, you wouldn't recognize them if you were standing in front of them. My guide pointed them out. Like everyone else, I just looked at where they are and moved on. Vlad must have sealed off the entrances after he hid the treasure there. He probably thought he could come back for it later."

"And no one ever wanted to clear the entrance and look inside?"

"Why bother? As far as anyone ever knew, it was just a link of empty caves."

"Then how do you suppose the Turkish captain found the treasure?"

"It's only a guess. He'd been stationed in that area with the Turkish army. He'd probably heard of the catacombs. He might have opened an entrance and used it as a refuge when the Christians were retaking the country around 1699."

I sat back and just stared at the ceiling. Thoughts were swimming until they finally melded into an idea.

"We have to go there," I said. "This is coming together. You have to show me where it is."

"I know. When?"

"Soon. I'll let you know. There's something I have to take care of before we leave. Maybe a few days. Will you wait for me?"

"A few more days? Why not?"

* * *

The pace was picking up. I was as anxious as George to play out the final scene as I pictured it. But first, there was business I had to attend to.

It was just after four in the afternoon. I was right in figuring that Mr. Devlin was back from court. He took my call in his office. He got Billy Coyne in on a conference call.

"What's the deal, kid? You ready to bring in Mickey Chan?"

"First things first, Mr. Coyne. I'm into something. If it works out, you won't need him. You'll be moving to dismiss the indictment."

"Yeah, sure. And when that hits the D.A.'s desk, she'll be taking my tonsils out through my anus. She's already counting on headlines for convicting Chan."

"She'll come around. Hopefully, you'll be substituting indictments for the top tong leaders. She'll get a parade through Chinatown."

"So you say, kid."

"Yes, I do. But it depends."

"On?"

"Witness protection for Ming Tan and her family. I can't wait any longer. Can you do it?"

"I'm working on it. I should hear from the U. S. Attorney by tomorrow."

"What are the odds?"

"They're feds. We're not exactly in the same Boy Scout troop. This is no buddy system. Besides, you didn't give me a whole lot of facts to base it on."

"It's the best I have at the moment. What's your estimation?"

"If I had to guess, slightly more likely than not."

I took a deep breath for thought. "Alright. Here are the odds on my side. I'm going to make a play to get Ming Tan out of the hands of the tong. It has to be done right now. I'm going to do it on blind faith that you'll come through with witness protection."

"I told you, kid. I'll do what I can. That's all I can offer."

"That's terrific, Mr. Coyne. Just so you understand the odds completely. If I can't pull this thing off, and I mean perfectly, you'll still be taking the train home to your wife in Lynnfield. The chances of my living to see my wife again, you wouldn't want to bet on. Under those circumstances, two things. One is you better do your *damn* best. The second, is . . . let that be the last time in this life that you call me *kid*. This game is not *kid* stuff."

Where I got the nerve to actually say it, I'll never know. But I did. Just like that. There was silence for three seconds.

Mr. Devlin couldn't hold it any longer. "Billy, I love you for the fine Irish lad that you are. But, by damn, if my partner is left swinging in the wind on this thing, I'll throw so much crap at the fan, you and that feather-brain you work for'll think it's midnight. I'd advise you *strongly* to get on the horn and nail down that witness protection. Have one hell of a day, Billy."

There was no better note to end the conversation. I hung up and thanked God for my partner, Lex Devlin, who had my back without the foggiest notion of what I was up to.

Next, I called my old Harvard buddy, Harry Wong. I thought it might be well to have someone who was familiar with the Chinatown underworld know where I was going in case it became a one-way trip.

I sketched a plan to Harry that might have seemed suicidal until I explained the leverage I'd be taking with me. I figured that would convince him that I was on solid ground.

Harry answered, "That is absolutely insane. Do you know who you're dealing with?"

"I think so."

"I don't think so. Dammit. How stubborn are you going to be about this?"

"I have no choice. My back's to the wall. I just want you to know where I'm going, you know, in case . . ."

"Where are you now, Michael?"

"The library. The big one. Copley Square. Why?"

I could almost hear Harry ruminating over a decision for about five seconds. "Meet me at the Chinatown Gate. Quarter of five. We can walk there before closing time at five."

"Harry, I just want you to know where I'm going to be. It's just insurance. I can do this myself."

"Really? How's your Chinese?" He poured out a sentence in flowing Mandarin. "What'd I say?"

"You said, 'Don't take any wooden fortune cookies.' It's a quote from Lao Tzu."

"Cute, Michael. But you're an ass. What if the conversation shifts to Chinese on their side? Exactly what creek will you be up?"

I had no answer.

"Right, Michael. Chinatown Gate. Quarter of five."

* * *

We met and walked from Beach Street. We were at the front door of the main bank of Chinatown at five minutes before closing. I grabbed Harry's elbow before we went in. "Truth told, I'm glad you're here, Harry. I owe you an excellent dinner."

"You owe me a week in Vegas for this one. Let's go."

"Wait a minute. Here's the play. I may need you for translation later, but let me take the lead. As long as it's in English, I'll do the talking. I really do have a plan."

"I hope so. After you, Tiger."

I took one deep breath. I led the way into what looked like any bank I'd been in except that all of the employees were Chinese. I walked with a confident smile up to a clerk who appeared to be in a management position.

"I'm here to see Mr. Chang. My name's Michael Knight. Would you let him know I'm here?"

He bowed with a smile, rapped on the door behind him, and entered. I could hear my name whispered. In about two seconds, Mr. Chang was in the doorway. His expression was halfway between puzzlement and shock that the prey would walk so willingly into the lion's den after the incident at Park Street Station.

He gestured for me to enter—no smile this time. A brusque word to the employee sent him back to his station.

I walked to the chair in front of his desk and sat down. Harry came in and closed the door behind him. He stood by the wall. When Mr. Chang recognized Harry, he shot him a glance that could have withered the flowers on his desk. Another reminder that

Harry's defection from the tong's youth gang in his teens was still an open sore. If it made Harry uncomfortable, it gave me a pang of delight. It confirmed my belief that Mr. Chang was a member of the tong, and probably at an extremely high level.

Mr. Chang finally focused on me and took his seat.

"You're a man of infinite surprises, Mr. Knight. I believe the last time we met you made a promise that remains curiously unfulfilled. I'm going to assume that's the purpose of your presence here."

I learned a principle in my first year at the bar. In an argument, never let your opponent set the agenda. "There are actually two issues on the table before us, Mr. Chang. First things first, yes?"

I could sense his reluctance to lose control of the order. "I'm listening."

"I made a promise to a certain elderly gentleman to share information regarding—shall we be open—a particular treasure, before I put a finger on it myself. I imagine you know the elderly gentleman. I assume you've heard about my commitment to him."

His expression revealed nothing.

"Ah, perhaps I'm wrong, Mr. Chang. I assumed your position in the organization entitled you to be kept advised. I also assumed that I could deal directly with you. Obviously I misjudged your position. Forgive my wasting your time."

I noticed a bit of puffing up in the chest area. My promise had been to the man from the Hong Kong triad who had stepped over Mr. Chang's head to take control of the treasure hunt. I had a strong feeling that Mr. Chang would relish gaining face when I presented the news of the treasure directly to him first.

His tone was somewhat more receptive. "You may talk directly with me. I'm ready to hear your report."

"I'm ready to give it. Shortly. One item has to be dealt with first."

The air held instant tension. "I was told that your promise was unconditional." He looked from me to Harry and back. "I would not advise gamesmanship at this point."

"No games, Mr. Chang. A simple ancillary matter. Strictly between you and me."

"Then why . . ." He gave a demeaning gesture of his chin toward Harry.

"Mr. Wong stays. Non-debatable. Shall we proceed?"

The venom in his glance toward Harry said this was a testing hurdle I had to get past. I gave it three seconds. I rose. "Let's go, Harry. We have an appointment in another part of Chinatown." I looked back at Mr. Chang. "It would not be received well by the gentleman in question if either of us were not to arrive there ready and able to do business."

I prayed that he'd assume the other appointment was with the man from Hong Kong and that his newly acquired *face* would slip away.

"Sit down, Mr. Knight. State your *ancillary* matter."

"It's business, Mr. Chang. I need something. You need something. All totally outside our agreement regarding the matter in Romania."

"And what exactly do you think I need?"

"You approved a loan from your bank. One million dollars. The security was nothing but a violin."

He shrugged. "It was within my authority. What concern of yours?"

"The violin was never within your reach if the loan was defaulted. In fact, I believe the person to whom you entrusted the million dollars, shall we be open, your Mr. Liu, had the money deflected to his own hidden account. With neither the violin nor the million dollars, you'll have a bit of explaining to do to your board."

"Your threat is empty, Mr. Knight. I have control of my board. I could always replace the money out of my own funds."

"And how about the federal inspectors? Your bank is insured by the Federal Deposit Insurance Corporation. Will their investigators be as pliable as your board of stooges? And when it comes out that the loan was made to a Chinese organized crime gang, with your knowledge? My, my. Some feathers might fly. Face won't be the only thing that could be lost."

"I have no—"

"Let me add one thought. This organized crime gang I mentioned. Once the federal investigations begin, how much of the business of the tong, how many of the people involved all the way to the top will be made public in open court? The press will love it."

His lips were pressed firmly together, either in anger or to keep injudicious words from reaching the ears of a tong traitor and a *weilu*.

"Let me relieve your anxiety, Mr. Chang. You asked what it is that you need that I can supply. Quite simply, I have the violin. Its value will certainly cover security for the million-dollar loan and whatever interest your bank chooses to charge. I will place the violin within your grasp. That solves the touchy issue of lack of security. Once the loan is repaid and cancelled, however you choose to do that, all of your troubles in this respect vanish. No one is the wiser. No public disclosure. No FDIC investigation. And you lose no face. An outcome surely to be desired. Would you agree?"

His eyes were now cold and searching. "And in return, you mentioned that you have a certain . . . need."

"My need will cost you no funds whatsoever. Since we're among friends here, shall we speak frankly?"

He had a wary look, but he opened his hands in a "Why not?" gesture.

"Good. Since we're here in the privacy of your office, might we assume for the sake of argument that you're intimately familiar with the inside workings of the Boston tong."

A questioning, semi-shocked expression came over his face.

"Without pressing the issue, let's just take that as a working assumption. For reasons of the tong's politics, your Mr. Liu, the one who involved me in this violin business from the start, was murdered. His throat was cut. Typical tong method. He was killed for betraying the tong in this violin, treasure business."

Mr. Chang slowly shook his head in apparent denial of any such knowledge.

"May I continue?"

Again, Mr. Chang gestured an invitation.

"Then the tong decided to kill two birds with one stone. You know that expression?"

"I have lived in this country for fifty years."

"Good. The tong decided it was a chance to avenge itself on Mickey Chan for his misguided loyalty to Mr. Liu. The tong compelled an innocent woman, Mrs. Ming Tan, probably by a threat to her life and her family, to falsely identify Mickey Chan as Mr. Liu's murderer. It takes the real tong murderer off the hook, and it punishes Mickey Chan. The tong took out insurance of her testimony by kidnapping Mrs. Tan."

Mr. Chang leaned back in his chair. "This story of yours is absolute fiction. But, only for the sake of argument, how is this a concern of yours?"

"Mickey Chan is my client. Cards on the table. This is my offer. I want Mrs. Tan released to me, in good health, by this evening. Nine o'clock. I'll give you the details later. In exchange, I'll place the violin where you will have easy access to it."

"And if this . . . request of yours is not granted?"

"If not, we both suffer the consequences . . . needlessly."

Mr. Chang went into a silent period of apparent wrestling with his options. He leaned forward. He seemed to adjust the position of his desk phone and stood up. He slowly walked to the window behind him.

He had me frozen for the moment. I had no idea if he was considering the proposition or just marking time.

In about ten seconds, I heard a slow whisper from Harry by the door. "Michael, *vocavit milites eius. Audio foris.*"

I looked back at Harry in disbelief. He nodded and whispered, "Professor Rothman!"

I almost smiled in spite of the situation. Harry and I had taken three courses in Latin at Harvard from Professor Rothman. I couldn't believe we were using it for anything but reading plaques on buildings.

Harry repeated the words. He was telling me that Mr. Chang had called out his troops. Harry heard them outside the door.

I nodded. Mr. Chang just looked confused daggers at Harry.

Harry said it, with considerably more emphasis. *"Pugnare aut fugire? Nunc!"*

He was asking me for the plan—*Fight or flight*? With the added urging to decide "Now!"

Neither of those options seemed to ensure that either of us would see the sunset. I'd learned from Mr. Devlin that when a slim chance seems the only positive option, go with the odds, no matter how long they seem.

CHAPTER THIRTY

I SHOT A quick word to Harry, "*Neuter!*", since "neither" of his options fit the bill. I stood up and walked to Mr. Chang's desk. Without asking, I took a sheet of blank paper from the top of his desk. I took a blue marker out of my pocket and wrote something on the paper, out of his line of sight.

I folded the paper and walked to the door with all of the false confidence I could muster. I opened the door. There were four obvious members of the tong's youth gang now assembled by the door, ready to burst in at the order of Mr. Chang. Each of them had weapon-like bulges in their clothing that suggested that our Harvard wrestling moves might not win the day.

I smiled warmly at the four thugs. My tone was one of gracious hospitality. "Come in. Come in, gentlemen. Don't stand on ceremony. You're just in time."

For all of their armed advantage, they seemed befuddled. They looked around the door to Mr. Chang for some confirmation of my invitation. Mr. Chang looked as befuddled as the four thugs.

I insisted. "Please, gentlemen. Mr. Chang is delighted to see you. Come in. He may be serving tea shortly."

Mr. Chang did not have it together enough to either join in or squash the invitation. He had summoned them in the first place, but this was no longer "the first place."

Under my enthusiastic urging, the four thugs skulked into the room. They stood around the wall, waiting for someone to tell them who the hell was in charge. It was not forthcoming from the silent Mr. Chang.

Since I still had my moment as master of ceremonies, I walked over to the desk. "I think you should be seated, Mr. Chang. You and I are still doing business."

I placed the folded paper on the desk in front of him. I picked up a jade paperweight and placed it on top of the paper to suggest secrecy. Mr. Chang was hesitant, but I had his curiosity. He looked at his army of four for reassurance and sat down.

I made a two-handed gesture of invitation to the note and walked back to my seat. One look at Harry suggested that he thought he'd fallen down the rabbit hole. I patted his knee for confidence. "Relax, Harry. I think Mr. Chang is about to extend an offer of tea. Unfortunately, business calls us elsewhere. We'll have to decline."

I looked back at Mr. Chang, who was now seated, looking with a blank expression at the folded note. I finally sensed the problem. The last thing he could do in his own office in front of his own men was to appear to take an order from me to open the note. On the other hand, I needed the four thugs right where they were for the note to work. I thought I'd grease the wheel. I oozed graciousness.

"Mr. Chang, I believe that note complies with what you wished me to do for you. I hope it satisfies your wishes."

That note was, if my prayer was answered, the last thing on this earth he wanted, or expected, to see. But at least now he wouldn't lose face by opening it.

I put on a benign smile as he reached for the note. He opened it slowly. I caught the slight quiver in his hand when he read the three characters I'd written.

I jumped into the silence. "We have no secrets in this room, do we, Mr. Chang? Why don't we just share what you've read with all these good men of yours? They are, after all, here at your invitation."

Mr. Chang could have been one of the terra-cotta figures. Silence reigned. His situation had gone from annoyance to a bed of nails in a matter of seconds. I thanked God that the assumption I was counting on apparently had legs.

It was time to give us all an escape hatch. "On the other hand, Mr. Chang, you and I are in the middle of a pleasant negotiation. Do we need to detain these gentlemen? It's your decision, of course."

I winked at him, just to enhance his confusion. It took a few seconds, but he finally saw his way clear to make a rational decision. He said something in a commanding tone in Chinese to the four men. They seemed eager to comply with his dismissal. Harry closed the door behind them.

Since I still had the ball, so to speak, I decided to make a final plunge for the goal line. The gracious tone in my voice had been spent. "Now that the fun and games are over, let's keep this clearly in mind. What I wrote on that paper is also in a note with a full explanation that will be delivered to the City Editor of the *Boston Globe* if Harry or I were to disappear or suffer an accident in any form."

His glare at me was at full intensity, but I sensed from his silence that there'd be no follow-up violent action on his part. That was enough. I wasn't there to make a pal.

"I'll assume that's a 'yes.' Then let's finish this business. The offer is open, but not negotiable. Let's not pretend that you don't have the power to accomplish the release of Mrs. Tan. We both know you do. That said, you can bet on this. I will hold up my end with the violin. It will be within your reach very shortly after Mrs. Tan is free. And with that, Mr. Chang, I have no more time to waste. It's a simple yes or no."

He looked from me to Harry and down at the note, still folded. I was sure it was playing on his decision. He finally just nodded. I stood.

"Done. Then understand this. Mrs. Tan will be delivered by your people this evening, at nine o'clock, to the parking lot of the Continental Restaurant. It's on Route 1 in Saugus. Is all of that totally clear?"

He was clearly chafing under the order. He kept his silence. But he nodded again.

"I'd like to hear that out loud, Mr. Chang. We don't want any misinterpretations."

He spat it out. "You have my answer."

"Which is?"

It took him a second, but the word "Yes" came out.

"Very astute. When the delivery of Mrs. Tan is successfully made, I'll send you notice of where you'll find the violin. So. If there's nothing further, I believe Harry and I will take our leave. Harry?"

Harry was out of his seat and holding the door for me. I deliberately took an annoyingly slow pace out the door, and out of the bank.

Harry was on my heels. "Michael, I have just two words."

"Would they be 'holy crap'?"

"You're psychic."

* * *

Harry had nothing more to say until we'd walked around the block. When we were out of sight of the bank, he grabbed my arm and pulled me to a stop. "Michael, what in the hell did you write on that note?"

I looked back. There seemed to be no one tailing us.

"I remembered what you told me, Harry. You said that the tong rules required that the identity of the number one man of the

Boston tong, the *shan chu*, be kept totally secret from everyone in the tong except the number two man. If it's like the rest of their code of rules, I figured someone would pay a high price in pain if the identity of the top man were revealed. Maybe even the *shan chu* himself would suffer. Was I right?"

"Yes."

"I thought of the cast of Chinese characters I'd met since this thing began. I was gambling on a hunch. I figured that the top man of the tong would want to be personally involved in something as big as this treasure hunt. Mr. Chang was certainly the ranking Chinese member of that dinner party at the China Pearl that started it all. I was guessing, hoping that our Mr. Chang might be the *shan chu*. If I was right, the last thing he could afford is to have that disclosed in front of those four tong goons. That's why I wanted them in the room. They actually gave me leverage."

"So what did you write on the paper?"

"You told me that the tong's secret code number for the *shan chu* was 489. I thought I'd spice it up by suggesting I knew more than I did. I just wrote those three numbers on the note. He couldn't afford to have me say it out loud in front of the troops. Anyway, he became agreeable."

Harry just shook his head. I started us walking toward our cars.

"What now, Mike?"

"If we get Mrs. Tan away from them, that's only half the game. We have to get Mr. Tan and their children too. I still need you, Harry. You in?"

"I wouldn't miss it."

"I'd like you to call the Tans' grocery shop. Put in a small order. Anything. Ask Mr. Tan to deliver it personally to the parking lot where you're parked."

"Alright."

"Then it gets tricky."

"Oh, that'll be different. In what way?"

"Mr. Tan doesn't speak much English. I need to have you explain to him in Chinese that we're getting his wife safely out of the hands of the tong. We need to have him join her. You can tell him that we're going to get both of them and their children out of the reach of the tong permanently. It's a major move, but from now on, they won't have that mob on their backs. They'll be safe. They'll have a new life. That should sell the plan, especially after his wife's kidnapping."

"Is this the witness protection program?"

"It is. And one last thing. When you have him safe in your car, will you take him directly to pick up their children at home? They need to be part of the relocation or the tong will still have control."

"I understand."

"He'll need time to pack some clothes. But make it brief. The sooner they all get out of the house, the safer. After that, would you just keep them on the road out of sight?"

"Of course. Then what?"

"Just as you heard in Chang's office. We'll all meet at nine tonight in the parking lot of the Continental Restaurant on Route 1."

"I know the place."

"I'm asking an awful lot of you, Harry. All I can say is that if it all comes together, the good guys will be on the scoreboard."

"Like I said. I'm in."

"I owe you. How about a week in Vegas?"

"Just a dinner'll do. These are my people. I'll treat you."

* * *

My last move before driving out of Chinatown was to call Mr. Devlin. Given my last words to Mr. Coyne, I welcomed Mr. Devlin's voice on the line when I spoke to him. We reached Mr. Coyne in his office. For better or worse, I led off.

"Mr. Coyne, in Sherlock's words, the game is afoot. The tong will deliver your witness, Ming Tan, to the parking lot of the Continental Restaurant on Route 1. We'll have her husband and two children there too. Tonight, nine o'clock. How about your end?"

"*Damn!* That's short. The U.S. Attorney is getting approval. He was going to call tomorrow."

"That's a day late. Lives are at stake. Can you get back to him?"

"I'll try."

"You can tell the U. S. Attorney for me that if he'll get his game in gear, he'll have one hell of a witness drop in his lap. I'll see you at nine tonight."

It was a brief but entire conversation, and not once did I hear the word "kid." That was a good sign.

I exercised every ounce of the optimism I inherited from my parents and acted on the assumption that, for the first time in this odyssey, a plan would actually work out according to my mental script.

I called George. He was still like a race horse in the starting gate, chomping at the bit. "It's a go, George. I can fly to Romania tomorrow. I'll meet you over there. How about a hotel in Ploiesti? We want to be close to the Targsor catacombs, but not too close."

"We're on. I'll get us rooms for tomorrow night in the Prahova Plaza Hotel. You'll like it."

"Good. I'll need two rooms. Can we rent a car? No, two cars. For the following morning."

"Of course. Anything else?"

"Yes. We'll need supplies. This thing is coming together."

"Excellent. What'll we need?"

I gave George as complete a list as I could pull together. "Can we get all of that over there?"

"I'll take care of it. I'll leave tonight."

"Done. Is there a restaurant in the hotel? We should meet day after tomorrow at, shall we say, eight a.m."

"Yes. The Piccolo Giardino Restaurant. I'll meet you for breakfast at eight. Anything else?"

"Just one thing."

"What?"

"Pray."

* * *

It was about six o'clock. I called my secretary, Julie, at home. Before she hit me with a litany of lawyers' calls that I knew I had no time to return, I asked her to book me a flight the next day to the Henri Coanda Airport just outside of Ploiesti.

Her response: "Why don't you just move to Romania and commute back here?"

"Because I think this is the last one."

"Good. You have clients that are—"

"No problem, Julie. Mr. Devlin said he'd step in for me. I'm sure the clients will think they've struck gold when he returns their calls."

"And is this one way or round trip?"

"One way. It depends on a lot of *ifs*. But I need two tickets."

With another dose of optimism, I gave her the name of the other passenger for booking purposes. "One last thing. How're you and Piper getting along?"

"Who's Piper? I don't know any Piper. I think you'll have to get yourself another dog. The only Piper I know won't want to leave me."

"You're a gem, Julie. I won't forget what you're doing for us."

"Just come back in one piece."

* * *

I was sitting in the parking lot of the Continental Restaurant on
Route 1 at quarter of nine. It was apparently a light night for business. There were only a few other cars in the lot.

I arrived with nerves on edge, but the first drop of perspiration
didn't flow until ten minutes later. By the time my watch said one
minute to nine, I was jumping out of my skin.

Just as the second hand was straight up, I saw a car pull into the
lot. There were four people in the car. I walked out to the center of
the lot to be clearly visible. The car slowly headed in my direction. It
was just twenty feet away when my heart rate shot up. I recognized
Harry at the wheel. He had one Chinese man and two young children in the car. When they came closer, I recognized Mr. Tan.

Harry pulled up beside me and opened the window. I smiled and
nodded to the whole crew. Harry stepped out of the car for a quick
consult.

"How'd it go?" I asked.

"Good on this end. Mr. Tan will go along with anything. He's
only focused on seeing his wife again."

"Okay. That's step one. The next two are the big ones."

The next five-minute wait took ten years off of my life. When I
saw a black Lincoln pull into the lot, my breath stopped. It slowed
to a stop about forty feet away in a dark corner. I said, "You wait
here, Harry."

I started walking toward the Lincoln. All the lights were off.
When I was ten feet from it, the back door opened. A small figure
got out and stood by the door. When I got close to the figure, I took
my first breath. I saw the fear-filled face of Ming Tan.

I took her hand. "It's alright, Mrs. Tan. Your husband's here. And
your children."

She didn't speak, but tears began flowing. I began to lead her away from the car when a voice from the back seat stopped me. I couldn't see a face in the dark, but I recognized the voice of the fat, pockmarked man I had seen at Mr. Leong's poultry shop. "First you owe your part of the bargain. You give me violin before you take the woman."

I thought of the violin ten miles away in a South Station locker. "I will do exactly what I said I'd do before the sun comes up in the morning. That's a promise."

"You'll do it now—or the girl does not leave."

His words were punctuated by what sounded like a handgun cocking.

I looked at the terrified face of Mrs. Tan. I could hear Mr. Tan outside of Harry's car yelling, pleading for his wife to come to him.

I cannot recall another moment in my life when my heart was so torn in two. I'd played my last card. I was out of tricks. Out of answers. I had no moves left. I was overcome with a feeling of responsibility and uselessness.

I was in limbo for five of the longest seconds in history. I could only pray—mostly for forgiveness for getting these people into this paralyzing situation.

I was so deep in borderline panic that I could barely grasp what happened. The literal blackness of that corner was suddenly ablaze with enough light to make a movie. The light was coming from three cars swooping in from three directions. A voice was blaring orders for everyone to freeze. The voice identified the men in the cars as federal marshals. It ordered the three men in the Lincoln, now awash in blinding light, to show their hands and get out of the car.

I was back in the game. I still had Mrs. Tan's hand. I pulled her at a dead run in the direction of Harry's car. We ran until I let her go into the arms of Mr. Tan. Their children ran to the two of them. The four of them looked like one large person.

I looked back at the scene in the corner of the lot. I recognized the pockmarked man and two other tong thugs in handcuffs. They were being led to the flashing cars by men I recognized as U.S. marshals.

By the time I looked back, another car, a black SUV, had pulled up beside Harry's car. I recognized Ben Styles, the Massachusetts U.S. Attorney. Two U. S. marshals were escorting the Tan family back to the SUV. I noticed Billy Coyne in his own car off to the right watching the whole show from the side.

I ran to his car. "Mr. Coyne. You came through. Come over here. Quick."

I half pulled him to the side of the SUV where Mrs. Tan was sitting. I called Harry over to translate.

"Harry, tell Mrs. Tan that she's completely safe from the tong. They'll never hurt her or her family again. Go ahead."

There was an exchange between Harry and Mrs. Tan in Chinese. She was nodding in tears. I took hold of Harry's arm. I said, "Now, Harry. Ask Mrs. Tan if the one who killed Mr. Liu was Mickey Chan. Ask her right now. Mr. Coyne, listen to this."

Harry asked a question in Chinese. Mrs. Tan was sobbing in gasps, but she was also strongly shaking her head. Words were pouring out in Chinese.

Harry turned to Mr. Coyne and me. "She said the tong forced her to say it. They threatened to kill her husband and children. It was not Mickey Chan."

"Harry, ask her if she knows who did commit the murder. Can she identify him?"

He asked, and the words poured out again. Harry translated. "She says she can. She heard them talking about it while they held her captive. She can identify the man who did it and the ones who ordered the murder."

I turned to Mr. Coyne. "You can take it from here. I'll bet the feds will cooperate. You'll both have a star witness."

"I'll admit it. You were right . . . Knight. The U.S. Attorney bought into it. The feds are taking the Tan family into witness protection right now."

"You did well yourself, Mr. Coyne. But before you move. I need a promise. Tomorrow morning, I want to meet you in the judge's chambers. I need a fast motion to dismiss the indictment against Mickey Chan."

"I'll take care of it tomorrow."

"It has to be first thing tomorrow morning. Nine o'clock. When the judge gets in. I have a reason. I'll have Mickey Chan in the courtroom."

He looked at me. "So now am I taking orders from you?"

"Yes. Just this once. And thanks for calling me 'Knight.'"

"You earned it . . . kid."

CHAPTER THIRTY-ONE

I WAS CLOSE to total depletion when I drove out of the Continental Restaurant lot, but I had one last mile to go before I slept. I'd promised Mr. Chang, the banker, that if he delivered Mrs. Tan, I'd put the Strad violin within his reach. I took the promise literally.

I left Harry with one last request—have Mickey Chan outside the judge's courtroom by nine in the morning.

* * *

My first stop was the South Station locker for the Strad. I drove from there to Boston Sympathy Hall. The old gentleman at the musicians' entrance let me in when I showed him what I was delivering.

The orchestra under Andris Nelsons was into the second movement of Beethoven's *Eroica*. I stayed to its completion and joined in the standing and prolonged ovation. The orchestra took a break to reset the stage between works. I caught the eye of the concert master, Lee Tang, from the left wing of the stage. I held up the Strad. He was at my side in four seconds.

I handed it to him gently. He received it as if the *Mona Lisa* were passing between us. The awesome joy in his face matched the sense of unburdening relief in my heart. It felt as if, after a six-century journey, the Stradivarius had finally found its true home.

Before leaving, I bought a ticket to the next evening's performance of the orchestra. I put it in an envelope with a written message addressed to Mr. Chang at his bank. I dropped it off at a twenty-four-hour service to be delivered first thing in the morning. The note said: "Mr. Chang; I promised to put the violin within your reach. This ticket will put you in the front row center for tonight's performance. You will be twenty feet from the Stradivarius in the hands of Concert Master Tang. I assume this makes us square. A distinct pleasure doing business with you. Your most humble and obedient, Michael Knight."

I figured that if that form of delivery didn't suit his complete pleasure, by the time murder, kidnapping, extortion, RICO, and other indictments started pouring out of the federal and state grand juries, based on the testimony of Ming Tan and that of any tong thugs the prosecutor managed to flip, the Boston tong house of cards would be tumbling down, all the way up to Chang's level. The violin would be the least of his concerns.

*　*　*

At 9:00 a.m. sharp the next morning, the judge's docket clerk showed the three of us—Billy Coyne, Mickey Chan, and me—into Judge Ev Albert's chambers off her courtroom. The judge and I had both started our legal careers in the U.S. Attorney's office as prosecutors. We'd been friends ever since. She granted the favor of scheduling this hearing before the start of her usual courtroom day.

I let Mr. Coyne make the formal motion to dismiss the indictment and explain the background. I thought it better coming from him.

Judge Albert looked to me. "Any objection to the motion, Mr. Knight?"

"Absolutely none, Your Honor."

"I'd think not. It's granted. Let's do this in open court."

With the formalities in order, I started walking Mickey down the steps of the courthouse. I stopped him halfway down.

"Where do you go from here, Mickey? I get the idea your former employers would be delighted to slice you up for stir-fry."

His silence said that his options were severely limited.

"Let me suggest something. I could use your help. It would involve traveling. This might not be a bad time for you to get out of Chinatown."

"So it seems. What did you have in mind?"

"Have you ever been to Romania?"

* * *

The second airline ticket and the second room at the Prahova Hotel in Ploiesti had been for Mickey. My hopeful presumption that he'd go along was not unfounded. He signed on without hesitation and without further explanation of the plan. His travels to his family home in China had caused him to keep his passport up to date. The last hurdle to his leaving the country had been his indictment for murder. That was now cleared in time for an early afternoon flight to Ploiesti, Romania.

* * *

The following morning, Mickey and I met at eight a.m. for breakfast in the Piccolo Giardino Restaurant of our hotel in Ploiesti. George was already at the table.

We fine-tuned the day's plan over a Romanian breakfast of om-
elet of *telemea*—sheep's milk cheese, and *zacusca*—eggplant and
pepper spread on *franzela*—Romanian bread. Three or four cups of
super-charged Romanian coffee and we were fueled for whatever
the day required.

We drove in one rented pickup truck with all of the supplies
George had mustered together the previous day under a blanketing
tarp. It was a twenty-minute ride to the ancient town of Targsor. As
we approached, George pointed out the outline of the shell that had
been the monastery of Targsor, erected and endowed by Vlad,
Dracula.

The closer we came to it, the faster my heart beat, undoubtedly in
synch with those of George, and even the newcomer to the adventure, Mickey.

As we drove close to the empty monastery, I was becoming awed
to be in the presence of an actual physical piece of the history of the
man who had been nothing more to me than a gripping legend. For
the first time, he took on a reality that I could almost touch.

We had the area to ourselves. As George drove us around the de-
serted, still imposing structure, the tension continued to climb.

"Where do we find it, George?"

"Patience. It'll wait for us. We're getting there."

Within seconds, George pulled off the road and headed toward a
massive stone hill on the south side of the building. He drove in
among a stand of trees and stopped in front of an uninviting cluster
of thickly grown bushes obscuring a rock face of the hill.

"Are you sure? There's nothing here."

"And so it's been for hundreds of years. That's the spot my guide
pointed out to me when I was over here a couple of years ago. It's
through that bramble bush. That's the entrance to the catacombs of
the fifteenth-century monks."

"Did you try to get through all this clutter when you were here before?"

"No. No reason then. By the look of it, no one else has either. Grab some of those cutters on the back of the truck. Let's get to work."

The sun blazed on our heads and backs as the three of us sliced and hacked a pathway through thick bushes. It was nearly eleven when the cleared path opened onto a solid rock wall fronted by a high pile of fragmented stones.

George handed us each a pair of leather gloves. "Now we work by hand. Let's go."

"Shall we take a break? We want to live to see what's in there."

"Break if you wish. I couldn't rest now if my arms were falling off."

If George in his fifties could press on, there'd be no rest for any of us. The two of us followed George in lifting and throwing rocks off to both sides.

It was another half hour of sweat before George removed a large stone that opened up a small hole into the black void that lay behind it. With the breath we had left, we gasped.

I brought us a round of water from the truck to fuel us for the final lap. We doubled our pace of lifting and throwing rocks. It was another half hour before we had opened a hole large enough for a man to slip through.

We stood back as if we were mentally drawing straws for the first man in.

"The honor should be yours, George. I'm right behind you."

We took battery lanterns from the truck and squeezed through the entrance in that order, with Mickey in third place. In spite of the opening to the outside, there was a stale, musty smell of unmoving air. My first relief was that the arid emptiness was unlikely to sustain the life of spiders, snakes, scorpions, or any Indiana Jones types of surprises.

The top of the narrow cave was just high enough to allow us to walk semi-upright with a fair bend of the back. I called to George in the lead. "Those monks must have been little, short guys."

I got a quick response in a whisper. "Keep it quiet. Look at the loose gravel falling on the sides here. This tunnel could cave in in a second."

I noticed that just my words had shaken loose rivers of dry dust and small stones on the sides of the tunnel. Even a mild case of claustrophobia was enough to suggest the possibility of an entombing cave-in. That ended the conversation.

George was careful to walk like he was on eggshells. The thought crossed my mind that if we came to the end of a dry, dusty, and totally empty cave, after the travails of the past three weeks, Prince Dracula would be somewhere laughing his butt off.

The air was becoming increasingly stale-smelling as we rounded one bend after another. Every time we rounded a bend, and our lantern light filled an empty chamber, there was a collective groan from the three of us.

After the fourth heart-dropping disappointment, the adrenalin that propelled our spirits into the cave was running low. George stopped for a breath. He looked back at me. His voice was a whisper. "Keep heart, Michael. There's more tunnel. Yogi Berra was right."

"You mean, 'It isn't over till it's over.'"

"Wisely spoken. Onward?"

My heart was saying, "No. I don't want to see the end of this thing with no pot of gold." I forced my mouth to whisper, "Damn the torpedoes, full speed ahead."

"What does that mean?"

"Nothing important. Let's do it."

George picked up the slow, agonizing pace. My mind was morphing from the expectation of an instantaneous "Eureka!" to an increasing desire just to ease the pain of keeping an arched back. Yet another heart-dropping turn of a corner left me with a full mind-consuming desire to just stretch out flat on the ground—if only for a minute.

I must have drifted into a semi-hypnotic focus on that last thought. I was looking straight down at the next step I was forcing my foot to take. The first shock was bumping headlong into the unyielding back of George. The second was the slow realization that George was frozen in position, just halfway around the next right-angle bend in the narrow path.

"What the hell, George? . . . What? . . . Damn it, speak!"

His low whisper was not to me. "My God in heaven. My dear God in heaven."

"George, I hate to interrupt a prayer, but I'm dying back here. Is it good or bad? Can you move?"

I doubt that he even heard my words. He never answered, but his body began slowly moving around the bend. He must have raised his lantern. The chamber ahead became filled with light.

I took a deep breath and rounded the bend. The stabbing pain in my back and the constant dread of being buried alive were suddenly blown totally out of my consciousness. I'm sure my jaw hung agape. Words flowed through my mind, but I couldn't get them past my tongue.

The first impression I can recall was of being nearly blinded by a million tiny reflected beams of light in colors ranging from ruby-red to cobalt blue and every shade in between. When my eyes adjusted, I realized that I was looking into a chamber filled with enough precious gems to coat the walls of a house. When my mind got around that reality, I was able to distinguish uncountable sculptures,

candelabra, art objects of every shape and design that could only be
of the very purest solid gold. When Shakespeare wrote, "All that
glitters is not gold," he was clearly not standing where we were.

In the back of my mind, I recalled George's telling me that
Dracula had not only spent years draining wealth out of the subjects of his own country, he had also received a steady flow of tribute
in magnificent gifts from powerful rulers as far away as Venice and
Istanbul. Those were just words when George had spoken them. To
see those words take physical form in that cave was to be . . . The
only word that comes close is *dumbfounded*.

The only sound in that tomb of everything the world values was
a faint ringing in my ears. I knew it was just the overload on strained
nerves. Our eyes were drawn beyond our control from one gleaming
object molded in solid gold or encrusted with pristine gems to another, and to another, and to another, and to another.

The next realization was that this eye-blitz of sculpted art was
surrounded by chest upon chest of coins, also of the purest gold and
imprinted with the crest of the dragon.

Time was frozen. Whether it was a minute, an hour, who knows
how long, we finally recaptured control of our eyes. George and I
looked numbly at each other. His face was drained of color, as probably was mine. What I read in his eyes was that he was as much in
the grip of the overwhelming reality as I was. We communicated
silently with nothing but the incredulous expressions on our faces.

When I looked back at Mickey, who I assumed had not been as
mentally prepared as George and I thought we were, I could see
our stunned struggle with disbelief reflected many times over in
his eyes.

George finally broke the silence with a whisper. "Michael, forgive
me. I have to ask this. I need the truth as never before. Are you still
committed to the plan? It's one thing to commit yourself when this

is just a dream." He held his hands out. "Now it's real. Does all of this bring out . . . a different side in you? It would in most men."

I think one would have to see what we were looking at to understand the question. It was perfectly clear to me.

I spoke back in a whisper, but George caught the depth of my words. "There is no different side, George. Only one side. I told you and the Russians and the Chinese what I want out of this. I want my life back. Nothing more. You and I agreed on something. That doesn't change."

We both looked at Mickey. He knew what we were asking. He just shook his head. "You gave me back my life, Mr. Knight. If you consider us even at the end of this, I came out ahead."

I looked at George. He nodded. I knew he meant that we wouldn't have to be looking over our shoulders for Mickey. I agreed.

For just that moment, I think the three of us found something in the others and in ourselves that outweighed everything else in that chamber. We shared it silently. It didn't need saying.

George broke the silence with a low whisper. "Then we have work to do."

CHAPTER THIRTY-TWO

MY FIRST CALL when we arrived back at the hotel in Ploiesti was to Mr. Lao, the man in the silk suit I met at the large-stakes gambling den in Chinatown. The older man from the Hong Kong triad with whom I'd actually dealt had said that I could reach him at any time through Mr. Lao.

The older man had apparently left orders. Thirty seconds after I gave my name, I recognized the older man's voice on the line.

"I'm fulfilling my promise."

"As I fully anticipated. I'm listening."

Without belaboring the mind-bending extent of the treasure, I simply announced that it did exist. I'd seen it. As promised, I was contacting him before I touched it myself.

He pressed me for specifics in a voice that was surprisingly animated by a lust for details of the treasure. I fed him just enough to ensure that his greed would drive him to follow the plan I laid down.

The instructions I gave him were simple. Fly into the Henri Coanda Airport in Ploiesti the next day. Come alone. Check into a reserved room at the Pik Elegance Hotel in Ploiesti. Be in the lobby at nine o'clock sharp the following morning. One more time for emphasis—*Come alone.*

He informed me that, in view of his advanced age, he would be sending his trusted assistant, Mr. Lao, the man in the silk suit. I was to treat him in every respect as I would the older man himself.

I made him aware that I would be fulfilling a like promise to Mr. Vasily Laskovitch, the head of the Russian gang. He took that with equanimity, if not joy.

My next call was to Mr. Laskovitch. I gave him the same limited description of the treasure. I could practically hear his saliva dripping into the phone. Again, the propulsion of greed gained agreement to my instructions. I told him to fly to Ploiesti the following day and check into the Vigo Hotel. It seemed the better part of discretion to have them at different hotels until I could chaperone their meeting. He was also to be in the lobby the following day at nine a.m. sharp. And, above all, *come alone.*

The one thing on which I would have bet my Boston Bruins season tickets was that neither of them would come alone. All to the good.

* * *

The following day, George and I split up the list of hotels within a fifty-mile radius of Ploiesti for a personal visit. At each hotel, we located a concierge whose loyalty could be bought for a hundred dollars' worth of Romanian lei. We slipped each one of them fifty dollars in lei with the promise of the other fifty for a cell phone call if a contingent of Chinese or Russian thugs checked in.

At seven that evening, George, Mickey, and I were at dinner in our hotel dining room. The first call came to me from the concierge at one of the hotels I'd visited. In a low voice he reported that six Chinese gentlemen "with whom he would not want to have a disagreement" had checked in.

Less than half an hour later, George got a call on his cell phone from a concierge at one the hotels he visited. He held up five fingers. It meant that five Russian-speaking thugs had just checked in.

That made thirteen seasoned warriors to our little band of three. No sweat. Theoretically. My anticipation was that the total predictability of their greed would even the odds.

* * *

George, Mickey, and I were up at six the next morning after a fitful sleep. At breakfast, we fed off of each other's tension. There was no discussion. And no jokes.

I took one rental car and picked up the Russian, Vasily Laskovitch, at his hotel at nine on the dot. At the same time, according to plan, Mickey took a second rental car and picked up Mr. Lao at his hotel. George drove a third car directly to the catacomb to wait. He covered the entrance we had carved through the bushes with a thin layer of branches.

Mickey and I each drove our passengers by a direct route and at a slow pace. As I hoped, the six Russians and five Chinese predictably followed their leaders from behind in separate cars.

The challenge of assembling that bucket of monkeys without open warfare would call for some fine-tuned diplomacy. Both Mr. Lao and Mr. Laskovitch knew that the other would be there. On the other hand, whatever tenuous agreement between their respective crime gangs had kept them off of each other's throats to that point would likely dissolve in the acid of greed when the actual treasure was within reach.

Lao and Laskovitch greeted each other and George at the entrance to the cave with all of the warmth of crabs in ice water. The real fun began when the two cars carrying the backup thugs of each gang pulled up. Every one of them displayed barely concealed bulges that signaled an arsenal on both sides.

It was an absolute certainly that if I left that little play-group to make friends on their own, all hell would break out within minutes. I took a quick lead, with Mickey translating for the Chinese.

"Gentlemen, here are the rules. George here and I will take Mr. Lao and Mr. Laskovitch into the cave. Alone. Unarmed. I'll show you what you've come here to see. Then George, Mickey, and I leave. How you settle things among yourselves after that is up to you. Then I'm out of it. Is that understood?"

At that point, the hell I predicted broke loose. Laskovitch demanded that he have his troops with him. The idea of being unarmed in any situation went against his nature. Lao spoke English well enough to say, roughly, "To hell with that. If his men go, my men go."

Voices began to rise. Some Russian and Chinese terms were thrown around that could have ignited gunfire if either side understood the other. The armed troops on both sides were moving in closer to a combat line. Weapons previously semi-concealed were making an appearance.

I climbed onto the roof of the car closest. I began pounding on the roof of the car with a heavy stick until I caught their attention. I grabbed a small break in the increasing hostilities to yell at the top of my lungs, "Do any of you bozos know where the entrance to the cave is?"

I yelled it three times for effect. It was a rhetorical question. George had effectively hidden the entrance with branches. They had no answer. I continued. "Well I do. Here's the deal. That tunnel is ready to cave in if anyone even raises his voice. So here's how we do it. Or not at all."

I checked their faces. I had their attention. "Mr. Lao. You and three of your men. Stand over here. Mr. Laskovitch. You and three of your men stand over there beside them. The rest of you people get the hell back in the cars. Nothing happens till you do it."

It took some grumbling and ethnic cursing, but as I'd hoped, the threat of a cave-in, plus the equality of guns on each side, made the arrangement borderline tolerable.

When the troops were finally lined up and the auxiliaries were back in their cars, I helped George pull away the branches from the entrance. George and I led the way in with lanterns. After an exchange of threatening glares, Lao and Laskovitch managed to squeeze though, Laskovitch winning the lead by virtue of size.

When the three thugs on each side came up to the small opening, the muscling for position escalated. I worked my way back to where I could be heard at the entrance. I said it in a whisper for fear of loose rocks, but it had all the steam I could put into it. "Listen to me, you boneheads! One loud noise in here and we all become part of this rock-heap. Pretend you've got half a brain. One at a time. You first."

I pointed to one of the Chinese. Then one of the Russians, then a Chinese, and so forth, until they were all inside and in line, and in silence. Mickey was the last in line.

George and I squeezed into the lead. No one spoke, but I could see rivulets of dirt and pebbles starting down the walls just from the footsteps of ten walkers. The more rapid the flow, the more insane that trek seemed for any amount of gold.

George and I were the first to round the final bend. When our lanterns filled that chamber with reflections off of a million gem facets, it was nearly as overwhelming as the first time.

I watched the faces of each man as he was struck full on for the first time by a brilliance more spectacular than anything he could have imagined. For the first few minutes, it was more than they could comprehend. They were stunned into silence.

When the stunning subsided, even just a little, their minds turned to the possibility of possessing it all. I could see the flame of greed ignite and burn in their eyes.

The Russian, Laskovitch, broke first. He yelled something to one of his troops. A gun was drawn, then another. That set off a show of weapons by the Chinese. In a fraction of a second, it could have been Dodge City, except that there was no stone cave to collapse in Dodge.

I jumped in between the two lines of handguns with my hands out. I tried to keep it to a whisper. "Easy. Easy. Settle down. The first shot any of you fires buries us all alive."

As if the hill were pressing my point, there was a loud rumble of rocks sliding down one side of the chamber. The panic that instantly wiped out the fixation with the cold treasure froze ten bodies in place. Guns were lowered. In the next instant, one of the Russians bolted for the exit. Another was on his heels. Two of the Chinese were at their backs.

The leaders, Lao and Laskovitch, who put up a fight to have their gunmen beside them, now found those bodies jamming the tiny way out of a rockslide entombment.

Mickey and I ran to the mass of shoving bodies. One by one, we grabbed bodies by the neck and threw them back from the return tunnel. Once it was cleared, we pushed each one of them in turn into the passageway. As soon as we let go of them, each one ran at the best speed they could make in a hunched-over position toward the entrance.

The clattering of footsteps brought more rivers of stone and dirt flowing down the walls. The debris was building up in the pathway. Rumbles of more seismic crumbling echoed in greater volume through the entire passage.

When all of the Russians and Chinese had cleared the treasure chamber, I started down the path, with Mickey at my heels and

George behind. It was too late to worry about the sound of foot-steps. We hit the best speed we could.

I was the first one out. The Russians and Chinese were huddled around looking back into the entrance. Mickey appeared briefly, but just as he was about to run out, we heard what sounded like an explosion, followed by rolling thunder from the inside. George's scream rose over the roar. "My leg! It's crushed! It's coming down!"

Mickey turned and ran back into the cave. Every eye was on the entrance. There was what sounded like another explosion deep inside the cave. What started as an earth-like groaning that came from the very belly of the stone hill became a thunderous pounding of rocks on rocks from deep inside the cave. The roar came toward us until as far back as we could see, the massive rock hill was collapsing in on itself.

By barely an instant, I saw a hunched figure covered in rock dust stagger out of the entrance. I ran to where Mickey collapsed on the ground.

"Mickey, are you hurt?"

"I'm alright. But George . . ."

*　*　*

For a long period—I don't know how long—the entire group of us stayed there, just gaping at what was formerly a cave, and was now a massive, hundred-foot high pile of rocks.

What was going through each of our minds depended on who we were and what we came there for in the first place. I suspect most of the mourning was for the loss of a treasure that may never be equaled.

I know that I was replaying in my mind every instant that I had spent in the company of a man the likes of whom I had never known before—and would probably never know again.

CHAPTER THIRTY-THREE

FOR THE NEXT three solid weeks, the most dangerous thing I did was to joust for position with other aggressive Boston drivers at the entrance to the Callahan Tunnel. I did it with a smile on my face a yard wide—which drove the other drivers to distraction.

I settled into trying my own cases, which took a burden off of the strong but aging shoulders of my senior partner. I answered phone calls and emails the day they came in, which made the life of my faithful secretary, Julie, livable again.

But at the top of the list, Terry and I picked up our life from where we had put it on hold. I was home every night to the scrambling, yipping greeting of our Sheltie and to the arms of the girl of my life. And both of us were consumed with plans for the arrival of one we loved even before he or she was born.

Three weeks to the day from the time I got off the plane from Romania for the last time, a letter came in the office mail. It held two tickets, third row center, to a concert of the Boston Symphony Orchestra. The soloist for Haydn's Violin Concerto in A major was to be Concert Master Lee Tang.

The note with it gave me the first jangle of nerves I'd felt in three weeks. It simply said, "Check under your seat."

My initial thought was, "Smoking crap! Another damn dose of intrigue." I was sorely tempted to turn the tickets back into the box office. When I told Terry about the tickets, I also told her about the note. In line with my commitment to her and the baby we were both determined to raise in peace, I also told her about my temptation to turn in the tickets.

When she asked who sent the tickets, I could only say, "I haven't the foggiest idea." She gave it a few seconds, and, as usual, she applied more logic than I did. "Michael, the concert is a beautiful gift. And you'll wonder for the rest of your life who sent them. Maybe you'll get an answer. If you don't like what's under the seat, we can just walk away from it. *After* we enjoy the concert. They're not going to catch you again."

So we went. We went early so I'd have time to check under the seat without an audience. What was really perplexing was that there was absolutely nothing under the seat. I finally figured that it was just a joke—quite possibly by Lex Devlin or Billy Coyne.

On that note, no pun intended, we settled into enjoyment of the violin concerto played superbly by Concert Master Tang on the Stradivarius that had had three criminal gangs dispatching victims with a reckless abandon.

We returned to our seats after an intermission of sparkling water for Terry and Famous Grouse for me. I happened to drop my program under the seat. When I bent down to pick it up, my hand hit something. I felt further and found a small box taped to the seat.

I showed it to Terry with a questioning look.

"Open it. Before they begin playing. You won't hear a single note if you don't."

I took off the wrapping paper slowly. There was a small felt box inside. I could feel the muscles in my stomach clench as I lifted the top of the box. What I saw flooded my mind with emotions I thought I had put to rest.

The box held a gleaming solid gold ring with a Christian cross raised on the top. Along both sides there was molded the twisting form of a dragon.

I knew I had seen it before. It had caught my attention while George and I were in that treasure chamber for the first time.

It just held me in a trance for four or five seconds until a thought drove me to my feet. I stood up and scanned the audience. I searched every face until I looked up to the first elevated box on our right. There was a man standing in the doorway to the box. He was looking in our direction. I couldn't make out his features, but he held out his hands as if he were holding them out to me.

It suddenly struck me. I held my hands out to him. I saw a smile light his face just a second before he disappeared through the door.

When I sat down, I could feel moisture running down both cheeks. I wanted to explain it to Terry, but my throat was too clogged to speak.

* * *

On the way home, we stopped at a late-night coffeehouse in Harvard Square. I needed time to explain something I had never mentioned to Terry in my determination to move ahead into a normal life. I thought I'd talk about it this once—tonight—and never again.

I forget the words I used, but what I told her was that at some point in that odyssey, I had sided completely with George and his Romanians over the other two gangs. He wanted the treasure as much as the others did, but for completely different reasons. His Romanian people had been plundered by one conqueror after another throughout history and by corrupt politicians ever since the fall of communism. His quest was to find the treasure to give it back to the descendants of the people who had been impoverished in the amassing of it.

The question was how it could be done in a way that would keep it out of the grasping hands of gangsters and politicians. That's when the plan evolved.

The day that George and Mickey and I first cleared our entrance to the monastery catacombs, we found more than the treasure. We were certain that the Christians who made the catacombs for protection would have made more than one entrance. We found the second tunnel leading from the treasure chamber to an exit in the opposite direction from the one we entered.

Before we left the treasure chamber on that first day, we covered that second exit from the chamber with a pile of rocks. We also freed the second exit where it led to the outside of the caves from the rocks and thick bushes and brambles hiding it from sight. We finally hid the exit to the outside with a light covering of branches.

We then used the supplies that George had gathered before Mickey and I arrived. We planted small explosives in the walls of the first tunnel we knew we'd be using when the Chinese and Russians arrived. The stage was set for one performance.

I was sure that when we brought that collection of Russian and Chinese thugs into the treasure chamber, their innate greed would stir up enough of a ruckus to start rocks and pebbles falling off the walls. I made my little speech when we arrived at the cave to prepare them to panic in fear of a landslide.

True to my prediction, within five minutes of the time the nine of us were all in the treasure chamber, their yelling and cursing at each other caused enough stone to fall to make it look like there'd be a cave-in any second. They stampeded out of the cave like the running of the bulls.

Once we had the gangsters outside the entrance, the playacting began.

Before Mickey came out, he detonated a string of small charges that sounded like a major cave-in and ran outside. That was when George yelled from deep inside about being trapped with a crushed leg. Actually, he was running safely back to the treasure chamber and out the second exit. He removed the branches we'd placed in front of the second exit and made his escape.

When they all heard George yell, Mickey played his part. He ran back into the cave as if to rescue George. What he was really doing was setting off the rest of the detonations in the front part of the cave. He made it sound as if the whole hill were caving in. Actually, the treasure room and the path leading to the second exit were still completely intact. Before leaving the area, George covered over that second entrance to the cave with bushes.

As far as the Russians and Chinese gangs knew, George and the treasure were now buried under a hundred feet of solid rock.

Terry took my hand and looked at the gold ring with the cross and the dragon. "And what about George?"

I thought for a few seconds before saying something I would never entrust to another human being. "You'll see. We'll be hearing news reports about things happening in Romania. There'll be hospitals built. There'll be orphanages. There'll be shelters and homes for homeless people. There'll be special schools. Parks and homes for elderly people. More than we can even imagine right now."

"And George?"

"All of these things will be done by an anonymous donor—one who seems to have unlimited resources. And no one will ever know who."

"Michael, that man you saw in the box at the orchestra tonight . . . I guess I don't need to ask."

* * *

The following April around Easter, Kimberly Anne Knight made
her entrance into our lives and raised the fullness and happiness of
every moment beyond anything Terry and I could ever have imagined possible. My life and practice of law with the other partner in
my life, Lex Devlin, remained within the parameters of a normal
lawyer—and happily so.

   Do I ever for the tiniest moment miss the nerve-clenching adventures that had seemed to seek me out before? . . . Mmmm.

AUTHOR'S NOTE

I have always been fascinated by the history behind the immortalization of Dracula as a fictional vampire. It's my hope that this work of fiction will shed light on the unforgettable, and yet almost totally forgotten, actual character out of the history of Eastern Europe.

When Bram Stoker seized on the folk legends of seventeenth-century villagers in the area of Transylvania to present Dracula as a fictional vampire, his classic novel totally overshadowed, to the point of nearly erasing from history, the existence of the actual, flesh-and-blood, famous or infamous, fifteenth-century ruler of a major province of Romania, Vlad Dracula.

The impact of the actual Dracula's rule by terror on the ebb and flow of the line of conquest between the Christian and Muslim kingdoms of Eastern Europe was immense. When, for example, Sultan Mehmed II's Ottoman army of Turkish Muslims drove the Christian forces under Dracula in retreat past the Transylvania border, the Sultan entered a narrow valley just beyond Dracula's capital city of Tirgoviste. The Sultan's advance was stopped cold. He and his army were totally dispirited by the sight of rows of corpses, executed on Dracula's command by his signature method of impalement of his enemies on high stakes—the bodies numbering in excess of twenty thousand.

Facts regarding the real Dracula that form this novel's background, which I found to be more fascinating than any that could be fictionalized, are as accurately incorporated in this novel as historical reporting over four centuries permits.

On the other hand, the legend of Dracula's amassing and secreting of a monumental treasure is of my own fictionalizing—although I would be astonished if such a fortune did not actually result from his demands on terrified subjects and tribute paid by rulers from Vienna to Istanbul.

Factual data regarding the other historical phenomenon that gives this novel its background, a violin produced in Cremona, Italy, around 1700 by Antonio Stradivari, is also founded in truth. The impact of the unique skill of Stradivari, using the wood of spruce trees available in Europe during that particular period, on the ability of musicians to bring an extraordinary tone, purity, and volume of sound to the performance of the works of master composers, will likely never be equaled. That part of the novel is also factually correct.

The code embedded in the particular violin for which people lose their lives in this novel, on the other hand, is as fictional as Michael and Lex themselves—although, at times, I do find myself in conversation with both of them. Just one of the pitfalls of writing fiction.